An Imperfection *in the* Kitchen Floor

HEATHER GREENLEAF

NEW YORK

NASHVILLE • MELBOURNE • VANCOUVER

AN IMPERFECTION IN THE KITCHEN FLOOR

Morgan James is a trademark of Morgan James, LLC.
www.MorganJamesPublishing.com

The Morgan James Speakers Group can bring authors to your live event. For more
information or to book an event visit The Morgan James Speakers Group at
www.TheMorganJamesSpeakersGroup.com.

Publisher's Note: This novel is a work of fiction. Names, characters, places, and
incidents are either products of the author's imagination or used fictitiously.
All characters are fictional, and any similarity to people living or dead is purely
coincidental.

ISBN 9781683506638 - paperback
ISBN 9781683506645 - eBook
Library of Congress Control Number: 2017910748

Cover Design by: Rachel Lopez
Interior Design by: Paul Curtis

In an effort to support local communities, raise awareness and funds, Morgan James
Publishing donates a percentage of all book sales for the life of each book to
Habitat for Humanity Peninsula and Greater Williamsburg.

Get involved today! Visit
www.MorganJamesBuilds.com

AN IMPERFECTION
IN THE KITCHEN FLOOR

for Trip and Alice
with all my love

TABLE OF CONTENTS

Prologue, 1920

Painfully detailed headlines landed on our porch: *Two Trains in a Deadly Head-on Collision… Passengers and Trainmen Mangled, Crushed, Scalded, and Burned Alive… Remains of Victims Carried Away in Baskets.* The daily newspapers piled up unread while we were at the hospital and, later, making funeral arrangements.

It was a long time before I could bring myself to read them, relive them. Eventually I cut out one of the articles, carefully preserving the victims' names typed in harsh black ink. I placed it deep inside his book on the shelf, pressing it like a flower and tucking it away.

CHAPTER ONE

Molly, 2005

The place was a dump.

I stared up at the dilapidated box that was our new house in disbelief. We left Washington DC for this?

"We're here," Corey said, standing next to me on the cracked sidewalk, his face proud and bright. "C'mon! Come inside and see it!"

I watched him lope up the bowed steps like an excited child. The house was three stories high and perfectly, unimaginatively, square. A wraparound porch with grayed and flaking columns surrounded the cracking stone facade. Pachysandra raced over most of the front lawn, dappled with fallen brown leaves. The sidewalk and walkway to the porch were littered with tree detritus from the two peeling sycamores that stood sentinel at the edge of the strangled yard.

Corey fiddled with the key, pulling on the knob and slamming his shoulder into the heavy wooden door a few times. The bolt finally fell, like a guillotine out of the lock. Then, without waiting for me, Corey rushed inside.

Two hundred miles north of our old apartment, its keys passed off forever to the landlord, regret clogged my throat. This practical and forlorn house had none of the beauty Corey had described—no, promised—in the months leading up to our move. My chest was tight with the finality of it all. This was it, where we would be living. Maybe forever.

Earlier that morning, I had awakened in our cozy one-bedroom apartment, stacked high with labeled boxes ready to be loaded onto the truck. The sun streamed through our slatted blinds, filling our bedroom with long, vertical stripes of light. I sat up and, with gentle fingertips, traced the line of sunshine that fell on Corey's bare shoulder. I was happy just being next to him, overwhelmed with love and excited for our relocation.

As we trundled along in the moving van, wisps of my long, thin, light hair blew in the breeze. I chewed on the hangnails forever plaguing my thumbs and watched Corey in the driver's seat. Scruff dotted his strong jawline. His brown hair flipped up at the nape of his neck like a duck's tail. Turning to me, he caught me staring. He reached out with a grin, exposing me to the full force of his dimples, and rubbed my bulbous belly.

"Almost home," he said.

Her home, this home, now our home.

In the truck, I had put my hand over Corey's where it rested on my belly, trusting him fully. Below our fingers, the baby rolled an elbow, or a perhaps a knee, and my stomach rose in a trailing arc. I grinned and looked at Corey. His smile let me know he had felt it too; our tiny creation saying hello.

We had discovered I was pregnant when I threw up at work. I was at my prep station in the kitchen of Aubergine, the French bistro in Georgetown, slicing Dover sole fillets cleanly off the bone. While the kitchen crew exchanged dirty jokes and tales of racy escapades from the night before, my head got heavy and hot and suddenly my stomach lurched. I dropped my knife and as it clattered to the cutting board, I raced out the back door, vomit rising and then spewing behind the dumpster. When I reentered, the guys applauded, assuming I was hungover.

I wasn't hungover.

Corey, who, until the moment the second blue line appeared, loved our late nights out drinking, dancing, and eating pizza in Addams Morgan, became an instant family man. His goals were immediately rearranged. He compulsively checked the balance of our savings account. He invested in more life insurance. He started talking about the house in Willow Grove.

I had never been there, but he painted the small Pennsylvania town and the large American Foursquare house with idyllic nostalgic colors. His Aunt Tish had lived in the house her entire life, some ninety-odd years, and after her death, she left it to him. He had let the house sit, generally ignored for years except in his memory. He told me stories of his summers there, picnicking under the pine trees in the backyard, running toy cars over the kitchen tiles, and relaxing in the rocking chairs on the front porch. His childhood days spent in Aunt Tish's house were full of happiness, and now he wanted to raise his family there too.

He described every aspect of the house, selling me on it with each gorgeous detail. It is old and charming, he said. It has a pocket door and leaded glass windows, he said. It is just sitting there waiting for us, he said. It is in a safe, suburban town, he said. There are four bedrooms and a backyard, he said. Aunt Tish would want us to raise our family there, he said.

Inside our cramped apartment, it was easy to get wrapped up in his excitement. Picturing something akin to Shangri La, I quit my sous chef job at Aubergine, packed up all of our things, and was ready to make a new life for our baby.

And now, standing in front of it, the reality was something quite different from the dream. Though I had conjured images of Frank Lloyd Wright beauty, the house was closer to Grey Gardens—once loved, but no longer. Corey's exaggeration of the house's glory was a betrayal. It pounded deep within, felt as surely as I felt the baby's swift kicks.

With a sigh, I lurched up the porch stairs. Once inside, it took my eyes a moment to adjust. A deep must filled my nose. I instinctively held my breath. I approached the windows, covered in lacy curtains that masked the sunlight, and threw open each one. The fresh air billowed fine cobwebs in the corners of the nine-foot ceilings and displaced the silt on the oak floors. Corey's footprints left empty spaces in the dust.

I followed his footprints until I found the kitchen at the back of the house. The room was a horizontal narrow rectangle with an old porcelain sink and precious little counter space. The stove had gas burners and I tested each one, fearing the worst, but they thankfully clicked and then burned blue.

Below my feet, one of the tiles had a long crack radiating from a dark crescent. I squatted down like a frog, knees bent and legs splayed out to the sides, my belly in the middle, and looked closer. I poked the tile with my finger. About two inches long, c-shaped, and deep, the crescent was an empty, dark recess. I shook my head in disbelief. Was everything in this house broken and crumbling? Feeling tricked, I continued to run my finger over the crescent's smooth edges.

The sound of rushing water began behind the pantry door. I turned and looked, certain that the plumbing had just given way. Suddenly the door flew open and Corey burst out. Before I could ask him what he was doing in the pantry, he stepped aside and I noticed it wasn't a pantry at all, but a very tiny bathroom.

"There's a sink, but no room to stand to wash your hands in there. I remember it being bigger! You have no chance of fitting in there!" Corey laughed. "Oh, I see you have found my racing track. I used that crack in the tile as the starting line, then raced all my toy cars to the other end of the kitchen. Our boy is going to love doing that too!"

I recoiled from the crack and stood, baffled by Corey's continued excitement. Couldn't he see this place for what it was?

"Corey," I began.

He ignored me and put his hands around my enormous belly, bending down to address the baby. "What do you think, little man? Want to race cars in here? Soon you are going to be running around this house, loving it as much as I do. Let's hope your mommy loves it too. She's looking pretty skeptical right now. But we aren't going to let that get us down, right, buddy?" He stood up, his face now level with mine. "I really think it is going to be great here. Let me show you upstairs."

He kissed my forehead, and after washing his hands at the kitchen sink, he took my hand in his and led me around the house, pointing out his favorite things. His chest was swollen with pride.

"Aunt Tish painted this landscape, and this painting was done by my grandmother," he said, pointing out a still life with onions and carrots on the dining room wall.

It was dark with age and though it seemed skillful, it wasn't my taste. I wrinkled my nose. "Do you like it?" I asked.

"Yeah, it's great, isn't it? I love it all. The house is already decorated and ready for us to just settle in! Don't you just love its charm?"

"Corey," I said slowly as we climbed the stairs even more slowly, "I'm not sure. It is already decorated, but the house isn't exactly how you described it."

"It needs a little work, but it will be great."

"A little work? It needs more than that," I said. I chewed the hangnail on my thumb. "It's dirty outside and in, and is the porch even safe?"

As Corey began to answer, a loud horn honked outside.

"Hank's here," he said and turned to thunder down the stairs, taking two at a time. I descended the stairs more cautiously and emerged out into the sunshine to see Corey greet his older brother with a hearty hug. Hank was burly, a jovial fraternity guy gone soft and nearly bald. I waved and called hello.

"Hey there, Suburban Lady! Are you missing the city already?" Hank hollered from the street. "Jocelyn will be glad to have you in town. She has tons of wisdom she'd like to impart about childrearing."

Hank and Jocelyn had been high school sweethearts. They married young, right out of college, bought a house, and now had two elementary-school-aged boys. Their family of four was part of the Hess contingent who had come to DC for our wedding. Hank stood as best man. Jocelyn had tutted around in her tight designer dress, fussing with the flowers, picking off the dead leaves, and straightening the silverware. Her boys ran around in their tiny suits, claiming to be ninjas, chasing each other and hollering. They were always hollering. And Jocelyn was always hollering for them to stop hollering. That Jocelyn "the Ubermom" was the only woman I knew in town made me cringe.

"Great," I muttered. Changing my tune, I said, "Hey, thanks for coming. I'm fairly useless right now." I patted my belly.

"Sure, use the baby as an excuse," Hank said, winking. "We all know you wish this van would turn around and drive you straight back to your little Dupont Circle apartment."

"Come on, Hank. This place is going to be great," Corey said. "Right, babe?"

"Well..." I began, unsure how to continue.

Hank let out a huge laugh. "Oh man, you didn't tell her what a dump this place is, did you?"

"It's not a dump!" Corey said. "You never liked this place as much as I did."

"Mom didn't send me here as much as she sent you. I was the good son, remember? She wanted me around," Hank said, winking again and grinning.

"Shut up and help me with this stuff," Corey said, giving Hank a slight nudge. He disappeared into the back of the van.

Corey didn't like his mother much, but hated to be reminded that she may have felt the same way about him. I first met her a few months into our relationship, when she visited DC. Corey had been reluctant to introduce her to me, almost embarrassed by her. "She's not your typical loving mother," he had warned me. We met her for lunch at a seafood restaurant on the Georgetown waterfront. She was a vegetarian. When we arrived, she air kissed Corey's cheeks and then moved on to me, her gold bracelets clanking together on her slim wrists. I returned her air kisses, embracing her lightly for fear that her thin frame would shatter under any embrace. She was glamorous but cold. Her hair was perfectly curled and framed her face. Her sharp nose and hollow, defined cheekbones were heavily covered in movie star makeup.

She insisted I call her Robin. She insisted that the waiter bring her fat free salad dressing, on the side. She insisted that her fish be broiled without "any butter whatsoever," and then sent that fish back twice, claiming that she tasted butter. I could just imagine what the kitchen staff was thinking about her.

Throughout lunch, she prattled on and on about her charity functions and the famous people who attended. She didn't ask Corey a single question about himself, and made very little effort to get to know me. She never mentioned Corey's father, who passed away shortly after Corey graduated from business school.

I didn't particularly like her. And soon she was off on a plane back home to New York, where she had moved a few years earlier.

From what little Corey would say about her, I knew she was much younger than Corey's father when his parents married, twenty-five years younger to be exact. "Having Hank and me negated some of the loss she would take in the prenuptial agreement," Corey often said with a touch of bitterness. "She never wanted to be a mother. Still doesn't." His parents had stayed together, though, until his father's death. Throughout Corey's childhood, it seemed that Robin was more than happy to let Aunt Tish, her spinster sister-in-law, take the boys for entire summers and long weekends.

And so, I understood the soft spot that Corey held for Aunt Tish and her house, but I was beginning to see that perhaps this love for her had clouded his view of her house in its current state.

Corey and Hank worked all day, placing our things amid the fragments of Aunt Tish's estate. She had left most of her furniture behind. Covered in sheets, the chairs and breakfronts stood like ghosts in all of the rooms. As I watched them bring in the pieces of our lives and place them in their permanent resting places, I tamped down my urge to scream, "Put it all back on the truck!"

Instead, I tore down the curtains, catching lungfuls of dust, as I pooled them on the ground in a musty heap. With the removal of each curtain, more sunshine entered the house, brindling the hardwood floors with light. Next, I busied myself pulling the sheets off the furniture, the dust motes taking flight and sparkling in the air. Hank and Corey brought in our sofa, cramming it in next to Aunt Tish's wingback chairs. They placed our flat screen television on top of what had to be an antique table. They dumped boxes anywhere and everywhere. The house was much larger than our apartment, but like a bomb, our things exploded and hit every wall. By the time Hank left, shrugging off our offer to feed him dinner, Corey and I were exhausted. Corey flopped down, throwing his leg over one arm of the wingback chair.

"Man, I'm thirsty," he called to me as I was puttering around, trying to organize the melee of boxes. Disappointment was still tangy at the back of my throat, but when I had everything unpacked, the place would be more like home.

"I haven't found the box with the glasses yet. Want to go out and get something?" I called back.

"I'll run to Wawa. Grab us some sandwiches too."

When he left, I sat down on our couch and propped my feet up on the nearest box. I looked around, sighing. It felt big, our new home, and I would focus on that. The sound of church bells trickled in the windows. It was a song I recognized, tinny and high, but kind in its familiarity. After a few moments, I climbed the stairs and located the box marked *Sheets* and made our bed.

Corey came home with two hoagies. "You have to call them that now. We are in Philadelphia," he said. "And, here, we call them hoagies."

"Got it," I said. "Hoagies. Wawa." The words felt silly in my mouth, but whatever they were called, Corey was right. They tasted good. After our sandwiches, Corey and I slept hard in our bed in his aunt's home.

• • •

The following Monday, Corey began his new job at his financial firm. I kissed him goodbye and was left alone to begin unpacking and settling in. I looked around. Years of dust fluttered in the morning light. The thought of our baby living here made me slightly ill. Though I felt desperately tired in these last weeks of pregnancy, I was compelled to clean the house. I started in the kitchen, wiping down all the counters and sweeping up the floor. Mouse turds turned my stomach and I made a mental note to call an exterminator as I splashed hot soapy water around with my mop. The recessed crack in the tile remained dingy and dark, a century of grime hiding inside.

I moved to the bathroom, banishing the stains from the toilet, sink, and tub. I wiped all of the baseboards and chased cobwebs and frighteningly large spiders with my vacuum.

I sat down, exhausted, fearing I was overdoing it. I rested my hand on my huge tummy. I fired up my laptop and entered our new Wi-Fi password. After sending a few emails and checking Facebook, I knew I couldn't stall much longer. I made the phone call I had been dreading.

I picked up the phone and dialed my father and stepmother in Florida. They had married shortly after my mother passed away. My stepmother had three sons, Nicholas, Joseph, and Michael. She had raised them herself, gritting through many tough times, and always called them by their full first names. Beware the person who tried to call them Nick, Joe, or Mike in her presence. Her relationship with them was almost Oedipal in its mutual devotion. There was no room for a daughter in the family; I was as unwanted as Cinderella.

My father, perhaps always secretly yearning for sons, was enamored with her trio as well. Dad was kind to a fault, and like milk toast, was absorbed easily into their life. But, without my mother, Dad was all I had, and so I called him now, hoping he or the machine would answer. My stepmother answered, breathless, annoyed before I had even said a word.

"Hello, Molly. Your father is out golfing, and I'm here with a repairman. I can't talk long. I have to get him settled and then go out soon."

"Okay. I won't keep you; I just wanted to give you our new address and let you know our phone is up and running."

"Yes, yes, let me get a pen."

After I relayed our new contact information, I ventured, "Only two weeks until the baby arrives. Maybe you and Dad could come up and visit once he is born? Last time I talked to Dad, he said he would talk to you about it."

A deep, overwrought sigh. "I wish you would discuss plans with me first. Your father always commits before knowing what is on our schedule. We are very busy with the boys."

I cringed. She said "the boys," as if they were children. Nicholas was over fifty with teenage children, and Joseph and Michael were close behind in age.

"Nicholas is coming down with our grandchildren," my stepmother continued, "and staying the entire month of July. We are traveling back to Maryland with them so we can stay with the kids while he and Barbara take a two-week vacation."

"Maybe after that?" I asked. "Philadelphia is just a few hours north of Maryland." I never seemed to beat "the boys" to the scheduling board; it was always full by the time I tried to add my name. Even now, with my baby arriving—my father's first actual grandchild—there was a six-week waiting period to see him.

"Maybe," she said. "We might have to head right back home to Florida. Joseph and Ann are talking about coming down sometime in August. And we're waiting to hear about Michael's vacation plans. I'll let your father know you called." And then she hung up on me.

When would I learn? She hadn't asked how I was feeling, or whether or not I was ready for the baby to arrive. I was certain they wouldn't come visit. Though she eagerly included my father when she said "our" grandchildren, I couldn't imagine her ever claiming my child as her own. She might not even tell my father that I had called. Though Corey and I joked about her often, the sting of my unimportance in her eyes was still there, and I missed the way my father was before my mother passed and my stepmother and "the boys" came into his life.

I had missed my mother throughout my pregnancy. When the doctors asked if there was any family pregnancy history they should know about, I had little knowledge and it was too late to ask. Though my colleagues clucked appropriately at the fuzzy black and white image, and what may or may not have been a foot on the ultrasound photo, I missed being able to show it to my mother. I wished she had been there to see my belly get rounder and my face flatten out. I wondered if the baby would take after her in any way. When shopping for baby items, I was nearly brought to tears when I passed a onesie that read *Grandma's favorite*. I put it in the cart and bought it, but didn't show Corey. It was still tucked away somewhere in one of the unpacked boxes.

• • •

Overnight, my water broke. Corey rushed me to Abington Hospital. After hours of Pitocin-induced horror, and then hours of epidural ease, the baby arrived. Corey and I wept. We named him Hayden and were overwhelmed by the enormity, the utter awesomeness, of this tiny baby.

The day we spent at the hospital was a quiet one. Hank and Jocelyn were away at a baseball tournament, and my phone conversation with my father was brief. Nurses bustled in and out to tell us what to do and when, and I was content for hours to just look at Hayden. I fiddled with his fingers, touched his cheeks, and felt relief when he latched on to my breast.

I looked at the nurse holding our discharge papers with disbelief when she said we could take him home. My eyes were no longer full of wonder; they were full of fear. The idyllic bubble of the hospital room burst too soon, and we were shooed out into the shocking sun as if newly birthed ourselves.

Back at the house, Corey took a week off and despite my self-doubt, the first few days were fuzzy and warm. Hayden slept most of the time. Corey seemed to take the dirty diapers, the late feedings, and the spit-ups all in stride.

At the beginning of our relationship, Corey and I took a camping trip. We went with a few of Corey's friends who were all fairly outdoorsy. Though I wasn't, I wanted him—and his friends—to think I was adventurous, outgoing, and fun. After pitching the tents, the group scattered, lounging on the rocky banks of a small stream. Corey sat next to me, casually hugging his bent knees. Exhausted from the tent-pitching effort, I laid back, propping myself up on my elbows, eyes closed and face turned up to the sun.

After a few moments, I opened my eyes and gazed over at Corey. There was a small blue and black salamander skittering over his shoulder blade toward his neck. I shrieked, startling both the salamander and Corey. The lizard froze in fear, and though Corey froze too, he was smiling. He glanced over his shoulder, just watching the shine of the lizard's blue spots on slick black skin. He stayed perfectly still, allowing the salamander to stay as long as it pleased. I was thankful that the lizard hadn't chosen me as a perch, as the presence of a lizard on my back would have brought me to my feet, frantically brushing it away, dancing and screaming until it was gone, exposing me as the opposite of adventurous, outgoing, and fun.

Corey was like this with Hayden too, calm and still. But too soon, the week ended and Corey went back to work. And Hayden began to cry. All of the time.

Through a thick veil of exhaustion and frustration, I roamed the house with a wailing baby in my arms, avoiding the unpacked boxes. The shelves held unfamiliar books. The rooms were crowded with strangers' furniture and dark still life paintings. And the baby, the only thing surely mine, was making me feel like an utter failure. I wondered if I had always been pretending to be more competent than I actually was—someone who could camp, someone who could revamp an old house, someone who was capable of caring for a newborn. The sun shone in the windows and the birds sang in the sycamores, but I couldn't appreciate any of it. This wasn't my house.

CHAPTER TWO
Tish, 1916

The March wind whipped down our narrow street, threatening to take my felt hat with it. I secured the buttons on my wool coat and gripped my cracked leather satchel. The lifting air rustled my bag and the metal tubes of paint inside the bag clinked against themselves. My chest seemed to close with the cold but I stood there, glaring at my fate, and my father, as he and a hired man carried a parade of our possessions down the steep steps of our row home.

Papa was a small, wiry man, and he grunted beneath the weight of my sister Ivy's large trunk. His mustache was wet with condensation, his serious brow wrinkled with the work. I shifted my weight from foot to foot on the cobblestones, trying to keep warm. My free hand fiddled with my long, dark braid, and I gazed up into the empty Philadelphia air knowing, no dreading, that the sky would look equally dreck at our new home only fourteen miles north. I wondered what the sky looked like out West today. Was the sun coming up and dying the horizon deep pink and gold? I exhaled, sending a plume of breath into the air that matched the titanium white atmosphere.

The front door of our townhouse stood ajar and when the wind calmed, I could hear snatches of what Mama was saying inside. "Gather your things... go outside with Tish... Stop moaning... you will be able to see William as frequently as ever..."

Ivy grumbled something that blew away on the cold breeze.

Mama appeared in the doorway, her tiny frame wrapped in a shawl. She continued, "The trolley can take William straight to Willow Grove each Saturday. You will be married by summer, and then you will have the rest of your lives to be together. You know your father is anxious to have the business up and running by the time the park opens."

Our new shop, Hess's Delicatessen, was, for my father, the culmination of years of hard work at the Navy Yard. Papa had arrived here from Germany in his youth and constantly talked about moving out of the crowded and dirty city. It showed prosperity, Papa said, truly proved that a man had made it. When he announced this past December that he had found not only a space for his delicatessen, but a building lot for a house, Mama jumped up and hugged him like it was the best present she had ever received. Ivy stormed out of the room. Papa stood proudly in front of our Christmas tree, decorated with cranberries and popcorn, arms stretched out to display the blueprint of an efficient floor plan that appealed to his everlasting German practicality. Papa pointed out the high ceilings and large windows, saying they gave a man room to breathe, as well as raise a growing family.

The house had all the modern conveniences, and now that it was finally ready, we would move to Willow Grove, despite the winter weather. It was a small town, interesting only because of world famous Willow Grove Park. With roller coasters roaring throughout the day and John Philip Sousa performing each night, the park attracted thousands of Philadelphians through its gates each week. And, Papa hoped, through his shop door as well. He, Mama, and, upon his insistence, I too, would be standing ready to serve them.

While I didn't indulge in *sturm und drang* like Ivy, it was no secret I did not want to move to Willow Grove or work in the delicatessen. It was Papa's dream and I did not begrudge him it, but it was not mine. I had little choice. I was only sixteen and stuck under Papa's strict rule.

I stood now in the cold, swallowing my resentment, and silently promising myself that I wouldn't be working at the shop for long. Willow Grove was simply a pawn's sacrifice on the way to checkmate. I only needed to wait to reach the endgame. In two short years, the shop would be up and running, successful enough to hire help. I would be eighteen, they would no longer need me, and I could pack up my easel and head west.

Papa's sharp call to Mama startled me. "Laurel, we are all packed and ready to go!"

Mama and Ivy descended the steps carrying small traveling cases. They were equally lovely versions of one another, one lithe and youthful, the other refined and wise. At nineteen, Ivy was well used to being lovely. Her auburn hair shone red even in the lowest light and her features were fine, almost birdlike. Mama had bestowed upon Ivy her Botticelli good looks, perhaps leaving too little remaining space to add her kind and generous nature. With Ivy's beauty came a laziness for everything except maintaining it, and when she didn't get what she wanted, her gorgeous indignation seemed to engulf our family.

"But Mama," Ivy whined.

Papa clapped the horse's hindquarters and said farewell to the man driving the cart. With it on its way, Papa turned and raised his hand to stop Ivy. "Enough. We will host a beautiful wedding out in the fresh country air. Our new house will have more room than here for a proper party. Now climb into the car. We should be on our way as well," he said.

"Oliver!" Mama called.

My three-year old brother, a brick of a boy, shouldered his way out the row house door. Clumsy and unaware of his own body proportions, he joined us on the street. Quickly, I grabbed his arm, his bulk squirming to be free.

"Isn't this exciting, Ollie?" I asked, opening the touring car door and gently coaxing him, and possibly myself, toward the backseat of our Ford. Mama settled into the front seat and Papa went to the front to wind up the motor.

Ivy huffed on the street next to me, "Aren't you worried? How will you ever meet a suitable man out in Willow Grove?"

Each engine crank echoed this oft-repeated conversation. Around and around. Again and again. My lack of suitors was distressing to Ivy, especially when it bolstered her own arguments against moving. I clenched my jaw against her insistence that my entire worth was wrapped up in to my ability to marry well. "If you don't find someone," she continued, "you'll have to work in Papa's shop forever. You can forget about painting anything else besides that roller coaster."

What did she know? The world was changing for women, and the country was opening up. More and more women were gaining independence, fighting to get the vote, putting off marriage, experiencing life for themselves, outside of the domestic realm. It was easier than ever to book a ticket on a westbound train, adventure deep into the United States comfortably and safely within a Pullman car. My life would be what I wanted it to be. I began to tell her this again, as I had countless times before, but she climbed quickly into the car. I sighed and followed. The engine caught and began bouncing. Papa climbed in also, shutting his door against the cold. Inside the Ford with rest of my family, I remained silent.

The few times I had ventured to discuss my plans with Papa, he had forbidden them. Because I was a girl, I was to meet a man, get married, start a family. It was unsafe, and unseemly, for a woman to travel alone out West, he argued, saying I'd be robbed and left for dead before I reached the great Mississippi. Ivy knew this, so she raised an eyebrow at me, daring me to refute her in front of Papa. Without a husband, Papa would never say yes.

Mama turned, reached over her seat, and patted my knee. "I would like to paint the roller coaster," she said. Painting was something she and I shared. She taught me, in fact. Mama indulged my desire in ways she could by purchasing me paint and taking me to art exhibitions featuring grand sweeping landscapes by American artists.

As Papa turned the car off our narrow cobblestone alley onto Broad Street, Ivy continued her well-rehearsed diatribe, "Will Tish have to marry some farmhand? Are there any people of means way out here?"

"Tish will be just fine," Mama said, turning to us again. "There are plenty of young people to meet in Willow Grove. More and more houses are being built every week, and many families come up from the city for the entire summer. Oliver! Will you please stop squirming!"

Removing his elbow from my side, I tried to turn Oliver's attention out the window. The view changed from row houses and leafless trees to yellowed fields and the occasional bright stone house. We trundled along the serpentine street and suddenly found ourselves in our tiny new village. Bumping along the plank roads, Papa began pointing out the sights.

"Welcome to Willow Grove. Welcome home. That is the post office," he called out, pointing right. We all dutifully looked at the building, its flag out front frozen to the pole by blown ice.

"And the train station." He pointed to a small station house with platforms flanking the tracks. "And here on the left is the entrance to Willow Grove Park."

The gates were closed during the off-season, and a heavy chain locked them tight. Through the wrought iron bars, flat expanses of land were visible, along with crystal ice flats of a large, frozen lake. Beyond that stood the skeletons of the rides—a circle of wires holding up floating airships, and crisscrossed wooden beams supporting the rising hills of the roller coaster.

"There it is, Tish. Your roller coaster," Ivy said, a sly smile parting her lips.

"And the shop! Our shop!" Papa said, slowing the car. A dark, unmarked storefront stood quietly between a barber shop and a bakery. The word SOLD blazed from a placard in the front window.

"There's the shop, Tish," Ivy said, her vicious grin growing larger.

We continued through town and past stately hotels and boarding houses, their pale columns and porches blending in with the graying snow on the ground. Heading up the hill, we followed trolley tracks that rutted the street below the ice. Within blocks, we turned off the main road into the Ferguson development tract. Newly delineated cinder roads squared off the lots, each empty hills of snow, except ours.

Papa parked in front of the house and we gazed up at it from the car window. It stood close to the road, tall on a hill, with three stories overlooking the area.

Papa spryly jumped out, instantly invigorated by the arrival at his new purchase. He ran around and opened the Ford's doors for Mama and Oliver. Mama's boot-clad foot stepped into the road, and then onto our sidewalk, holding the top of her hat against the wind as she tipped her head high to take in all that was newly ours.

"It's lovely, Julian. Truly lovely," Mama breathed.

Papa let out a sigh, as if he had been waiting for her confirmation.

And it was lovely. So different from the city, where house after house lined the crowded, dirty streets. Willow Grove had an openness, a lightness, so much air to call our own. I had to admit, there was green here, even in the dreck winter. Three verdant evergreens towered over the back of the house, and the trunks of the two sycamores out front were a mottled sage. I let the cold fill my lungs, breathing it in, fresh and crisp. It burned clean my nostrils and I felt like this was the first true breath I had ever taken.

We followed Papa up the five stairs to the porch. Mama lugged Oliver, thirty pounds of ornery, the two of them both tired from the journey.

Papa brandished a shiny key from the pocket of his wool trousers and approached the wide front door. Leaded glass windows with a diamond and square pattern lined the doorframe, and the pattern on the big brass knob disappeared beneath Papa's hand. The door swung open to reveal a receiving room and stairs leading up to the second floor. The dark wood floors were warm and rich like maple syrup, and the white plaster walls shone bright like whipped cream.

We all stood in the foyer, looking around, waiting on Papa to lead us in further. Sweeping ceilings and tall windows allowed rays of light to pattern the floor. Tiny rainbows danced like enchantments from the leaded glass.

"Look at the light in here, Laurel," Papa said to Mama, spreading his arms out wide. "We'll set up your easel right over here."

Tentatively, trying to hold on to my refusal to like the house, I looked around. Ivy followed me and we could hear Papa calling to us. "The third floor is your bedroom, girls!"

We took a cursory glance at the second-floor bedrooms, and then Ivy and I walked the circular staircase to the third floor. The top revealed a large single room with three dormer windows.

"Look, Ivy," I said, enthusiasm creeping up on me. "You can see the whole countryside from here! And the park."

"Hmmm, yes. Wonderful," Ivy said, wandering around the space, lost in her own thoughts and, as usual, likely not truly listening to me.

I heard the clip-clop of the horse and cart arriving and went downstairs to collect my trunk and easel. Ivy and I lugged our trunks up the stairs, first hers, then mine, and set our room up to our liking. I unpacked my spare canvases and books, stacking them within easy reach of my bed—Kafka's *Metamorphosis*, Frances Hodgson Burnett's *Secret Garden*, and Harold Bell Wright's *The Eyes of the World*. I had finished school in the city last June, and though I had done well and enjoyed it, Papa said there wasn't any money for college until the delicatessen was established and earning. I suspected he thought I was educated enough, as a woman, preferring that I marry well and start a family.

I tacked up some of my Currier and Ives prints with a certain defiance and determination, so that I could keep the Great Salt Lake and the Coast of California near.

• • •

The rest of our belongings came in the next few weeks by way of orders Mama made from the Sears catalog. Dishes, candlesticks, rugs, even the stove arrived on trucks and furnished our new nest. Papa spent the days at the shop in downtown Willow Grove while we went about cleaning and organizing the house. We hung curtains and leveled our clock on the wall in the foyer. The pendulum ticked loudly in the mostly empty rooms, chiming the hour and once each half hour, soon becoming the sound of home.

The new house felt grand and expansive. We had been so used to being packed in like oily canned fish in the row home. During the first few weeks, Mama would often arrive at the top of the stairs in our bedroom quite in a huff. "Girls, I have been calling for you to come help me in the kitchen with dinner."

"Mama, we can't hear you all the way up here," I would respond and promptly leave my reading or sketching to go help.

With a house this much larger, there was also much more to be done to keep it clean. More floor space to sweep, more area to dust, more cobwebs to dismantle, so many more windows to keep sparkling. Mama, Ivy, and I spent the days cleaning and organizing the house, but finally we had a chance to relax and paint. Mama set up her easel and began a new still life. Onions and carrots, the only things we had in the larder, served as her subject.

Eager to paint as well, I took my opportunity to sit with her, sharing the burnt sienna and yellow ochre she had doled out on to her palette. Light streamed in the windows, casting highlights on the onions and shadows below the carrots. I looked at Mama, deep in concentration next to me. Lit up by the sun like a Rembrandt painting, she was beautiful, all fine features and grace. We sat in silence until I worked up the courage to talk to her about the only thing that really mattered to me.

"Remember that painting we saw at the Academy of the Fine Arts, the one with the lake and the mountains that disappeared into the clouds?" I asked.

"Mmm-hmmm," she assented, her gaze switching between the canvas and the onions, brush hovering over the palette she now held in her hand.

"The Dougherty, I think," I said. "Wouldn't it be wonderful to paint that in person? Really be there? I bet it is like nothing we've ever seen before."

"Mmm-hmmm," Mama said.

I continued musing this way as my brush recreated the onions on the canvas and the carrots began to take shape. Despite painting the same subject matter just in front of us, our paintings were quite different.

She put down her brush and looked at me, the look she gave me letting me know she wasn't as distracted as she seemed. "Tish," she began, in her lecture tone, "I think it is wonderful that you have dreams and plans for the future, and I hope that one day you get to achieve them all. But don't forget to be happy in the meantime. If you focus completely on being happy later, you'll miss all the wonders that are in your life now. We only have so much time here on this earth. Don't wish it away by looking ahead so much. Keep sight of your future, but be sure to find happiness in today." The clock chimed five o'clock and Mama plunked her brush into the mineral spirits. "Well, time to begin real life again. What shall we have for dinner?"

Papa arrived home from the shop, declaring that the countertops and the front sign had been installed. We sat at our new long dining room table, so used to bumping elbows that we laughed at how far we had to reach to pass the meal to one another. Papa was in a good mood, king of his castle, and Mama beamed as if she were his queen. The final gasps of the winter wind ripped past our windows, and I tried to be happy within our new walls.

• • •

The winter soon thawed and the sunshine of April and May came to Willow Grove. Emerging from our cocoons like city butterflies, we reveled in the small patch of land we now called our own. During the week, we all went down to the delicatessen to help Papa in his preparations, but on the weekends, we spent time outside planting blackberries, apple and peach saplings, and digging beds for fall vegetables. Papa built a chicken coop. Bud bundles appeared on the forsythia that grew wild, and buttercups sprouted brightly in the grass along the roads. We flung the windows open to the scented springtime air and could listen to the sound of nearby church bells tolling noon. Their song floated in on the warm breeze, complimenting the chimes of the clock in the foyer.

Oliver and I had been sent down to the shop with Papa that morning. We worked hard, wiping clean the new cold cases, mopping the floor, and working on price lists. Papa tested the scale, practiced punching in a few sales, and reviewed his order from the purveyors. Oliver and I began unloading the canned and jarred goods from wooden crates. I pried a crate open and lifted out glass jar after glass jar of gherkins. The last jar slipped from my grip and shattered all over the floor. Glass shards gleamed in a splash of brine and shiny green gherkins rolled away from me like logs on a river.

"Tish!" Papa yelled as he came running.

"Papa, I'm sorry..." I gingerly stepped over the mess to get the dustpan.

Papa got there first. Exasperation colored his face vermilion and with a tight mouth, he shooed us out of the shop with his broom. Oliver and I trudged up the hill toward home.

I berated myself the entire way. "See, Oliver, that is why I shouldn't be working in the shop." He just skipped ahead, nonplussed.

At home, Mama had the table set for her and Ivy. Forced to explain why we were home earlier than expected, she shook her head but patted my shoulder and set another two spots at the table. We ate cream of celery soup, sopping up the dregs with crusty slices of buttered bread. Ivy ate little, and when Mama prodded her, she protested. "I'm too nervous to eat, Mama. William will be here in the morning," she said, her voice tinged with anticipation.

They would spend Saturday together before he returned on the trolley to Philadelphia. Papa had given them permission to stroll about Willow Grove Park and even watch the electric fountain and fireworks after Sousa's band played its final show that evening.

Ivy had been putting off the visit until we had the house in order. William came from a wealthy family in the Chestnut Hill section of the city, and Ivy was certainly marrying up.

"Mama, will you please make sure that everything is perfect when William arrives? It is his first time here and I want him to be pleased with the house." Ivy continued, "I'm certain his parents will ask him all about it, especially since we are hosting the wedding party. I want to show him all around, even out back. Oh, I am so excited to see him, Mama! I have never been away from him so long! I hope he missed me as much as I missed him. Everything must be just right when he arrives."

"Yes, Ivy," Mama sighed, taking her final spoonful of soup and dabbing her mouth with the linen napkin from her lap. "We will do the sweeping today and begin the washing right away to ensure that everything is off the line by tomorrow morning. The weather looks fine for drying tonight, so perhaps we should get started. If you help me, we can accomplish nearly everything today and we will have more time for your hair in the morning."

"But, Mama, I need to iron my dress and..." Ivy trailed off, seeing the stern look that Mama was giving her.

"I'll help you, Mama," I said. I gave the last hunk of my bread to Oliver, who took it greedily in one big chubby-cheeked bite.

"Thank you, Tish. And Oliver, please, that is too much in your mouth at once." Mama began clearing the dishes.

The doorbell rang, the single chime still unfamiliar to us. Our first visitor gave Ivy the distraction she needed to sneak upstairs and begin her primping preparations. Mama continued clearing the table and headed to the kitchen, nodding at me to answer the door.

"Come on, Ollie. Let's see who it is," I said, encouraging Oliver up out of his seat. His little hand in mine, together we walked through the foyer to greet our visitor.

On our front step stood a girl about my age, brandishing a pie. I could see her through the large panel of glass on our front door. She was swaying slightly, perhaps impatiently, but she turned her head and smiled at our approach. Her blonde hair was softly pulled back into a twist at the nape of her neck and she wore a straw hat embellished with small red flowers. Her eyes were bright and friendly and I got the feeling that she would boisterously wave at me by way of initial greeting, had she not been holding the pastry.

We opened the door and she immediately started talking, rapidly and excitedly. "Hello there! I'm Virginia Howerth. My mother sent over this Montgomery Pie to welcome you to the neighborhood. We live down on Cherry Street, and your new shop is right next to ours. The barber? Anyway, Mother wanted to come last week, but our shop is so busy. Even today, well, she wanted to come, but she had to stay and help Daddy, so she sent me up. I hope that I didn't interrupt your luncheon..." She finally took a breath and held the pie out for me to take.

"No, we are finished. Thank you for the pie. Please, would you like to come in?" I asked, taking the pie in my free hand and shuffling backward with Oliver, who clutched my hand tighter and sidled halfway behind me, peering around at Virginia. "Mama," I called toward the kitchen, "A Miss Virginia Howerth is here, and she has brought a pie from her mother."

Mama emerged into the foyer, still carrying a dish towel and wiping dry her hands. "Oh, how very kind of your mother, Virginia. This looks wonderful. Thank you very much."

"You are welcome, Mrs. Hess," Virginia smiled.

"Seems you have met my daughter, Tish. She looks to be about your age, sixteen, correct?" Mama asked and Virginia nodded with a grin. "And this is our son, Oliver. My eldest, Ivy, is upstairs in preparations for a very important visitor tomorrow. Perhaps you'll have to meet her later." Mama took the pie from me and ushered Virginia into the dining room. Oliver and I closed the door and followed the sound of Virginia still chatting to our mother, answering her polite conversation starters.

"We are happy to have a new business next to our shop. I see it will be a delicatessen?" she asked. "How wonderful! It's a good location. Daddy's barbershop gets all the business from the Mineral Springs Hotel. When a guest needs a shave or a haircut, Mr. Ehrenpfort—he's the owner of the Mineral Springs Hotel—sends them right over. In fact, all the local businessmen come down for a cut from Daddy. Mr. Robinson, you know, the newspaper man, was just in last Saturday, and Mr. Malcolm, who owns the lumber yard, stops in for a trim every Wednesday on his way to work. Perhaps Mr. Hess needs a new local barber now, too?"

"I will certainly tell him there is a very capable barber in town, thank you," Mama answered, offering her a seat at the dining room table. "Tish, please refresh this pitcher of lemonade and bring in a glass for our guest." Oliver settled on Mama's lap and I went into the kitchen, listening to Virginia's continued chatter.

When I arrived back, Virginia was saying, "There sure are, Mrs. Hess. In fact, tonight there is a dance over at the park. My mother is chaperoning. Perhaps Tish might be able to join us." Virginia raised a mischievous eyebrow at me, but lowered it as soon as Mama's gaze fell on her. I handed Virginia a glass of lemonade and sat back down at the table.

Though it seemed Mama wanted me to socialize, perhaps she had sewing circles in mind rather than dances. After a long draught of her own lemonade and some thought, Mama looked at me and said, "Well, I think it would be very nice for you to attend, Tish. A fine way to meet other people your age. And since it will be chaperoned, if you wish, you may go."

Not waiting for my answer, Virginia stood and rushed around the table to my side, clutching my arm as if we were already great friends. "Wonderful! It will be so much fun! Shall we walk over together? My mother and I will meet you downtown at the trolley entrance to the park at seven. Have you ever been to the park? It's marvelous at night. You'll love it. We'll walk you home when it's over." She rushed to the door. "Thank you, Mrs. Hess, for the lemonade. And Tish, I'll see you later this evening. I simply must get home. Goodbye!"

Stunned, we remained at the table listening to the front door opening. "Please thank your mother for me, Virginia. I look forward to meeting her!" Mama called nearly too late; the door slammed and Virginia was gone. To me, Mama said, "She certainly has a lot of vigor. If you do not want to go to the dance, I can call 'round the barbershop and decline for you."

"No, Mama, it's fine. But thank you. I do want to go. It would be exciting to see the park, and perhaps I would meet some new people. It sounds like Virginia knows everyone in this town."

"Yes, I'll say she likely does," Mama said with a smile. "I'm glad you are going to attend. It will do you good to get out and meet some people who exist right here. We've been cooped up inside too long this winter. Let's get started on today's chores and we'll see what we have for you to wear."

• • •

Papa walked in the door at five-thirty and loosened his tie. With a chaste kiss for Mama on the cheek, he settled himself in his wingback chair with the day's newspaper. I greeted him and received in return the briefest of smiles before he returned his attention to his reading. Perhaps he was still angry about the broken gherkin jar. Oliver jumped onto his lap, peppering him with questions and observations of the day. Papa did not tolerate his boisterous squirming long and once the paper began to crinkle and become unreadable, he sent Oliver off to the kitchen with the task of discovering dinner's start time.

Tonight, Mama and I had prepared a ham pie. Ivy attempted to help, but mostly she fretted and wandered, picking up a carrot, then placing it back down, distracted and anxious. Finally, Mama sent Ivy out to the dining room to set the table, and she and I finished in companionable silence.

"Tish, thank you for helping. Here now, all ready. Please take this to the table, eat quickly, and then go up and put your dress on. Arrange your hair in a tidy braid, and then perhaps your Sunday hat?" Mama bustled and planned seamlessly, perhaps a little too excited.

After dinner, I raced upstairs. With Ivy still at the table pushing her food around on her plate, I had the room to myself. From the front window of our bedroom, I could see the lights coming on at the park. The tall Ferris Wheel spun in a lazy circle, its cars stopping and swaying at intervals. The roller coaster's peaks crested above the trees and the cars rattled as they raced on parallel wooden tracks, the cries of the riders like the distant crash of ocean waves. There was music, and if I strained, I could hear a few distant notes. A swell of excitement found its way from my stomach to my throat and caught there. I put on my white dress and tied the black sash around my waist. Brushing through my long, thick hair, I secured it in a fat braid trailing down my back. I found a ribbon among Ivy's things, hoped she wouldn't notice that I borrowed it, and tied it to the bottom of my hair.

I descended the stairs and found Papa pacing in the foyer. Mama had asked him to walk me down to meet Mrs. Howerth and Virginia, and although he agreed, his face now showed consternation. I hesitated, my bouncing gait slowing, and cautiously asked, "Ready to go, Papa?"

"I just don't know about this, Tish. You are only sixteen, I don't know the Howerths, and the park is known for its riff-raff," Papa said, moving back and forth across the floor and worrying his hand through his thinning and greased-back hair.

Mama entered the foyer just then and, taking my arm on one side and his arm on the other, walked us toward the door, saying, "Julian, the park is known for its superior police force, in place for the specific purpose of women feeling safe there unaccompanied. She will be fine. Have a lovely time, Tish."

Sighing, Papa walked out the front door and down the porch steps. Smiling gratefully at Mama, I quickened my step after him, my braid bouncing against my lower back at each step. Papa and I walked together toward town. It was a clear night, warm and calm. Quietly, twilight was falling and the stars were beginning to peek out. The streets were nearly empty, and the few houses we passed along Easton Road were glowing yellow from within. At Papa's pace, I double-stepped to keep up.

He was still very quiet, so I ventured, "Papa, I'm sorry about the gherkins this morning."

Papa sighed. "Tish, if you are going to be working in the shop, you need to be more careful, more present of mind. Those gherkins cost money, and we can't afford to waste before we even get started."

"I know, Papa. I'll try to be more careful. But honestly, Papa, maybe it is best if you hire someone else? Someone more permanent?"

"We cannot afford that right now. I need you to help the family," he said with finality.

Everything inside me screamed to further declare my independence, insist to him that I wouldn't stay and help the family, how I would go, and soon. Instead I just nodded and kept quiet. It was a fight for another time.

We approached the center of town. Mrs. Howerth, a stout, stern woman with a military air, was waiting next to Virginia at the triangular meeting of streets that was the middle of Willow Grove. Both mother and daughter were dressed in fine clothing, though Virginia wore white and Mrs. Howerth a dull gray. Both wore straw hats, Virginia's the one I had admired earlier in the day.

When we approached, Mrs. Howerth extended her hand, palm down, for Papa to grasp. He did, cordially, and thanked her for her pie Virginia brought earlier. "I am sure the family is enjoying it right now," he said with a nod back up the hill toward our house. "And thank you for taking Tish with you tonight. I expect that the dance will be over by ten o'clock, and that you will come right home afterward?"

"Yes, Mr. Hess. I will be with the young ladies the entire evening. We will go to the dance and then come home directly. There is time enough later in the season for rides and such," Mrs. Howerth said, shooting a sideways look at Virginia. I gleaned that there may have been a debate about this earlier that Virginia did not win. Virginia pursed her lips briefly and then smiled at me.

"Well, then. All right. Tish, have a nice time," Papa said with thinly veiled reluctance. He handed me a little spending money and with a brusque pat on my shoulder, turned to walk back up the hill toward home.

"Well, ladies, it is getting late. Shall we be off?" It was a question, but seemed more like a command, as Mrs. Howerth's back was already turned to us as she briskly walked toward the park entrance.

"Yes, ma'am," Virginia and I chimed together, falling in step behind her. Virginia smiled at me and we entered the park.

The main entrance sat just past the superintendent's stone house, and we walked along a landscape lined path. Along the flat green expanse, other paths diverted to the left and around small ponds. Mrs. Howerth walked straight ahead with purpose, and we followed after her. Crossing over Moreland Road, we continued along the path and past the large lake with the electric fountain. It was too early for the lights to illuminate the waters in color, so we marched on toward the casino building. The bandstand, looking just like an open clam shell, was on the left. There was another pond to our right. I swiveled my head in both directions to see it all while staying closely on the brisk heels of our chaperone. The same faint music I could hear from my bedroom was loud now, tinny and repeating in a short loop of song as the carousel horses circled. Lights blinked from the games, and vendors called out their wares.

Mrs. Howerth abruptly stopped and turned, entering a large hall with a blazing sign reading *Dance Land*. Virginia and I entered through a wrought iron arched doorway that opened into an empty and cavernous space. There were stairs on either side of the entrance leading to a balcony that surrounded the entire room. Seating lined the outer wall. The ten-piece band was just setting up, and Mrs. Howerth left us to approach them, her heels clacking loudly across the floor.

Alone now, Virginia said, "Tonight is going to be such fun!" She turned to face me full on and grasped my arms.

"Are you looking forward to seeing someone in particular?" I asked, aware I was, perhaps, prying a bit, but interested in getting to know my new friend.

"Oh, no. Certainly not. There will be lots of boys here tonight, townies mostly, but they are too young and unestablished. I intend to marry someone who has already amassed some money and influence." She lowered her voice conspiratorially. "There are plenty of men who come in to Daddy's shop and have their eye on me, you know. Most are married, but some..." She trailed off, unwilling to give any more. "But, before I marry an old man with lots and lots of money, I intend to have a little fun with the young boys!" Virginia grinned and quickly checked to be sure her mother was out of earshot.

I was amused, and liked the bright boldness of Virginia. It was suddenly easy to open up when she asked me, "What kind of boy do you like, Tish?"

"I don't really like the idea of settling down right away." Virginia looked at me as if I were joking. "No, really," I insisted. "I'd like to travel a bit, maybe live in a few different places. Do you know anyone around here who thinks like that?"

"I'm not sure." She looked thoughtfully at the ceiling and continued, "Most of these boys are just going to do what their fathers do, right here in Willow Grove. I had my eye on Paul Robinson for a while; he lives around the corner from you. His father owns the newspaper. Now, he would have been a good man for either of us. His family travels abroad all the time, sometimes for half of the year. But he married a girl he met in college." Virginia sighed wistfully at her opportunity lost.

"Hmmm, well, I certainly don't have to meet the man I am going to marry tonight. In a few years, I can travel west on my own, paint the mountains out there..." I suddenly fell silent. I had never actually expressed this wish to a stranger before. And here I had said it, right out loud, let it echo in this cavernous hall. Perhaps the dream was getting so big it couldn't be contained any longer.

"West? Like Colorado or California?" Virginia asked, only half listening, slightly twirling her hips and, I guessed, imagining the dancing to come later that evening.

I nodded casually, trying in vain to make it seem less important. "It can be anywhere that is new and exciting and full of color. I was just recently reading *The Eyes of the World*, and it is all about California, the mountains, the palm trees, the orange groves. I have never seen anyplace like that. Wouldn't you love to live in a place so interesting, or at least experience it?"

"I suppose I might, but I am happy right here. This park makes our town exciting enough, and there are lots of new houses being built every day. Important people come here all the time, sometimes to live. Willow Grove is going to be something. You'll see. And I am going to be one of the most influential ladies here." With a big spin, Virginia opened her arms wide and looked almost theatrical in her declaration.

We stopped chatting as other young people started filing in. The girls entered arm in arm, twittering in each other's ears and quietly giggling under hand-covered mouths. There was not one among them so bold as Virginia. She and I watched them file through the arch. I stood silently observing and she called out friendly greetings, waving her hand high in the air and flapping her wrist. Wearing white dresses with dark stockings and boots, most girls took off their simple straw hats upon arrival, revealing softly secured low buns or long braids. They collected like fish caught in a small pool, despite the cavernous room. Gathered tightly in one area, there was safety in numbers.

The boys were raucous and pushing, their hair slick under their straw and banded hats. Most wore high-waisted three-piece suits, a bit loose, as if they were borrowed from an older brother or father, and lace-up boots. The park had a strict dress code, but Mrs. Howerth seemed the type of woman to require refinement at an event like this, even if the park didn't.

Despite their attire, there was little formality about these boys. They all seemed to expect a loud and boisterous evening. Seeing them arrive, and hearing their echoing voices race around the space, Mrs. Howerth left her post instructing the band and approached the swell. She clapped her hands, hard and loud like a schoolmarm.

"Gentlemen, please," she bellowed once she had enough of their attention. "The band will begin to play in just a few moments. I trust that we will all behave like the ladies and gentlemen we are while we dance. I will be watching from the refreshment table." A stern look completed her speech, though when she turned her back, the volume level rose again quickly.

Soon, the band began to play and couples formed on the expansive dance floor. I watched as Virginia paired off with different boys, song after song. There were a few fellows who looked my way, but just momentarily before their eyes found a partner that they wanted.

Wishing I had brought my sketchbook to keep me occupied, or at least help me feel like less of a wallflower, I gazed around the room. Across the hall, my eyes fell on a man standing alone. He was particularly tall and slightly older than the rest of us. He showed no interest in anyone there and I couldn't shake the feeling that he was lurking. I continued to look around the room, but was drawn back to him suddenly. I could feel his eyes on me. He held my gaze, almost wolfishly, but without menace. He wore a blue jacket and untailored pants. His face was handsome, with dark brows and deep eyes, and I was unable to look away.

Virginia arrived, bouncing, at my side. Her firm grasp of my arm broke my eye contact with the man in the blue jacket, and I turned to be dragged to the refreshment table.

"Have you danced yet, Tish?" Virginia asked, not stopping but craning her head and neck back toward me.

"No, I haven't been asked yet," I replied, embarrassed to have to say it aloud.

"Let's get a glass of punch, and after that, I will introduce you to people. They may not be world travelers, but they'll do for a dance," Virginia winked at me and with her standing next to me, it didn't take long. Two fellows sauntered up as one song ended and both seemed in pursuit of Virginia. Arriving at the same time, she guessed their intentions and didn't allow them to speak. Holding out her hands to both of them she said, "Joe, Frank, this is my friend Tish. She recently moved here, and this is her first dance. Joe, I'll dance with you first while Frank and Tish dance. Then, next song we will switch partners." Without giving anyone the chance to object, she dragged Joe onto the dance floor, leaving Frank and me awkwardly behind.

"Tish, is it?" he asked politely. I nodded. "I'm Frank Leeds," he said. "Would you care to dance a bit?"

Clearly, I was the consolation prize, the duty that needed to be undertaken to curry favor with Virginia, but I nodded again and we entered the dance floor. We struggled for small talk, and though Frank was handsome and kind, he seemed simple and I was barely interested. I was grateful to be dancing, but now that I was, I enjoyed myself less than I expected. As we spun around the floor, my eyes continually found the man in the blue jacket. And he was watching me. I felt uneasy, but thrilled somehow as well.

The song ended and Frank dropped his arms, turning to find Virginia quickly. Joe joined me, somewhat reluctantly. Joe was not as attractive as Frank, but he was gregarious and funny. He cracked jokes and we laughed.

Perhaps because Joe and Frank had danced with me, the other boys began to warm up and a few sidled over and introduced themselves. We danced to a few songs and then moved on to other partners. Everyone was very cordial, but none were worth a repeat performance. The man in the blue jacket never moved from his place against the wall, but every time I looked at him, he was looking at me. I waited for him to ask me to dance, but the evening began winding down. As Virginia and I prepared to leave, I looked at him once more, only to find that he was gone and that I was disappointed.

The night was dark, the stars blocked from view by the electric lights that illuminated the vendor stands along the midway. We walked past the fountain, now lit and dancing, its colors changing from red to green as we strolled by. Further, the moon shone its perfect circle reflection off the lake. There was a chill in the air, and Virginia and I huddled close to each other a few steps behind Mrs. Howerth.

Hoping we were far enough back that she couldn't hear us, Virginia asked me, "Did you fancy anyone you danced with tonight?"

"I thought Joe was very funny, and Frank was handsome, but I think they both preferred dancing with you," I answered without the slightest feeling of jealousy.

"How about the other fellows that you danced with. Anyone memorable?"

"Honestly, no." I hesitated, curiosity getting the better of me. "Did you see that man in the blue jacket? He wasn't dancing, just, well just sort of standing at the edge of the dance floor."

"No, I didn't see him. Why? Was he handsome?"

"Yes, but, well never mind. I just thought you might have known who he was." I wanted to stop thinking about him. "How about you? Who did you enjoy dancing with the most?"

"Well, Frank certainly is handsome, but his father only has about six acres of farmland up in Hatboro. He has an older brother, also, who is sure to inherit the farm, so Frank will likely just work under him there. That isn't what I want out of life, so while Frank may be handsome, he's not for me. Joe is so funny, isn't he? Too funny, perhaps, though. Not serious enough about anything to get very far in life. Like I said, this was just a fun Friday night. I don't want anything more from any of these young boys than a dance and a laugh."

Mrs. Howerth turned back to find us straggling quite far behind and called to us to catch up. "Mr. Hess will likely want his daughter back before dawn, Virginia. Please stop dawdling."

We quickened our step to catch up, and turned our conversation to less private matters. The park was still full of visitors getting refreshments, playing games, and awaiting the nightly show. Fireworks streaked the sky and crashed through the night as we exited the park. I gaped at them over my shoulder, but Mrs. Howerth and Virginia barely gave them a glance.

When we arrived at my house, the electric lights were still on in the front room. I thanked Mrs. Howerth for allowing me to attend the dance and gave Virginia a quick squeeze before alighting the stairs to the porch and the front door. With a quick backward wave, I entered the house.

Papa was seated in his chair, his black notebook of recipes on his lap, pencil furiously scratching down new notes.

"How was your evening, Tish?" he asked.

"Fine. Thank you for allowing me to go."

"Good, good. I'm glad," Papa said, stifling a yawn. "You can thank your mother. I would have preferred that you stay here and not risked any trouble down there at the park. Now up to bed, both of us. I suppose the perfect potato salad recipe can wait until morning." He rose slowly from his chair and stretched. He closed the recipe book and motioned for me to go upstairs.

● ● ●

The next day was warm for May. Sunlight streamed in the tall windows and woke the house early. Ivy, suddenly alert and full of instructions, sat across from me at the breakfast table. She quickly forked eggs into her mouth, muffling her constant directions.

"Breathe, Ivy. Please slow down. We will get everything accomplished before William arrives," Mama said, a lilt of amusement in her voice. Her eyes found Papa's over his steaming cup of coffee, and she gave him a wistful smile. He grinned, a bit foolishly, back at her. After all these years, I could see love in their eyes, even over shirred eggs at a formal breakfast table.

At eighteen, my mother had married my father, twelve years her senior. When they met, he was new in town, but he worked hard to make a new life for himself in Philadelphia. Desperately trying to shake his German accent and prove his loyalty to his new homeland, he was happy when a gentle American girl showed interest in his serious demeanor, and he made her his bride. It had taken him nearly twenty years, but now he had provided his family with their own business and home.

Ivy shoved her plate back and pushed her chair away from the table, announcing, "William's trolley arrives at ten forty-five, and his letter said he would walk right here. It is nearly eight thirty. I should be getting ready."

Attempting to delay her retreat, Mama quickly instructed, "Please remain at the table while everyone is still eating. And then, after that, you can help me with the morning dishes. We certainly cannot have dirty dishes lying around when William arrives."

"Yes, Mama," Ivy sighed.

I continued to eat my eggs and griddle cakes, thinking about my own plans for the day.

Mama turned to me and asked, "How was the dance last night, Tish?"

"It was lovely, Mama. The music was very nice, and Virginia has a lot of friends to whom she introduced me."

"What was the park like?" Ivy asked. "I can't wait to take William there. First, we'll ride the rides, then we'll stroll through the gardens..." She droned on and I tuned out. I would be happy to have Ivy out of the house. Once William arrived, this flurry of activity would calm down and then, perhaps if it were warm enough, I might be able to find a spot outside to set up my easel. The forsythia blooms were beginning to wither and I wanted to capture their sunny stalks before it was too late. I had some Cadmium yellow left that could be mixed with Titanium white...

Ivy's shriek brought me back from my daydream.

"Why, Mama, you can't be serious!" I heard Ivy complain. "I haven't seen William in two months and now you are going to make me take Tish along for the entire day?"

Confused, I tried to piece together what had just happened. I had no intention of spending the day with Ivy and William.

"Papa, please," Ivy implored, turning her entire body toward him.

"No, your mother is right," he said. "Perhaps, for appearance's sake, it would be better if Tish accompanied you today."

"But William and I are to be married in a month. There is nothing improper about the two of us being alone together," Ivy protested.

"All the more reason—you will have your entire lives together. What is one afternoon with your sister?" Mama's insistent tone finished the discussion.

In a boiling fury, Ivy excused herself from the table and brought her plate into the kitchen. I followed her in, carrying the remainder of the plates. I stood next to Ivy at the sink, feeling the heat of her impotent wrath. Silently and cautiously, I began to help her wash up.

"I'll stay out of your way today, Ivy," I ventured quietly, lest Mama and Papa hear. "I'm really sorry that Mama and Papa are making me come with you. I'll bring my sketchbook, walk down to the park with you, and then find a bench. When you are ready to go home, swing by and fetch me. If we walk back together, Mama will think we were together all day."

She remained silent, fuming, passing me clean dishes to dry. When we finished, she went upstairs to our room to get ready. I reluctantly followed her, supposing that I, too, should be ready to go out for the day. While Ivy brushed her silky hair and twisted it softly up at the nape of her neck, she hummed to herself, clearly calmed by the sight of her reflection. I plaited my dark hair down my back. Deciding it looked juvenile, I took out the braid and rewove it to resemble something closer to Ivy's coif. Though I could never attain her natural beauty, I was pleased with my appearance and went downstairs, leaving Ivy and her humming behind.

• • •

It was a grand reunion. William rushed in the front door, squeezing both of Ivy's hands in his and declaring earnestly how much he had missed her. He was classically handsome, dressed in a high-waisted brown suit and straw hat.

He removed the hat when he stepped inside, shaking Papa's hand in a friendly greeting and then smoothing his side-parted blond hair. He presented Oliver with a small chocolate while gently grinding his knuckles into Oliver's plump cheek.

Mama invited him to sit down in the parlor, but Ivy insisted on a tour, showing him the highlights of where the wedding ceremony would be held, and where the food would be set up, and the musicians, and the punch. Papa trailed behind them, eagerly receiving William's compliments on the spaciousness of the home and the land that was contained within our double lot. It was improper for William to go upstairs, so Ivy told him all about the amazing view from our window, how we could see the fireworks from the park, and sometimes even hear the music wafting in. It was as if, given the opportunity to brag, she suddenly liked our home.

"Well, don't get too settled, my darling," William said to her. "Soon we'll have our own space, though not quite this impressive, I'm afraid." With one statement, he had deftly pleased both Ivy and Papa. We all sat in the parlor, and Mama appeared with tall glasses of lemonade.

"How's business, William?" Papa asked from his chair. William regaled us with stories from the bank in the city where he was quickly moving up in management. His father was a banker, and they had a grand old house in Chestnut Hill. Though his parents had offered him a nest egg when he and Ivy got engaged, William had turned it down, along with the seven-bedroom starter house down the block from his parents' fine estate on Seminole Street, preferring to make his own way in the world. I admired that in him, especially since I knew Ivy desperately wanted that well-appointed Colonial.

"The talk abroad about the European war is a little unsettling to our big investors," William said, "but we're counting on Mr. Wilson to keep his promise of America remaining uninvolved." Ivy beamed in pride next to him on the chaise lounge. "And how is the shop coming along, Mr. Hess?" William asked.

"Good, good. A little delayed in the opening, but it is planned for next week."

"Wonderful. And what a beautiful setting we will have here for the wedding! My mother will just love it, and she has asked me to extend her offer to help any way she can," William said, attempting to sound sincere.

Of course, his mother was going to look right down her nose at this relatively humble house. I had only met her once, but I envisioned her haughtily floating around the reception party, quietly judging behind her pinched face and greeting people only after they spoke to her. Some of the Chestnut Hill society would be invited, of course, and so they would likely tightly pack together, afraid middle-class lower earning potential might be contagious.

"We are looking forward to seeing them again," Mama said, genuine and self-secure.

The conversation continued over the particulars of the wedding and finally Mama excused herself and pulled me with her to prepare the luncheon. Oliver tagged along and occupied himself near our feet, zooming wooden cars along the floor of the kitchen. We laid out the thinly sliced meat and cheese. Mama brought out her bright orange gelatin salad. It was stippled with peaches and Bing cherries, a blizzard of coconut on top. I carried a tall sweating pitcher of lemonade to the dining room as Mama announced that the meal was ready.

Over lunch, I listened as my family discussed the wedding, the honeymoon plans and the newlywed cottage, subjects that held my interest only slightly. I made myself a sandwich and ate, almost knowing what was going to be said next. Everything was always so familiar. Even in this new house, the furniture and its configuration was the same. Our familial habits and the intonation of their voices had an invariable lilt. I knew exactly what this bread, this meat slathered with mustard, was going to taste like. The bright tang of the mustard would always be muted slightly by the greased turkey breast, and by its absorption into the deep crevasses of the pillowy bread. Mama's signature gelatin salad, which people loved for its consistency, turned my stomach in its familiarity. I yearned for something new. I lost my appetite and left most of my sandwich untouched.

"Tish... Tish..." Somewhere distant, someone was saying my name. I brought my mind back around to the conversation at the table.

"Yes, I'm sorry. What were you saying?" I looked up, hopeful that my face feigned interest and that I could sustain it for the entire afternoon.

• • •

The air was warm and muggy as we walked toward the park. I trailed a safe distance behind Ivy and William. She clung to him like he was a raft in a storm, her arm linked in his. Bored, I kicked up the cinders on the road, making a scuffing sound and dirtying my stockings with clouds of dust. Ivy's face grumbled at me with each glance back. We entered the park at the same place as last night, right past the superintendent's house, but this time, I followed William and Ivy as they wound around slowly on the various paths, past the flowers and the paisley-shaped ponds.

The park sounds weighed heavy in the humid air. Through the song of the carousel and the chiming of the games, I could hear the flirtatious lilt of Ivy's voice. We joined the swarm of people on the midway, the large open space lined with games and vendors, and William paused at a booth to buy some popcorn. In the crush of people, I had to stay closer to them than any of us wanted. They did not share their popcorn with me, and shot ahead as often as possible. I kept my eyes on them and followed through the well-dressed crowd.

Soon, the park guests diffused, floating in various directions and filtering around the grounds. We passed the Dance Land where the dance had been held, and approached the rides. Ahead of me, I could see the entrance to the rides: The Coal Mine, Venice, the Toboggan, and The Scenic Mountain Railway roller coaster. As we wandered by the Mirror Maze, I searched for a bench and wondered what Ivy and William would ride first.

"Ride one with us, will you Tish?" William asked, earning a frown from Ivy.

I nodded and followed them to the line and then through the turnstile of the Flying Airships. The man collecting the coins at the front wore the uniform of park employees, with a metal change-maker strapped around his waist. The skin on his face glistened in the heat, and it had a sun-beaten olive tone. He was tall, with dark hair. He turned and I saw blazing brown eyes that I recognized immediately. He was the man from the dance last night. A crooked grin softened his stare as he seemed to recognize me too. I was startled, and self-consciously smoothed my hair. I held his eyes for a moment, but looked away first.

He took William's fare for the three of us and then ushered William and Ivy into an airship. He pressed a button at his control panel and they moved slowly away. An empty airship, hung from two cables, floated toward me. He said nothing, but offered his hand in assistance. I took it, feeling a shiver of electricity in the depth of my belly, and climbed onto the ride.

There was a heavy click and the airship raised up into the air, elevated and swinging around in dizzying circles until finally slowing back to earth. We disembarked on the other side and Ivy turned on me. "I'd really like some time with William. Alone," she hissed under her breath.

"Alone?" I asked, incredulous, and spreading my arms out wide to illustrate my point. "There are thousands of people here!"

Ivy audibly sighed. "You know just what I mean, Tish. Mama and Papa made you come with me, but you promised that you wouldn't hang around all day. You promised!"

"Yes, all right, I did. Enjoy the park. Come find me when you are ready to go home."

Ivy grabbed the popcorn box out of William's snacking hands and held it out to me as some sort of consolation. "Here, you can have this."

I took the popcorn and wandered toward a bench out of the sun. Watching Ivy and William walk away, I grabbed a handful of the warm popcorn and shoved some into my mouth. The slick butter and salty coating instantly made me thirsty. I should have asked William to get me a drink before they left. Placing the popcorn down on the seat next to me, I pulled my small sketchbook out of my satchel and began to draw the roller coaster. I enjoyed the task, but grumbled at how Ivy had fulfilled her prophecy of me painting the roller coaster by abandoning me here at the park. The sounds surrounding me were distracting at first, the crowd chatter and the clacking roller coaster crashing in on my concentration, but soon I was well into the drawing and I might as well have been alone.

"That's pretty good," someone said.

I was startled, and looked up. It was the man in the blue jacket, which I now understood to be the park's uniform. As he looked down at me, I noticed that his dark hair had a slight wave to it and, despite the hair tonic that shone in it, yearned to be free.

"Thank you," I said. I wasn't sure I wanted to start a conversation. I turned back to my drawing, bringing out the shadows cast by the trees.

The man helped himself to the seat on the bench next to me and began to read a book. I recognized the dust jacket of *The Eyes of the World*, the same as sat on my bookshelf at home.

After a few moments, he looked up. "Have you read this?" he asked, holding it out to me.

"I have," I said.

"It takes place in my home state," he said. He sighed and stretched his arms across the back ledge, his legs out straight in front of him, crossing them at the ankles.

"You are from California?" I asked, my voice pricking with interest and something I recognized as jealousy.

"Yes," was all he said.

There was so much I wanted to know! How did he get here from there? Why did he choose to leave a state that seemed so full of color and adventure? Did he spend time in the mountains? Were the mountains as big as they seemed in the paintings? Was it always warm? What did the Pacific Ocean look like?

This man sitting inches from me on the bench had lived in a place that I so desperately wanted to explore; he had lived a life I so desperately wanted to live, but we had not been introduced and I couldn't simply pepper him with all of my questions.

"Have you been there? To California?" he asked.

"Not yet."

"Not yet?" He sniffed. "How's a girl like you, who gets dragged around a dance by her friend, and dragged around the park by—who was that—your sister, going to ever get to California? Did you pick out a husband at the dance last night to take you there?"

I was aghast. "You don't know what kind of girl I am. You don't even know me. And how could you, lurking in the corner all night long?"

"Ah ha. I knew you were watching me."

"It was you who was watching me!" I cried, but instantly regretted it. I flushed deep crimson. How could I be so bold? I had to turn the conversation to something more civilized. "There are some wonderful paintings depicting California on display downtown at the Pennsylvania Academy of the Fine Arts.

Huge sky and sprawling mountains. There just seems to be so much air. Do you know the art work of Albert Bierstadt? Or Paul Dougherty?"

He laughed and stood up. Instead of answering, he stretched his arms out wide and arched his back, letting out a groan. "I'm Ellis."

"I'm Letitia, but everyone calls me Tish," I said.

We shook hands and he said, "Let's walk around a bit. I'll tell you everything you want to know about California. Besides, I bet that popcorn is making you thirsty."

Popcorn surely makes everyone thirsty, but I couldn't help feeling that maybe he did know me.

• • •

After getting a boysenberry juice from a nearby vendor, Ellis and I strolled the grounds of the park, finding ourselves back around the big lake. The grassy areas surrounding the paths were lush and ripe in the early spring, but quite manicured and forced. I sipped my drink and brushed aside a flowering branch that was hanging over the path. Its delicate blossoms were just beginning to burst forth, their pink the darkest they would ever be.

"That's a pretty tree. I've never seen it before." Ellis said.

"It's a cherry tree. These all are," I said, pointing out the ones that surrounded it. "They come from Japan. I've seen them at Morris Arboretum. I read in the newspaper that they have them in Washington DC now, too, but I haven't been there. Yet."

"There is that 'yet' again," he said.

I fiddled with the branch, gently turning it to look at the buds. "In a week," I continued, "these trees will all bloom at once, raining down petals like fairy snow. The flowers don't last long. I bet Mama would love to paint them. I'll have to bring her back to show her."

"Your mother paints?"

"Yes, mostly still lifes. Fruit, vegetables, flowers."

"Do you paint also?" he asked with a nod toward my sketchbook, now closed and tucked under my arm as we walked.

"Yes. Do you like art?"

"Can't say I know much about it."

"Well, there are lots of great museums in Philadelphia. We used to live in the city and Mama would try to take us to a museum once a month. Either the Academy of the Fine Arts or the Philadelphia Art Museum. She likes to get ideas for her still lifes. The Peale Family is from Philadelphia and are quite famous artists, you know. They paint the most realistic still lifes. But I prefer the grand landscape paintings. There was an incredible exhibition a few years ago, all landscapes. Mama let me see it twice. America is so vast, I want to be there, paint where those artists did, experience it for myself. The colors take my breath away. I can't imagine how intense the view would be in real life."

I knew I was rambling, but it filled the space between us with safe territory. We drifted further along the path.

"Why not enjoy the view right here? Compared to the city, this is practically countryside," Ellis asked.

"How easy for you to say, since you have already seen it all. I am fairly familiar with everything here. It still has the same sort of feeling. I have seen almost all the types of trees that grow here, and the flowers. I want to experience something new."

He pointed at a cluster of yellow flowers near the ground. "How about these? Seen these before?"

"Daffodils are just about everywhere you look, each springtime of my entire life," I laughed. "The Victorians say they represent new beginnings."

"Oh, really? Fancy that." He looked around to see if anyone was watching, then leaned down and plucked one, using his thumbnail to cut through the stem. He handed it to me with a grin.

CHAPTER THREE

Molly

In that first week home alone with Hayden in Aunt Tish's house, I felt the loss of my mother acutely. Every question I had went unanswered, every doubt doubled. I felt like a bear cub abandoned in the woods. I stumbled endlessly through the wilderness.

My mom had been sick when I was in high school, but we thought she had beaten the cancer. One Tuesday afternoon, a few weeks into the fall semester of my sophomore year of college, I was lying on my dorm room bed, clumsily undoing the buttons on my boyfriend's shirt and kicking the largely ignored textbook to the ground, when the phone rang.

"Let the machine get it," I mumbled between fervent kisses.

My boyfriend, Jeremy, was very cute. Though if I were being completely honest, he was a little dopey. We had gotten into the same college, so he must have been book smart, but he was scattered. He was always losing things and didn't seem to understand the jokes our friends made. But, he had strong, defined shoulders and the most adorable cleft in his chin. At nineteen, what else mattered?

The phone rang and rang as I gave up on the buttons and lifted Jeremy's shirt over his head. Finally, the machine clicked on and my roommate's voice announced, "You've reached Caroline and Molly. We're out having more fun than you! Leave us a message and we'll call you back!" The machine beeped loudly.

My shirt was nearly off too when my father's voice filled the room. Reflexively, I covered myself up, as if he could see me.

"Molly, it's Dad. I really need to talk to you. It's about Mom. Please call me back as soon as you can."

When he clicked off, I moved away from Jeremy. "You'd better go," I said. He reluctantly put his shirt back on.

"You going to be at Poli-Sci today at five-thirty?" he asked, turning back as he walked out the door.

"Yes," I sighed as I shooed him out. Our Political Science lecture actually started at five-fifteen. Despite being weeks into the class and repeated reminders of this, Jeremy always wandered in after the professor had begun.

I grabbed the portable phone off its cradle and dialed home. Dad answered on the second ring and after exchanging pleasantries, I asked him why he'd called.

There was a long pause on the other end.

"Dad?"

"Molly, it's Mom. She wasn't feeling great, so she went to see her oncologist, and it turns out that the cancer is back. It's pretty aggressive, and it has spread. I think you should come home this weekend, if you can. I'll come get you, or you can take the train, whatever works best…"

"How aggressive, Dad? Do I really need to come home this weekend?" I interrupted, anger flashing inside me. Going home that weekend would mean I would miss Jeremy's fraternity's Luau party. It was going to be the first big party of the semester, and I wanted to be there. Awaiting his answer, I stomped to my closet and twirled my finger around a few of the strings of the grass skirt I had found at a party store.

"Yes, Molly, I think you should be here as we decide what to do. Mom is scared and I'm sure she'd want you here. She asked me not to call you, but …"

I yanked the grass skirt from the hanger and threw it into the trash can. I was sure Dad was overreacting. Mom would be fine. She had beaten this once before; why would this be any different? "Okay, fine! I'll get a train ticket and call you with the schedule." I jammed the phone's OFF button.

I skipped Poli-Sci that afternoon and pouted in my dorm room.

• • •

Mom was on the couch when Dad and I arrived home from the train station that Friday evening. The house was a mess, and the air inside was still and thick with the humid fog of her illness. A metallic medicinal smell filled my nostrils when I went to sit next to her. She opened her arms for a hug and, as always, she squeezed me tightly, not letting go until after I did.

Dad had filled me in on the details in the car, how she had refused chemo and radiation this time, how the doctors thought it wouldn't help much anyway. We had weeks, months if we were lucky. Though I had been reluctant to come home, I could now feel the severity of the situation deep in my stomach, churning with worry. I chewed on a loose hangnail, ripping it free and drawing blood. I hollered at my father from the passenger seat, demanding he tell me why he didn't call me earlier. They didn't know earlier, he had said simply.

Now he stood forlornly in the middle of the living room, his light hair greasy, my overnight bag in his hand, looking clueless as to what he should do next.

"Go on and take that upstairs for her, Richard," Mom said. "Then call over to Panda Garden for our dinner. I'd like some Moo Shu Pork."

Dad nodded and shuffled up the stairs.

"Oh, Molly, I'm so sorry," Mom said. The skin on her hands was translucent and I could trace the path of her veins.

"Stop it, Mom. What are you sorry for? You didn't choose to be sick."

"I'm sorry that we can't fix it this time. I'm sorry to put you and Dad through this."

"Geez, Mom, stop it! What about you? Are you scared?"

"A little. But mostly about you two. I have taken care of Dad for so long, I'm not sure he can do much himself."

"He'll be fine." I wanted to reassure her, but looking around the messy house, I started to have my doubts.

"I was hoping to see you finish college," she said, "See you do something you love, start a family." Her voice caught in her throat and she closed her eyes. She paused a moment, then groaned as she sat up straighter, pushing back her long frizzy hair. It was hippie hair, unchanged, along with her wardrobe style, since her days in college spent marching for civil rights. "I loved being your mother. I want you to be sure of that," she continued, holding my gaze. Slowly, haltingly, she continued. "Being a mother and a wife is wonderful, but I also want you know that you can do more. I never had a career, really. I wanted one, but I was so young when you were born and I stayed home with you and took care of Dad. I simply never went back to work. You can do more. I know you can."

"Okay, Mom. Okay." I wanted her to stop talking like that, like it was the last opportunity to tell me these things. It was too much. I didn't want it to feel this real. I wanted to be at the Luau party with the rest of my friends, none of whom were thinking about their parents or their future beyond who they might be making out with later in the evening when the spiked punch kicked in.

"Honey..." Mom tried to continue, but I cut her off.

"Mom, I know. I get it."

She sighed. "Okay."

Soon doorbell rang, announcing the take-out delivery man. Dad and I sat around Mom, eating right out of the containers. She picked at her dinner, not eating more than a few bites, and abandoned it altogether when Dad and I were finished. I carried her container to the fridge, but found it too full of casseroles from friends and family who had heard my mother was sick. Dad joined me in the kitchen.

"Mom wants her cookies," he said, pulling a package of iced oatmeal cookies out of the pantry.

Back in the living room, Dad opened the outer cellophane and we all ate a cookie. It was silent except for our crunching. Sweet and our only source of comfort, we all helped ourselves to another.

She didn't eat much in the next few weeks and her strength declined rapidly. A hospice nurse came to the house each day. Dad sat by her side while I cleaned up the house and made us meals.

I couldn't leave them. I missed two full weeks of classes altogether before calling the dean's office to explain to them why I would be withdrawing for the semester. I talked to my roommate, Caroline, a few times, but she didn't know what to say and the conversations were awkward. Jeremy called, sweet and concerned, but I couldn't talk to him either. I tried to explain the details of Mom's diagnosis, but he asked too many questions and I was too sad and too tired to repeatedly explain. When he asked me if I thought he had left his Communications and Media textbook in my dorm room, I yelled that he should call Caroline or go over and look himself. After that, I stopped answering his calls, essentially letting him go. Someone else could take care of him; it wouldn't be me. I needed to take care of things at home.

The cancer took Mom overnight a few weeks before Christmas. At the funeral, the church was full of poinsettias, and our dark drive home from the cemetery twinkled with holiday lights. My limbs were heavy and numb, my eyes burned out and dry. I had no appetite, but I shuffled inside to get Dad something to eat. In the kitchen, I noticed a sliver of diagonal light along the floor. The fridge door stood slightly ajar, blocked by an abundance of prepared food people had dropped off. Getting closer, I could feel the cool air oozing out.

Suddenly, I was furious. I slammed the refrigerator door shut and watched as it bounced slowly open again. I started hauling out the food. Snapping open a trash bag, I tossed in the tin containers, each flimsy in their fullness. I dumped out Pyrex dishes, ignoring the names and notes attached to the foil on top. Into the bag went quart containers of soup, wrapped banana breads, and bags of bagels. Frenzied, I hauled the full trash bag out to the garbage cans in the yard. The air was frozen. My breath hung in heavy clouds like a horse's after a hard run. Tears ran down my cheeks and I felt empty.

When I came back inside, I found Dad standing in front of the fridge, the interior light illuminating his face.

"Where is all the food?" he said.

"I threw it away," I grumbled, pushing by him.

"Why, Molly? Lots of people made that food to show that they care about us. And Mom."

"I will make you something, Dad," I said, and I started cooking.

• • •

I dropped out of college and took the first job any kitchen would give me. I worked my way up through the back of the house ranks, got my own apartment when Dad married my stepmother, and eventually became the sous chef at Aubergine. Night after night, sweat dripped down my back at my station near the flat top. We sent gorgeous, upscale food out through the swinging door and used ugly, raunchy language behind it. The guys plated slices of beef tenderloin underlined with a balsamic glaze to the constant lurid chatter describing their sexual escapades from the night before. Each dish was more beautiful than the last; each storied girl more beautiful than the last. Listening to them made it easier to not think about my mom. I focused on each order, putting the finishing touches on a masterpiece meal before the plate went out the customers. It was an escape.

One slow Saturday night, Corey was one of those customers.

Halfway through the dinner service, a waiter pushed through the door to the kitchen and called, "Chef, the couple at table 16 wants to see you!"

Girard, my overweight and grouchy French boss, just grunted, a sign that he had no intention of dealing with customers that night. As he headed out back for a cigarette, he raised his hairy forearm and pointed at me and then at the dining room. I would have to go see table 16 and take the credit or the criticism. I did most of the work on the line anyway, so it was my praise or criticism to receive.

Removing my soiled apron and tossing it in the laundry pile by the back door, I washed my hands and pushed through the swinging door that separated the kitchen from the dining room. Once through, I was expected to be polite and courteous, leaving all the bawdy behavior of the kitchen on the inside of that door. I approached table 16 with a smile. An attractive couple sat there, each finishing their plate of Steak Frites.

"Good evening. Thanks for coming to Aubergine," I said, suddenly aware of how handsome the man sitting there was. He was about my age, though much older than his female companion. His brown hair was side swept and long enough so that he had bangs and a short up-flip at the back of his neck. He wore a crisp white Oxford shirt, open at the neck, the sleeves cuffed halfway up his forearms.

"We wanted to tell you how good this is!" trilled his young female companion. She was cute, with a bob of blond curls. I always kept my hair long and pulled back tight at work. I was intimidated by women who had the confidence to don short tresses. "When I was studying in Paris," she tittered, "I ate steak like this every night. I don't usually allow myself the calories now, of course, but this was worth the extra three miles I'll have to run tomorrow."

"Thank you. I am glad you enjoyed it," I said, my hands clasped behind my back. The man said nothing. He just stared at me, making me self-conscious of the sweat on my brow, the lingering hard-to-wash-off smell of the twenty-five flounders I had filleted that afternoon. Both scents certainly mingled and surrounded me like a toxic cloud. His companion babbled on about IM Pei and Notre Dame, and while I was nodding and half listening, he caught my eye and smirked just slightly.

Afterward, back in the kitchen, I wasn't even sure I had actually seen him do it, his cute, thin lips turning up at the right corner for a fraction of a second. Business picked-up, orders came in, and I forgot about him. I finished up that night's service, cleaned up my station, and packed up my knife bag. Through the streets of Georgetown, crowded that time of night with college students ready for an evening at the bars, I made my way home.

Later in the week, after the kitchen closed, I wearily pushed through the swinging doors and walked through the dark, empty dining room to the bar. On the way, I unbuttoned the top two buttons of my white chef coat, revealing a sweaty t-shirt underneath. Not expecting any customers to still be there, I hollered out, "Gin and tonic please, Garrett."

I flopped down on a bar stool, exhaled long and slow, shaking off the tension that built up in my shoulders during the evening rush. When I looked up, I saw the handsome customer from the week earlier. He was seated near the middle of the short bar. His arms were up on it and bent in a semi-circle surrounding his wine glass, an empty plate in front of him. He was watching me. I would find this quiet observation to be a hallmark of his, getting the measure of other people and letting them begin any conversation. In another man, this might seem odd, but there was no threat in his stare, no leering interest, just a comfortable waiting.

"Oh, hello," I said. "I didn't realize anyone was still here. Thought it was just me and Garrett." My head swiveled around to find my co-worker. "Where is Garrett?"

"He went in search of the 1998 Louis Latour I wanted," he replied, not initiating any further, turning back to his still-full wine glass.

Struggling for conversation to fill the empty and quiet space, I continued, "You were in here earlier this week, weren't you?" He nodded. "Did you eat again tonight?" I asked.

"Yes, at the bar. I had the mussels. They were good, but a bit too briny." There was that smirk again, though harder to see because I could only see his profile.

Jerk. "Oh yeah? I assure you they were fresh. I received them myself from the purveyor just this morning." He shrugged and we sat in silence for a while longer, both looking at the mirrored back wall of the bar lined with liquor bottles, waiting for Garrett. Finally, Garrett appeared, wine bottle in hand.

"Found it! Hi, Molly. I see you have met Corey," Garrett said, putting the wine bottle down in front of Corey and picking up his rag to start wiping down the bar.

"Actually, not officially yet," I said, turning to face him head-on. "I'm Molly." I leaned over toward him and extended my hand.

"Corey," he said simply, and after we shook hands, he returned his focus to Garrett, who poured me a gin and tonic as he chatted away with Corey.

I listened intermittently, sipping my drink, trying to relax and unwind from my shift, surreptitiously stealing glances at Corey. Though he never engaged me in conversation, sometimes he would look at me and smile. His teeth were slightly crooked, tilted back almost, and he was cuter for the imperfection. After his second glass of wine, he paid Garrett and pushed his stool out. I expected a nod of goodbye, but instead, he walked the short distance over to my stool.

"Want to go get a drink somewhere? Garrett is ready to close up. Says he's meeting someone soon," he said.

I was surprised at the invitation, and overly conscious of my sweat-slicked hair, hounds-tooth baggy pants, and post-work perfume of garlic and fish guts. I took a deep breath while Corey waited, and decided that, yes, I would go get a drink with him, despite my appearance. I pushed down all the insecurity threatening to float to the top, grabbed my bag, and, with a wave and a shrug, left Garrett to close the restaurant.

• • •

We walked down M Street toward Foggy Bottom and stopped into a tiny piano lounge with old stained-glass windows and a copper bar. A nattily suited singer crooned at the piano. Corey led me to a small table toward the back. When our bored-looking waitress arrived, she took our drink orders, and slowly walked away. Corey and I sat facing each other. Dean Martin's "You're Nobody 'Til Somebody Loves You" pounded on the piano.

"So..." I began fruitlessly, lost completely on how to get to know someone. I hadn't dated since Jeremy.

"You know, your food is amazing," Corey said, leaning back in his chair.

"Thanks. Do you come in often?" I asked. Besides with dates, I thought, but didn't say.

"Sometimes," he replied vaguely, shrugging. "It's a good place to take a... a..." he trailed off.

"A date?"

"Yes, but tonight I came back to see you," Corey said, looking up and straight at me.

Suddenly uncomfortable and fidgety, I joked, "Oh yeah? Even though the mussels were briny?"

"I do like how you pair them with Gorgonzola. It makes it an interesting dish," he said, ignoring my jab. "I know about food. My aunt used to run a delicatessen up in Pennsylvania. Nothing as fancy as Aubergine, of course; no mussels on her menu. I could eat them every day."

"Me too."

"The girls I bring in never order the mussels, though," he said with a shrug. "They seem to like your salads. What is it about girls and salads?"

"I don't know. I'm not really a salad girl," I said. Corey raised his eyebrows. I continued, "Oh, don't get me wrong. I love a good salad, but it has to have bacon, or a soft-boiled egg, or both."

"Okay, so tell me what you would order at Aubergine," Corey said, his eyes bright with mischief even in the low light of the bar. He was hard to figure out. Was he interested in me or did he just ask me here to find out what the sous chef considered the best menu item? Either way, he was pretty cute, if arrogant, so I figured I'd play along.

The waitress dropped off our drinks, saying nothing and sloshing some over the side of my glass upon impact with the table. I picked up my gin and tonic and took a long sip. Corey held his glass, swirled his red wine around in aeration, and waited for my answer.

"To start, I'd order the escargot..."

Corey interrupted, suddenly intrigued. "Snails, huh?"

"Definitely. We make them with lots of garlic and morel mushrooms, and they are divine. Of course, I'd make my date—presumably you—try them too, so that we both had dragon breath and he wouldn't mind kissing me goodnight, should he be given permission," I said, stabbing the lime in my drink. "Then, for the main course, I would order the Steak Tartar..."

"A bold choice, raw meat. Not what I'd expect," he said.

"I love raw beef. Especially the way we make it, mixed with a single golden egg yolk, minced onions, and the bright pop of capers. And I'd need lots of bread to spread it on."

"Naturally," he grinned.

"Finally, I'd have the cheese course."

"Not something sweet?" Corey asked, unconvinced.

I shook my head. "Nope, cheese course. We have an amazing selection of soft cheeses. For me, the runnier the better."

Corey seemed to consider this. He smiled at me, as if I passed a test.

CHAPTER FOUR

Tish, 1916

Papa opened his shop to great fanfare.

Every day for the past few weeks, we all walked downtown, rolled up our sleeves, and worked hard to be ready. Papa met the purveyors at the back door and we hauled in various cheeses and canned goods. He forced pounds of meat through the grinder, before stuffing it into white casings that waited patiently in bowls of water like snakes. Papa's black recipe book, stained now with spills and ink, stood open in front of him as he added spices to the sausage meat. That book was his constant companion in those early weeks, but today he handed it off to me to prepare the cucumber salad saying, "Use the recipe that I wrote down in the back. Follow my notes precisely. That is very important. I want everything to be consistent."

I poured and measured as his notes instructed, Papa's precious book flayed out before me. I struggled to stay focused on the tedious task at hand. With hopes of opening the doors for the first time that morning, we had begun work just as the sun was rising. The sky was streaked a deep mauve, beautifully distracting. I sliced the cool onion, but gazed out the window at the way the light fell on the theater marquee across the street. It lit it up as if electrified.

I peeled the cucumbers and began slicing them, my fingers itching to sketch or paint instead. Clumsily, I fumbled the cucumber. When I looked down to grab it, I saw that many circular slices had missed the bowl and landed wet on Papa's book. With a groan, I picked them off the page. The ink below had run, making the recipe illegible. Mama watched as I threw the black-stained cucumber slices into the trash bin. With a look of reproof, she fetched me another cucumber.

"Please be careful," she said. "That is money wasted."

"More's the better, then, that I won't be working here very much longer," I muttered under my breath, raking the peeler across the new cucumber, flailing away its green skin.

When I had finished, I took the mixture to Papa for tasting. "Yes, just as I thought, it needs more vinegar. Add just a quarter cup. Then write it down here in my book so that we can be consistent moving forward." He looked down to where I had laid his book open, the page now a wet blotch.

"What has happened here? Tish! Please pay attention." He snatched the book away from my space with a sigh. He tended to it like a wounded animal, patting the page dry with a cloth and carefully writing the recipe again.

When I was finished with the cucumber salad, he and I prepared and adjusted the recipes for a few other dishes he intended to offer—tasting, considering, writing down corrections—but he guarded his book carefully against my carelessness. Frankly, I was glad to be rid of it. The sooner Papa got used to doing the tasks the shop required on his own, the better.

A few hours later, content with his recipes for potato salad, coleslaw, cucumber salad, tomato and celery salad, perfection salad, and tuna fish salad, Papa was ready to open the doors to the public. He consulted his book a few last times, then slapped it shut and tucked it into his back pocket. Papa looked around his kingdom. The countertops gleamed and the cold cases displayed the various meats and cheeses on offer. A basket of bread, freshly delivered from the bakery next door, sat on top of the counter. Cans of sardines and tuna were stacked on the back wall. Six varieties of sausage hung in the front windows.

Everything seemed perfect—except the tiny fingerprints that dotted the inside of the glass where Oliver stood to watch the street.

"Do you want me to take him home, Julian?" Mama asked.

"No, of course not," he said, rushing over to shoo Oliver away and wipe the glass clean. "This is a family business. Besides, Laurel, you know that I need you here." She touched his arm and went to straighten the already straight chairs around the tables.

Though I was happy for Papa and wished him every success, I felt tied to the floor. Now that the shop would officially open, what if I never convinced Papa to let me go West? What if I was forced to stay here forever? I went outside to escape the weight of it all. Above my head, the new sign bearing our surname gleamed. The trolley car dinged on its way by, full of passengers ready for a day at Willow Grove Park. I followed its journey longingly with my eyes and then went back inside to put on my apron.

"You're a good girl, Tish," Papa said patting my arm, "when you focus on your work. I need to be able to count on you to help me run the business."

"But Papa," I began. Dread was rising again in my throat.

He held his hand up. "No, not today. I will not hear a single word about painting or mountains or oceans today. Today we open the shop, as a family."

I nodded. Papa donned his apron, put on his white butcher sleeves, and straightened his bow tie. "All ready to open the doors to Hess's Delicatessen?"

We were. Ivy stood unenthusiastically behind the register, surely counting the days until she was married and wouldn't have to work. I unbuttoned and folded up the sleeves of my blouse, silently counting my own days left here at the deli. Papa turned the sign from CLOSED to OPEN and went behind the counter to stand vigil.

• • •

It took about a half hour, but soon word spread on the street and customers trickled in. We began taking orders. I sliced a half pound of roast beef. Mama wrapped six sausages. Ivy called out the orders when they were ready and collected the money. Oliver was underfoot the entire time, but overall quite well behaved.

The voices of the customers filled the shop and we were doing a bustling first day of business.

Things quieted after lunchtime. Papa let out an audible sigh and wrapped his arm around Mama's shoulders. He was grinning.

The bell on the door chimed and Papa straightened up. He greeted the lone customer, a man in a white shirt and bow tie, his hair parted down the middle.

"Just open, did you?" the man said.

"Indeed, just this morning," Papa said.

"Well, welcome to the block. I'm George Howerth, the barber next door. I believe you have met my wife and daughter. My apologies for not stopping in sooner."

"Pleasure to meet you, Mr. Howerth. Julian Hess." Papa wiped his hand on a rag and offered it to Mr. Howerth. Oddly, the gesture was not returned. Papa let his arm drop.

"Yes, Hess, is it? I saw the sign. Are you German?"

"Yes," Papa said warily. "From the Schwartzwald. That's the Black Forest. Have you heard of it?"

"No," Mr. Howerth stated. The word fell flat onto the floor. He crinkled his nose as if catching the scent of something foul.

Papa plowed on, his pride beginning to falter, "Really? It is quite beautiful there. This here is my wife, Laurel, and our children Ivy, Tish, and Oliver."

"Pleasure to meet you." Mr. Howerth's smile was thin. I wondered how a girl as boisterous as Virginia ever came from such parents. As if conjured, Virginia appeared in the doorway.

"Oh Tish, the shop is wonderful!" she cried, walking around the counter to the back side with us.

"Virginia, please," Mr. Howerth said. "Come out from behind there this instant!" Then to Papa, "Pack me up a pound of pastrami."

"How about some sausages? We made them right here; old family recipe. Our gift to you, one neighbor to another," Papa offered, trying hard.

"No. That won't be necessary. Just the pastrami."

Mama turned and began to fill his request. Papa's fingers were flexing, his arms tight at his sides. Mama lightly touched Papa's shoulder, words unspoken between them but conveyed nonetheless. Papa wrote up a ticket.

"Would you like to start a tab?" Mama asked, her voice perfectly friendly and smooth. "Since you are right next door and will likely come in often, we would be happy to bill your total at the end of each month."

"That certainly won't be necessary," Mr. Howerth said. He held his hand out for the receipt, considered it, and then took money out of his billfold. The clang of the register's drawer echoed through the silent store. Mama handed him the paper-wrapped meat.

"Well," Mr. Howerth said, "best of luck in your new business venture." His insincerity was thick.

"If you enjoy the pastrami, please feel free to recommend us to the customers in your shop," Mama called to Mr. Howerth's back as he walked silently out the door.

Virginia looked at me and smiled sadly, shaking her head. She turned to my parents and said, "It really does look great in here! I'm starving! Can't wait to try your pastrami. See you soon!"

When she left and we were alone in the shop, Papa smacked the counter with his rag.

"Julian, please," Mama said.

"I have been in this country for twenty-five years. I have an American family. I work and live in America."

I felt cold. This was the first time I had experienced anyone showing anything other than respect to Papa. I could see the pain on his face, the frustration mingled with fallen pride. He had worked so hard to get to this day, years at the Navy Yard, years of dreaming. My face flushed in embarrassment for him, for us. The newspaper headlines were saying awful things about the Germans, but we weren't them. Papa was making sausages here, in Willow Grove. He had nothing to do with the assassination of that Archduke or the war that was tearing Europe apart.

"It's all right, Papa," I said. "One taste of your pastrami and he's sure to recommend the shop to everyone who comes in for a haircut."

Papa fixed a sharp eye on me but said nothing.

"Let's get back to work," Mama said. "The afternoon rush will be here before you know it. Folks will want something when they come in to the park for the fireworks."

We all quietly resumed our tasks. Our first day of business was successful, but somehow tainted. From then on, I never heard Papa tell anyone he was from Germany. When asked, he answered that he was from Philadelphia, new to Willow Grove, but happy to serve the fine people of the town. People surely knew, though. Our surname—the name of our shop—broadcast it out.

We worked hard those first few weeks, figuring out our rhythm and responsibilities. The sooner the shop was a staple in the community, a well-running delicatessen popular with regulars and day trippers, the sooner I could leave my parents to it. I focused on the shop, for my sake, but also for my father.

• • •

On Mondays we closed early, and this Monday's weather was particularly gorgeous. I raced through my preparations for Tuesday's business day, wiped down the counter, and slapped the soapy mop around the floor.

"I'm all finished! I'm going to the park to paint a bit, Papa!" I hollered back to him. Without waiting for his approval, I secured my hat, grabbed my satchel, and raced out into the sunshine.

The street noise didn't muffle the bird songs and I felt my spirits lift with each step I took away from the delicatessen. Headed for the park, I passed Mr. Howerth's barber shop. He hadn't come in again, and I pushed past his windows in refusal to let him dampen my day.

The trolley trailed me as I walked up York Road. A mass of people disembarked and we all walked as one toward the entrance to the park. Once inside the gates, I serpentined along a garden path. It was lined with boxwoods. Their herbaceous fragrance greeted me at every curve. Around a bend, there was a small pond with floating water lilies. Behind it stood a willow tree, its long wisps of branches blowing in the breeze and brushing the grass below.

I settled on a bench. I had brought along two small pieces of particle board that had separated jars of olives in the last delivery. Making one my canvas and one my palette, I squeezed out phthalo green, veridian, and raw sienna from their tin tubes. Couples strolled by, arm in arm, and I could hear the tinny carousel song chiming in the distance. It all fell away as the willow tree began to appear on the board. My brush rendered the tiny leaves, shadows in the bark, and highlights on the branches. Soon I was happily lost inside the painting.

I worked until the afternoon light turned orange. Sweat slicked my brow and strands of hair escaped my hat. I tamed them back and stretched my back into a deep arch. I rolled my neck around to loosen it. What a pleasant afternoon. How I longed to spend each afternoon like this, painting out in the open air, rather than stuck behind a deli counter, making silly mistakes and displeasing Papa. Of course, leaving forever to paint would displease him infinitely more than a broken jar of gherkins or a wasted mess of cucumbers. Free labor, no matter how clumsy, seemed, for now, to be his highest priority.

My fingers were spattered with the colors I had used, and I gingerly propped my painting up against the back of the bench while I prepared to go. I wiped down my brushes and packed up the tubes of paint. With a firm zip, I closed my satchel and began my walk home.

I wound around the paths slowly, knowing it was nearing supper and sure that Mama would want my help in preparing it. I was in no rush to be back in a kitchen again and stopped a few times along the way to appreciate the gardens and pick out future painting sites.

I was admiring a wild rose bush when I saw him. It was Ellis. He was on another path, shoulders and chest leading the way. He struck a strong profile and I liked how confidently he walked. I froze, unsure if I wanted him to see me or not. He was intriguing, but his boldness was also intimidating.

Perhaps he was heading to work. Perhaps he was late. Perhaps he was meeting someone. I knew so little about him and found myself wanting to know more.

Just then he looked up, as if called by my thoughts of him, and he saw me. His steps hitched up a bit and a small smile parted his lips. He waved and I waved back, a timid little one from my waist. Ellis looked around for a way to walk over to me, but our paths were separated by a large patch of greenery. After a moment's thought, he stepped over the little stanchions meant to keep visitors off the grass and marched through toward me. This was exactly what I liked, and didn't like, about him.

"Hello," he called as he neared me. He stepped over the stanchions and off the grass onto the path next to me. He had left a row of footprints in the perfect lawn and I ached to move away from the evidence lest a park police officer happen by. I nodded in greeting, picked up my painting, and started walking slowly away down the path.

"Tish, please wait," he said, quickening his pace to catch up. "How are you? It's nice to see you."

"And you."

"I'm on my way to work. You?"

"I had the afternoon free so I decided to come here and paint for a while."

"You have paint on your cheek," he said, pointing.

Embarrassed, I let go of the painting with one hand and cupped my cheek to hide it.

"Just a bit of green," he continued, and then reached out to touch me.

I pulled back, almost in reflex, though the thought of his hand on my face sent a thrill through me. He reached out again and I lowered my hand, letting him wipe at the paint. The skin of his fingers was rough, but his touch was gentle.

He frowned. "I think it is dry." Then he looked down at the particle board hanging at my side. "Can I see what you were working on?"

"Oh, it's nothing. Just that willow tree over there."

"Don't do that. Don't demean your work. Please, may I see?"

I held up the board, image out, in front of my chest like a shield. I held my breath. I wasn't sure I wanted to hear what Ellis had to say. He seemed to be so brutally honest, and I suddenly feared that he wouldn't like my work. Ellis turned his head from side to side and put his chin in his hand. As he considered my painting for what felt like an interminably long time, I vacillated between being eager for his praise and brazenly ambivalent. I needed him to love it. I didn't care if he didn't. Oh, of course I cared. I cared more than I was willing to admit. I couldn't wait a moment longer for his critique.

"Well?" I spat.

He just laughed. "It's wonderful."

"Thank you." I exhaled the words. Pleasure and pride brought a smile to my lips. I walked further down the path and he tagged along like a puppy at my heels.

"You are quite skilled. Do you intend to sell these to save money for a transcontinental ticket?"

He remembered my plans. "Perhaps. And I am working at my father's delicatessen as well. As soon as business picks up, I'm sure he'll be able to pay me and I'll save up enough to go."

"And how about when you get there? You'll need enough for room and board. And food, too."

"I'll have enough. And if not, I can always get a job out there."

Ellis ran his hands along the tops of the bushes that lined this part of the path. A chuckle escaped his lips.

"What?" I asked.

"It's just that I've been living the type of life you are talking about—moving from place to place, trying to find work as I go—and it isn't that simple. It is gritty and hard. Jobs aren't necessarily easy to find, nor boarding houses. You won't have your family to fall back on once you are out there. Painting won't..."

"I know that!" I said, cutting him off. "I'm not a fool. You think because I am a woman that I am incapable of surviving on my own. You are just like him!"

"Like who?"

"My father!" I quickened my pace toward home.

"Now wait a minute," Ellis said, matching my runaway speed. "This has nothing to do with you being a woman. I'm trying to be realistic."

"I'm going," I said, setting my lips. "And there isn't anything you or Papa can do to stop me."

"That may be true when it comes to me, but I can think of a few ways your father could stop you."

"Such as?"

"Hmmm, let's see. First, maybe never agrees to pay you a salary."

"He wouldn't do that. He knows I want to travel and need money to do so."

"Your father likes the idea of you leaving, then, does he?"

"Well," I stopped walking abruptly, forcing Ellis to stop short and nearly plow into me. "No, you're right. Papa doesn't actually want me to go." I looked at the painting in my hands. A willow tree from Willow Grove. Would I ever paint the trees in the Grand Canyon Forest Reserve? I felt tremendously foolish. And it had been such a pleasant afternoon.

"Tish, I think it is wonderful that you..."

I held up my hand to stop him. "It was nice seeing you, Ellis. It is time I got back home."

He reached out his hand to grasp my arm, but I turned away avoiding it and his arm fell to his side. I began walking again, out of the park and back up the hill toward home.

CHAPTER FIVE

Molly

During our quiet moments, Hayden's newness amazed me. His hooded black-brown eyes and bulbous belly were things remarkable, special, about my child. I loved holding him, loved his way of pulling his knees to his chest and snuggling into me like a tree frog. But then he would wake up.

If he wasn't sleeping, Hayden's squall gusted day and night. He wailed and I answered with ineptitude. I had no idea how to keep him happy. Corey headed to the office and Hayden sucked on my breasts, screamed in my ears, pooped on my arms, and threw up on my chest. Without my complete attention, Hayden hollered for it, and once he was crying, it was hard to pull him out of the fit. I hadn't cooked a meal since his arrival. I yearned for bed by seven-thirty, ready for the day to be over but knowing I would be awakened again in too few restful hours.

A few nights after Corey went back to work, I found myself sitting up, my mind emerging from the depths of dreams slowly, slowly. What day was it? What was that sound? Before I was fully awake, I was moving out of the warmth of the covers and across the cold floor of the bedroom. As my cognizant mind caught up with my unconscious one, I realized where I was and why I was awake. The baby was crying.

The clock read 3:42 and my stomach sunk, realizing I had only fallen back to sleep two hours ago. As I moped past Corey's side of the bed, I heard him snore.

In the nursery, I fed Hayden and settled him back in his crib. I don't even remember how I got back to bed.

The next morning dawned like all the rest, Hayden as alarm clock, my breasts full and leaking at the sound of his cries. I looked at the clock. 6:21. He had slept only two more hours since the last feeding and my body felt like lead. With a quick good morning peck, Corey jumped out of bed to shower, peppy and ready for work. I stumbled and swayed into Hayden's room to change his diaper. I settled back in my own bed and he latched on.

I heard the pipes creak as Corey turned off the water and padded back into our room, a towel around his waist. His hair was streaming and his chest dappled with drops of water. I had no sex drive but could still see how good-looking he was. I cringed at the comparison of our appearances. My hair felt heavy with grease and I felt the sag of my once-perky breasts with every pull from Hayden.

"Going to do some unpacking today?" Corey asked.

"Uh-huh. I'm sure going to try."

"Don't throw away anything of my aunt's just yet, though, okay? And, it would be awesome if you could find my golf gloves. I need them for Sunday."

"Wait, you're not going to be home on Sunday?" I asked, panic rising. "For goodness sake, Corey, can't we just see how I do by myself this week? I thought I could at least count on you this weekend."

"Not this weekend. I have a golf outing. Boss mandated."

He came over to me and kissed the crown of my head, no doubt smelling my dirty hair. He then kissed Hayden, who became distracted and fell off my breast. A wail escaped his little mouth.

"Get out of here; he has to concentrate! We don't quite have this down yet," I said as my free arm shooed Corey away and the other latched Hayden back on.

Corey tromped down the stairs and out the front door. I heard his SUV back out and drive away. Eager for a change in scenery, Hayden and I moved downstairs.

Because my body was so used to constant motion—hustling in the kitchen during the rush, hauling pots full of water, and pulling large pans out of the oven—all of these new sedentary hours felt slothful. Lethargy overwhelmed my limbs, perhaps from inactivity and boredom even more than my sleepless nights. I had never been at home much during the day before; I'd go to the gym or out for a run, and then head into the restaurant kitchen to make prep sheets or complete purchase orders before service that night.

Shackled to Hayden, I was imprisoned. And there were so many boxes to unpack. We shuffled around them as I bounced my ornery bundle. I examined the ancient dark paintings that hung on the walls in gilded frames. Curious, I tilted up a small panel painting depicting an unidentifiable European town and peeked behind. Beneath lay a stark white patch of painted wall, a precise square that hadn't been faded by sunlight over the years. I sighed, adding fresh paint to my mental list of things in the house that needed improvement.

After twenty more minutes of swaying and bouncing up on the balls of my feet, Hayden finally fell asleep. I climbed the stairs, each one its own Everest. Easing Hayden slowly away from my body, I lowered him down at just the right angle, like all the books said, with his head higher than his bottom so that he wouldn't feel like he was falling and startle awake. I stood stock still for a minute after letting go, anticipating the wail, but he stayed silent. Hayden was asleep. Victory!

Afraid to breathe, I tiptoed out of the room. A loud creak filled the space. The throw rug Corey had put down hid a minefield of creaky wooden boards beneath. I quickly picked my foot up, but the board groaned louder upon release. At a run, I escaped.

In the hallway, I grabbed hold of the doorjamb and craned my upper body around the wall to see if Hayden was still sleeping. Thankfully, he was. I let out my breath and went down the stairs. At the bottom, the Jack and Jill stairway split and I followed them to the right and into the library where boxes sat waiting to be unpacked.

Locating the baby monitor, I flicked it on and set it atop some boxes. Hayden lay still and I could hear the soft cadence of his breathing. I ripped open a box nearby and found my books inside. The shelves in the library were already crammed with Aunt Tish's books. Where would ours go?

I looked around at all she had left behind. To Corey, everything here held a special memory from his childhood. Everything. The rocking chair they sat on together as Aunt Tish read him a story, the table where she would rest her coffee and his hot chocolate, the old knickknacks, the old books. Some, or ideally all, of it would have to go if we were ever going to fit our life into this house.

I hauled my books out of the box, stacking them on the floor. Then, one by one, I pulled down Aunt Tish's books, filling the empty box and making room on the shelf for mine. Corey could go through hers before I donated them. Volume by volume, the books came off the shelves, along with ancient dust. I glanced over the titles, familiar with some. Classics like *Wuthering Heights* and *Uncle Tom's Cabin* went into the boxes, along with shelves of travel photography books and thick hardback art museum catalogs.

A small black bound book, tattered and faded, was tucked in among them. I contemplated its shabbiness for a long moment, running my fingers over the ragged leather, feeling rather kindred. I opened the book. A piece of paper fluttered out, the inner edge torn loose from the binding. It was a recipe, handwritten and titled "Perfection Salad." What in the world was that? Gelatin, cabbage, celery, and pimentos. Yuck. Mixed, solidified, and cubed. No, thank you.

I placed it aside and flipped through the rest of the book. A folded menu tucked inside caught my eye. *Hess's Delicatessen*, it read. This must have been Aunt Tish's place. The left listed take-out meats and deli salads, including that Perfection Salad, and the right listed sandwiches and light meals for fifteen cents. It must have been the menu when the place first opened. I wondered when that was.

There were more menus inside, the prices steadily increasing, I assumed at pace with inflation, and pages of recipes for the dishes listed as offerings. The food was so old-fashioned and strange—Oyster Salad, Orange Feather Cake. I wanted to linger and imagine the outcome of each of these recipes, remember what it was like to lose myself in the process of cooking.

But just then, I heard Hayden on the monitor. My enthusiasm turned quickly to annoyance. I searched through the box maze and found the device, green lights blinking the staccato of his screams. I could see on the screen that he was flailing his arms and ready to be picked up, needing to be comforted.

With a sigh, I set the black book back on Aunt Tish's shelf and climbed the creaky stairs up to Hayden. The foyer clock said it had been only twenty minutes since I first placed him into his crib.

• • •

Later in the week, Jocelyn stopped by. Colten and Rowan were in camp, and so she arrived unencumbered by my raucous nephews. When I answered the door, she sauntered in, wearing a royal blue velour tracksuit and running sneakers, her tight abs hinted at under the white baby tee peeking out from her unzipped jacket. Her hair and makeup were perfect, and I wondered if she was heading to the gym that way.

"Hi, Molly. Are you still in your pajamas?" In her French manicured hands, she held out a casserole. I greeted her with a half-hearted kiss on the cheek, trying to take her comments in stride.

She leaned in to accept my greeting, but then away suddenly.

"You have spit-up on your shoulder. Looks like you have lost almost all of your baby weight, though! You are so much skinnier now than you used to be, even before you were pregnant. Motherhood agrees with you!" I took the casserole and the backhanded compliment. How heavy must she have considered me before I was pregnant?

"Where is that beautiful baby?" she asked. Finding him in his swing, she walked over, bent down and cooed to him for a few moments. Then she stood, glanced around and said, "It doesn't look like you have settled in much."

"No, I guess we still have a lot of boxes to empty," I sighed, resolving myself for a long afternoon of criticism.

"Doesn't all of this clutter drive you crazy? And Corey? He likes things neat, right?"

"I suppose he'd prefer it if we were fully unpacked, but when we got here, there was so much cleaning to do, and then Hayden arrived..." I stopped myself, refusing to make any more excuses. I changed tack. "Thank you for the casserole."

"Oh, sure. It isn't restaurant quality, like Corey is used to from you. It's just something I whipped up after my Pilates class. Are you cooking much these days?"

"No."

We settled onto the couch. A moment went by in unpleasant silence.

"Oh, well," she recovered, "just focus on the baby. Aren't babies just wonderful? Enjoy every moment. He'll never be this sweet and tiny and helpless again."

Thank goodness! A short guffaw escaped my lips. If Jocelyn noticed, she didn't react. She plowed right on. "How is Hayden sleeping?"

"Not very well, actually. He's up every few hours."

"In a few more weeks you should absolutely try the Ferber method. There's no other way. My boys didn't need it—they slept right through the night by six weeks all on their own—but I have friends who swear by it."

"Maybe," I said, not yet sold on the idea of letting Hayden cry it out. "I can't even get him to sleep in the Pack 'n Play for his naps yet."

"Oh, you just have to! Put him down. He'll get used to it. No wonder your house is in such a state. He is in his crib at night, isn't he?"

I hesitated, wondering if I should be honest with her. Why not? She'd judge me either way. "Most nights...though sometimes I fall asleep nursing and he ends up with us in our bed."

"Oh no! What if you roll over on to him? Co-sleeping is very dangerous. And Hayden will get used to sleeping with you and never want to sleep anywhere else."

She spoke with such authority on the matter, I thought maybe she had to put an end to her boys sleeping in the bed with her and Hank, so I asked, "Your boys didn't have any trouble sleeping in their cribs?"

"No, no." She waved her hand as if my question were ridiculous. "What diapers are you using?"

I sighed. Of course her boys slept through the night, in their own perfect cribs, in their perfectly clean house, and they probably also woke up cheerful and full of smiles. They were monsters now, though, and I found some comfort in this.

Without waiting for my answer, Jocelyn continued, "You must not get the diapers with the blue dye. They made Rowan break out in the worst hives. And don't use anything but Quadruple Cream. The others are just a waste of money. Do you have a place figured out yet for swimming classes? Or maybe music? I'll send you an email with all the places Colten and Rowan loved. You should get registered soon. They fill up quickly." She looked me over again. "You'll actually have to get dressed, though. What will the other mommies think?"

That I was drowning. They would think I was drowning. And I was. Though maybe there were some other "mommies" out there who were feeling lost too? It didn't seem like it. If idyllic Facebook feeds were any indication, it was possible that all new mothers were exactly like Jocelyn. In her presence, I felt like the only woman alive to struggle with motherhood.

Although I was sure that Jocelyn had sniffed out my incompetence the moment she walked in the front door, there was no way I would ever admit it. Especially not to her. I refused to let her see how defeated I was, outmaneuvered by an infant. So I shut up tight like a clam for the rest of our conversation, and pretended to value her sage advice. I nodded. I listened. I smiled. Everything was under control. When Hayden started arching his back, a sure sign he was about to wail, I picked him up out of the swing. A distant version of my voice told Jocelyn that I loved motherhood, it was hard, but worth it. Holding Hayden, I started bouncing around the room. Yes, I was getting used to living in the suburbs. Yes, I would sign up for a few of the classes, thank you for suggesting that. Yes, I would, of course, take a shower before taking him to them. To prove that I would heed her advice about Hayden sleeping out of my arms for naps, I walked him over to the Pack 'n Play and settled him down. The moment he left my arms for the cold cradle, he began to wail.

Part of me felt vindicated. My mind screamed at Jocelyn, "See this isn't so easy. Hayden is a hard baby! He isn't an automaton like your kids. He needs more. I'd like to see you handle Hayden for the day!" I held my tongue, though, too tired to stand up to any further barrage of her opinions.

"Well, that's my cue!" Jocelyn said, jumping up. "Your little man may need to eat again! Make sure he is gaining weight! If you ever want to switch to formula, let me know. I'll tell you the best one to buy. Enjoy the casserole! I'm glad that both of your men will get real food today!" And with that, she air kissed my cheek, staying far away from the spit-up shoulder, waggled her perfect nails in the air at Hayden, and rushed out the front door.

• • •

I hated to admit it, but Jocelyn's casserole tasted good. I sneaked a bite before putting it into our nearly empty fridge. It was cheesy and rich in carbs, just the way I liked it. There was no way we were going to eat it though. I wouldn't let the first home-cooked meal Corey and I shared in this house post-baby to be cooked by Jocelyn.

Because we had nothing else, I resolved to go the grocery store. I worked up my determination between bites of buttered toast—the most exciting thing I had recently summoned the energy to prepare. As I mumbled to myself about the things I needed to get, crumbs fell into Hayden's fine hair. I brushed them away.

After tummy time, I changed his diaper and settled down on the couch to nurse him. I flipped on the television—just while he nursed, I told myself. I was one episode of *Golden Girls* away from fresh air and human contact, even if it was just the checkout girl. I was one half hour away from supplies for a real meal.

Everything went according to plan. Hayden finished eating without falling asleep and was still happy. A little dance around the room produced a good burp and I started to get him into his onesie jacket. Chatting non-stop in that high-pitched just-for-babies ridiculous voice, I buckled him into the seat, grabbed the handle with a heave, and hooked the carrier seat into the crook of my bent elbow. I turned toward the front door feeling accomplished. I was going to make it out the door!

And then I heard it. A low rumble that kept escalating and mutating into a loud spurt. I knew right away what the sound was: an up-the-back poop.

"Okay, little man, you aren't going to deter this trip. We're just going to quick change you, and then right back on the road. We still have time to get to the store and back before you will want to eat again." I continued my incessant burbling as I moved him to the changing table. Out of the jacket, which had been hit and stained, out of his outfit, which had been smeared and was likely unrecoverable, and out of his diaper, which threatened to continue its overflow on its way to the pail. A few once-overs with wet wipes would be good enough for now.

Soiled clothes went in the hamper. A new diaper, outfit, and coat went on the baby. The baby went back in to the car seat. I went to the sink for a good hand-washing. Twenty minutes later, we were finally out the door.

• • •

The grocery store was worse than I imagined it would be. Hayden cried the entire time we were there. I cooed at him and stroked his face as I walked and pushed the cart, his seat nestled deep inside. By the third aisle, I was gritting my teeth, pasting on a pained smile and plowing through.

A few older women offered a sympathetic word and other mothers trudged along, tugging their own children behind, nodding at me in understanding. I paid for, bagged, and loaded the groceries in the trunk to the soundtrack of Hayden's unending unhappiness.

I pulled into the driveway, barely missing the trash cans, completely frazzled. I turned off the ignition. I could see Hayden, though he faced backward, via the baby mirror. Strapped into his carrier, his little face was puckered red with anger, his mouth wide open in an angry howl, bare gums and back of his throat visible. I rested my head on the steering wheel in front of me and tried to take a calming breath.

I reached over between the seats to engage the parking brake and found the handle already locked in the up position. Confused, I looked again. As the realization dawned on me—I had driven all the way home from the grocery store with the parking brake on—a dark, rubbery smell began to seep into the car. No. No, no, no! I didn't know how much damage I had done to the car, but I knew it wasn't good. A small wail that echoed Hayden's escaped my lips, and the tears began to trickle down my cheeks. I picked at a hangnail, drawing a small bead of blood. I was acutely aware of how tired I was, how frustrated, how distracted. Soon I was full-on crying. Hayden continued his protest from the backseat.

Guessing at the shapes before my tear-filled eyes, I climbed out of the car, unlatched Hayden's seat, and carried him up to the porch, allowing Hayden a full vocal assault on the neighborhood. I heard my voice wavering as I continued my futile attempts at soothing him. Sobbing and snotting everywhere, I unloaded the grocery bags and carried them, two at a time, up the porch steps to the front door, calling out quaking reassurances to Hayden. I desperately wanted to get inside and hide my inadequacy from the world. My prison had become my sanctuary.

I heard the front door of the house across the street open. A woman walked out, followed by her young daughter.

"What's that stinky smell, Mommy?" the child asked. I stole a furtive glance across the street and saw the little girl crinkling her nose and bringing her pudgy fingers up to pinch it shut.

"I don't know, Kayla, probably a car," the woman with her said. She called out, "Can we give you a hand?"

My neighbor was a few years older than I was, with full brown curly hair and a fuller figure. Without waiting for my answer, she took her child's hand and led her across the street toward me. In one swift, practiced motion, she produced a tissue out of her pocket and held it in my direction.

Pulling myself together with a deep, snotty inhale, I accepted the tissue. "Thank you," I said. "I'm sorry we have to meet this way. I'm Molly. That is my baby, Hayden." I gestured up toward the porch.

"He's noisy, Mommy," the little girl chirped. "And her car is really stinky."

"Hush, Kayla. Kind words only, please." The woman let go of the child's hand, now that they were standing on my sidewalk, and extended her hand with manicured nails toward me. "I'm Liz," she said. "Welcome to the neighborhood."

We shook and her hand felt so soft, comforting and friendly.

"I am sure it is a much noisier place now that we have moved in," I said. "No matter what I try, he cries most of the day," I heard the self-deprecation in my voice and I hated it. Self-consciously, I covered the pulled-back portion of my greasy ponytail briefly with my hand and wiped at my eyes with her tissue.

"Are you kidding me?" Liz joked. "Kayla, this overly honest one here, is my fourth, and they all cried like that when they were babies. Colic is the worst. It won't last forever, though. Soon he'll be using real words to sass you." She winked and smiled. "My second one was a real pain in the... when he was a baby," she continued, lowering her voice to a mere whisper and letting me fill in the blank. "If he had been my first, I wouldn't have had any others! Kayla arrived on the scene after one too many glasses of wine on my birthday, if you know what I mean!" Liz looked down at Kayla and continued reassuringly, "Not planned, but not unwanted." Kayla just nodded, as if she had heard that line many times.

"Let me help you with these groceries," Liz said, grabbing a heavy bag from my trunk and marching up my front steps, Kayla straggling behind her.

I watched this confident woman stride into my house, very capably handling a heavy bag of groceries and her own child. I really was the only one who couldn't do this. My eyes pricked with tears again but I resolutely pushed them back down and hustled to unlock the door for my neighbors.

"Kayla, grab this and take it to the kitchen," Liz instructed. I gaped as Kayla walked right toward the back of the house. By way of explanation, Liz said, "Oh, we were over here a few times when the previous owner was here. Nice old lady."

I unstrapped Hayden from his car seat, snuggling his struggling, angry body to mine. I started bouncing in the foyer, keeping an eye on Kayla in the kitchen. I was strangely uncomfortable with Liz and Kayla's level of familiarity here. Even though it didn't feel quite like it yet, this was my house now, and shouldn't I be the one to show people where the kitchen was located? In an odd reversal of roles, I felt like the guest and Liz and Kayla the hostesses.

"She was my husband's aunt, actually," I said. "I never met her. Did she take care of the house at all?" I asked. "It's kind of falling apart."

"She was fairly meticulous. The inside was always clean and nice, and for the outside, I think she hired a landscaper or handyman when she needed it. Don't worry. You can bring the house back to its former glory."

I sighed, overwhelmed with the idea. "Hopefully. I can't seem to make much of a dent. She left everything behind—clearly—and it's all still here."

Liz looked around. "Wow, you aren't kidding," she said, letting out a low whistle. "It's like she never left. Are you going to haul most of her things out to make room for yours?"

I shrugged, genuinely unsure that Corey would allow that.

"Do you want help organizing the house? My older ones are still in camp for a few more weeks," Liz offered.

"No. Thanks, though." I did want help, knew it in fact, but I held back unable to admit defeat. "I'll get the hang of this motherhood thing and get some things done while Hayden is asleep. It is just really hard to put him down, and that makes it really hard to accomplish anything." I decided to let her in a little, test the waters of our early friendship. "Taking care of him is much harder than I expected. I am going a little crazy, actually."

She looked at me sympathetically and said, "Of course you are. New babies are hard. Especially the first one. Plus, you are alone here all day."

I looked up at her sharply, surprised at how aware she was of our comings and goings.

"It's okay, honey, I know you are," she continued, "I hear your husband's SUV pull out pretty early and I don't notice it back here until pretty late each night. Try to get out more. Even the littlest bit of fresh air would help you. Do you have any family in the area who could help you out?"

I shook my head. Just Jocelyn. No thanks.

I missed my mother. If she were alive, I knew that she and my father would be fawning over Hayden. Missing my mother was heightened by my exhaustion, her absence more acute now that I had a baby myself. Tears threatened, but I didn't want to start crying again.

"As you can see, I tried the grocery store today," I said to Liz, trying to change the focus on our conversation. "What a nightmare. All I want to do is cook something, but I don't have any groceries, and my kitchen stuff is all still in boxes. Aunt Tish left some kitchen items behind I could use, but it is so hard to do anything when I can't put Hayden down."

"The grocery store cannot be considered getting out," Liz insisted. "The grocery store is always a nightmare. Be prepared for years and years of that being true, even when the kids get older. Especially when the kids get older. The screams get louder and the other customers get less sympathetic. Okay, so new plan. You need to find something just for yourself. What is it that you like to do? What did you do before you had Hayden? Did you work?"

"I was a chef in a restaurant," I said, feeling like that was a very long time ago.

"Well, there you go. That's what you will do. The first thing you need to do is unpack your kitchen. And then start cooking. Get a seat, put Hayden in it in the kitchen with you, maybe even up on the counter. If he cries, he cries. But I bet he'll get used to it. I'll come over and hold him if you want. Trust me, doing something for you is really important. Even if it is just an hour each day."

She had four kids to back up her advice, but I still wasn't sure. Part of me would feel guilty if I didn't focus all my attention on Hayden. Isn't that what a mother is supposed to do? How could I just let him cry while I did something else?

"Well, we will get out of your hair. It was very nice to meet you, Molly. C'mon, Kayla, let's go. We have to pick up your brothers in a bit." She stood to go, and I made a motion to stand too. "Trust me: Find those kitchen boxes," Liz instructed. "Get back into something that makes you remember who you are."

"Thank you for your help with the groceries," I called as she and Kayla closed the door and headed back across the street. I thought about the black book with the menus and recipes. Maybe I would surprise Corey by making one or two from there.

CHAPTER SIX
Tish, 1916

The weekend of Ivy's wedding, Papa closed the shop with a merry sign in the window, "Closed to celebrate the nuptials of Ivy Hess and William Wonderling. We will re-open Tuesday morning!"

The sun was bright and climbing. Thin clouds wrote calligraphy across the blue summer sky and the heady scent of lilies drifted up into our bedroom. I dressed quickly and silently so as not to wake Ivy who continued to snooze as I descended the spiral staircase. Mama was at the front door directing deliveries, motioning the men, arms laden with goods, to the correct place in the house or backyard.

The caterer had delivered the chafing dishes and Mama and I went to work on the Welsh rarebit. I added cheese to the eggs and cream and slowly stirred it with the golden butter until it was melted and molten. I was under strict instructions from Mama not to let it boil so I stirred and stirred, and as it thickened, I gazed out the kitchen window.

In the backyard, the men were setting up chairs. They wafted a crisp white cloth over a table. As the fabric settled atop, a corner caught the breeze and it inflated underneath like a marshmallow. Men scuttled to tamp it down, smoothing it with broad sweeps of their hands. They placed a heavy vase on top and moved on to the next task.

I heard a popping sound and looked down at the pot. Fat, heavy bubbles were rising to the surface. I had let it boil! The eggs had scrambled and what was meant to be smooth was now chunky.

"No!" I hollered and pulled the pot from the heat.

Mama appeared at my side and shook her head. "Start again, Tish. Pay attention. In fact, never mind. Just go see if Ivy is awake."

I removed my apron, rinsed my hands, grabbed some toast points from the rarebit tray for Ivy, and trudged up the stairs to our room. She was awake now, her face flushed with a full night's sleep. Still in her dressing gown and seated at the vanity, she held her hairbrush aloft.

"Today's the day, Tish," she said breathlessly. She smoothed her hair for what may have been the hundredth time, taming flyaway strands that seemed to only exist in her mind. Her hair looked perfect, swept softly back from her face in waves, parted in the middle and gathered at the back. I nodded, already sick of this wedding, and placed the plate of toast in front of her on the vanity. Ignoring it, she gazed intently at herself, pinching her cheeks and puckering her lips in a kiss that would soon be delivered in front of our closest family and friends.

"Today I marry William and we begin our lives together. Oh, everything has to be just perfect," she mooned, maybe to me, maybe to the lovely girl in the mirror. "He's wonderful, isn't he? I am so happy. So very happy."

Ivy was getting everything she wanted: a charming, handsome, well-off man who adored her and wanted to make her his wife. And what's more, in a few hours, relatives and friends would arrive by train and touring car to witness his public declaration of her worthiness. The Chestnut Hill contingent of William's family would descend upon Willow Grove in their finery, and after the ceremony, they would claim Ivy as one of their own. I had no doubt that she would fit in perfectly. Beautiful and well-mannered, Ivy would gracefully slip into her life as William's bride. Their house would be ready for them upon their return from their three-week honeymoon in Maine. It was a quaint bungalow just off Germantown Avenue, already full of fine furniture cast off by William's mother.

And this room would be mine. I considered filling it with books and creating a cozy nook where I could paint, perhaps placing a chair close to the window so the morning sun could ignite my imagination. But, no, why bother? I would not be here much longer either. I, too, would be off soon, on my own adventures.

Though I knew full well Papa wanted me to follow in Ivy's footsteps—nice husband, new house, eventual family—somehow I needed to make him understand what I wanted. How could I impress on him that my vision of life didn't stay stagnant, it was always moving, flowing in new directions, bright with new experiences. I thought of that tablecloth, yearning to blow away, and felt as though it was Papa's hands forcing me down, letting the air out from under me, straightening me into a life that was orderly and smooth.

But why would he even want me to stay? Thinking of the curdled rarebit that I had dumped into the bin this morning, I knew I was truly terrible at food preparation. My heart wasn't in it, never would be. Mama would fix the rarebit, make a new one easily. She would make it right.

Though Ivy was meant to be packing for her honeymoon, she sat at her mirror, lost in her own reflection. With a sigh, I began picking up the clothing strewn all around, wishing it were my suitcase that was being loaded in anticipation of departure. I folded dresses and stockings, rounded up matching stray shoes and hats. Ivy began talking at some point, idle chatter, and I assented at the pauses as necessary.

When the room was tidier and Ivy was nearly packed, I flopped down on my bed. Staring at the ceiling, I listened as Ivy prattled on about the guests, the honeymoon, and all things wedding.

Mama came upstairs, now dressed in her finery, and helped Ivy put on her lace wedding gown. When dressed and veiled, Ivy's loveliness caught in my throat. She was just as striking as the Lady Lilith painted by Dante Gabriel Rossetti, but more delicate, with a fragile grace.

Feeling clunky, I dressed in the white dress and baby blue sash Ivy had chosen for me. Though I could never match Ivy's beauty, I saw approval in Mama's eyes as she reached for a barrette and fiddled it into my dark brunette bun.

"Let's leave the bride, shall we? I need some help with a few last-minute things," Mama said and bent to gently kiss the top of my head. Turning toward Ivy, she said, "Tish and I will go down now and greet the guests. Papa will come get you when it is time. Oh, Ivy, you are so lovely today. I hope you have a wonderful marriage." With a peck on Ivy's cheek and a squeeze of both her hands, Mama let go of her oldest daughter, and cast her off into adulthood and matrimony.

• • •

William, looking dapper in his dark suit, hair slick and shining in the afternoon sun, stood in our backyard near the minister, awaiting his bride.

The musicians began to play and the lilt of the notes danced through the guests as we all stood and turned to watch Ivy. Her arm slung through Papa's, they stepped down off the back steps and began a slow procession down the aisle. Ivy glowed from within and her happiness burst through in a smile she could not contain. Papa looked serious but happy in his brown suit. Mama, Oliver, and I stood at our seats in the front row, our bodies turned to face Ivy and Papa, welcoming them to the altar, to a new beginning.

With all eyes on my sister, I began to daydream and glance through the crowd. There were many faces I didn't recognize, wizened grand dames surely from Chestnut Hill, distant cousins in fine suits and flowered hats. Along with them, our Philadelphia family and new Willow Grove friends were here. Mr. Ferguson, the man from whom Papa bought the house, and his handsome wife stood together, tall and proud. Mr. Malcolm was in the row behind them, as reedy as Ichabod Crane, fussing over his handkerchief, attempting to make it behave in his breast pocket.

Beyond the guests, the waiters moved silently, readying the tables for the luncheon. One in particular caught my eye. There was something familiar about him. It was Ellis. He looked up and gave me a slow smile. Embarrassed, I darted my eyes back to Ivy and Papa. What was he doing here? Heat climbed up my neck.

The minister spoke of wine and Canaan, but I had trouble concentrating on the sermon. I was still annoyed at him because of our last encounter but I could feel Ellis' presence balloon and consume the backyard. I was conscious of my every movement, a tuck of my hair behind my ear, a kind gaze down at Oliver, a smile in Ivy's direction, knowing he was watching me. Eventually, I could no longer fight the urge to look in his direction. Like holding my breath, there was only so long I could struggle, and my head turned in sharp exhale to seek him through the crowd. When I found him, his eyes were shifted sideways and on me, silently awaiting my glance. I swiveled my head around, a grin sneaking its way up my cheeks, and vowed not to look again.

• • •

Ivy and William were wed and the band exchanged their string instruments for lively brass horns. Celebratory blasts peppered the party as the guests helped themselves to food and wine. The ceremony chairs were whisked away, leaving the backyard open for mingling. People collected in small groups, plate or drink in hand, hearty laughter and raucous regaling in their conversation. Though I was meant to be helping Mama socialize with the guests, after the ceremony, I was overwhelmingly tired and embarrassed by my own bold stares at Ellis. I stayed in the house, briefly greeting the guests that freely moved about, and trying to look busy. The back door squeaked its opening and I knew it was him. I felt Ellis walk across the kitchen toward me more than actually seeing him, my eyes locked on the floor and heart racing.

"Hello, Tish," he said.

"Oh, hello Ellis."

"You look lovely."

I fiddled with my necklace and looked all around the room, anywhere but at his face. I knew he was seeking eye contact. My stomach fluttered. Finally, with a deep breath, I looked up at him, and there they were, his melted chocolate eyes, waiting for mine.

"Your home is lovely too," he continued, "and not a far walk from the boarding house where I am staying."

"Are you a waiter here today?" I asked, looking at his uniform and tray of punch glasses.

"I pick up odd jobs on days off from the park. Would you like some punch?"

I nodded, and he lowered the tray for me to take one of the pink-filled cups.

"I can take a break now if you'd like to show me around," he said. Without waiting for my answer, he put the tray down, braced my elbow and led me out to the front porch. Casually, he propped his shoulder on one of the posts, balanced on one foot, and crossed his ankle over the other. I sat down in one of the rocking chairs.

"I'm surprised you are so eager to leave this place," he said. "Like Dorothy says, 'There's no place like home.'"

"I do like the house. I just want to see more. I want to see everything!" I said.

Slowly Ellis said, "Then I think you should."

He had said this before, but this time it felt like an invitation. I looked at his hands, strong and wiry. They were big hands, hard and used, with dirt under his short fingernails. So unlike Papa, who, despite hard work, kept his nails meticulously clean. I could hear Papa now, his voice booming from behind the house, bursting with pride at his eldest having made such a fine match.

"You were right about one thing, though: I don't know how to convince my father that I can go," I lamented. "I have mentioned it a few times and he always says the same things about it being unwise for women to travel alone. He wants me to stay here, make a life in the delicatessen. But it simply isn't what I want. I can't imagine my life here, without experiencing other places, other scenery. Reading about it in books is not enough for me. The more I read, the more I yearn to experience it for myself."

"Maybe the solution is simpler than you realize. Maybe you don't go alone," Ellis said. Though his words were confident, his chin was turned down and his eyes were hesitating, looking up at me through his thick eyelashes.

"Pardon me?" I blushed.

He waited a moment, looked up at the porch ceiling. "Would your father be happier if you traveled with an escort, someone who could earn money as well?"

A shocked laugh escaped my lips. Ellis was so bold, too bold. I had no answer for him. There were footfalls on the porch steps and Oliver appeared. He tugged at my skirt, saving me from yet another inappropriate conversation with Ellis, but one I desperately wanted to continue.

"Time to say goodbye to Ivy!" His little hand grabbed mine and pulled. A crowd passed by us on the porch and gathered along the street's edge. Ivy, now changed into her honeymoon suit, made a grand exit from the front door with her new husband by her side. They descended the porch steps to the street without a sideways glance at us. William opened the door of his touring car to allow Ivy to get in. With a grand salute toward the guests, he climbed in himself. A moment later, the engine roared to life and they jostled down the road, away from the waving crowd.

I looked back at Ellis only to find that he was no longer standing on the porch with me. Oliver was hanging halfway off the railing and the two of us watched the other guests disperse. Mama exchanged kisses with many people, her own cheek lightly brushing cheek after cheek. I took Oliver's hand and led him to the backyard.

"Did you have a fun day, Ollie?"

He nodded, his hot hand sweaty in mine. His eyelids were heavy and we sat down in the shade.

"Tell me a story, Tish," he asked. He leaned against me and fiddled with the blades of grass to our side.

"Once upon a time there was a little girl named Alice," I began. "She was sleepy like you and so settled down in the grass for a nap, when all of a sudden she saw a white rabbit."

The wait staff, including Ellis, busied themselves cleaning up the yard. They whisked away the dirty dishes and removed the tablecloths and chairs. Oliver's eyes got heavy, Alice met the Cheshire Cat, and soon the backyard was just as it was before.

Groaning, I hoisted Oliver up and brought him inside the house and up to bed. I settled him and went downstairs to help Mama. Back in the foyer, I felt a hand on my elbow. "It's time for me to go," Ellis said, his voice close and soft in my ear.

I stood still, hoping he would ask to see me again. When he remained silent, I said, "Yes, of course."

"I was glad to spend the afternoon with you."

I smiled. "Me too."

The swish of layered skirts announced Mama's arrival. "Well, hello. I don't think we have met. I'm Mrs. Hess, Ivy and Tish's mother. And you are?"

"Ellis Cassidy, ma'am. Your home is beautiful."

"Thank you," Mama said, looking a bit confused.

"Well, we are just about finished here. I met your daughter at the park a few weeks back, and just wanted to say goodbye."

"Lovely to meet you Mr. Cassidy. Thank you for your assistance today." With a nod and sideways look at me, she took her leave.

"Right, well. Tish, I must be going," Ellis said, placing his straw boater hat on his head. Quickly, and catching me completely by surprise, his lips brushed mine in an exquisitely tiny kiss. My shock was bright, like lightning, intense and brief, leaving me unsure if it had really happened.

Ellis closed the front door behind him and I turned to see Papa standing there, his eyes cold.

• • •

Papa slowly folded his arms across his chest. He waited. My heart pounded in my ears.

"Local boy?" he asked. His words sliced straight through me. My ears were suddenly hot.

"No, but he works at the park," I said.

"Seems to me he works for the caterer. How do you know him?"

"I met him the day I went to the park with Ivy and William. That is his usual job—he said he gets odd jobs on his off days," I explained. "I suppose that is why he was working here today. I don't know." My words came out too quickly. They sounded like excuses. I was flustered by the kiss and by Papa witnessing it. Papa was not impressed with my explanations.

"It occurs to me that if you don't know a man very well that you should not be allowing him to kiss you," Papa said. His voice was gaining anger.

"Yes, Papa, I know. That was too bold of him."

"Indeed." He nodded. A decision had been made. "I don't want you to see him again."

"But, Papa!" I swallowed hard. My jaw set stiff and I tasted iron. I couldn't go West, I couldn't see Ellis, I couldn't find my way out from under Papa's thumb. His rules were infuriating.

"I'm not going to stay here and be your spinster daughter, working for you in the shop forever!" I shouted. "One way or another, sooner or later, I'm leaving."

"Oh, that's rich. What a daughter you are turning out to be, kissing strangers, forsaking your family!"

His disappointment in me cut like a knife, but I soldiered on, afraid if I gave up now that I would lose the battle forever.

"Papa, why can't you understand that I don't want what you want, what Ivy wants?"

He waved me off with both hands. "You're too young to know what you want."

"I'm not, Papa," I said, getting quiet now. "I don't want to work at the delicatessen."

His eyes were steel. "You will work at the delicatessen and you will stop seeing that man. I've raised you better than this." I began to protest again, but he cut me off. "I've said my peace."

I fled upstairs to my bedroom, grateful to have it all to myself. I paced back and forth, furious and impotent, my hands in fists at my hips. Rage colored my cheeks and furrowed my brow. Mama arrived in the doorway, soft as a cat.

"I heard what happened," she said.

I waited for her reprimand, but it didn't come.

"Oh, Mama!" I cried, flying into her arms, my tears breaking the dam and spilling over. I leaned into her, my chest heaving and spirit broken. "I'll never be allowed to do anything, Mama, ever."

Mama smoothed my hair and led me to the edge of the bed to sit. She made hushing sounds to calm me. They merely reminded me of how much of a child I still was considered to be and I cried even harder. I was locked in this life, trapped by the mere happenstance of being born a girl.

I didn't know if Ellis was my way out, or if I even wanted him to be, but I wasn't going to let my father dictate my life choices anymore. I snuffled and swallowed my tears, pulling out of Mama's embrace. I squared my shoulders but let Mama wipe my cheeks. Her smile was soothing, and I'd miss her when I was gone.

• • •

Tension remained between Papa and me, but I worked hard and stayed out of his way. A few days later, Papa flipped the sign on the shop door to CLOSED and fetched the bucket. He handed me the mop and disappeared into the back. Suds glistened on the floor and the mop squelched as I pushed it back and forth over the tile. Outside the window, fireflies lit pinpoints of fairy dust, and I tried to predict where they would light up next. A man in a blue jacket walked by and I instantly recognized his profile. Ellis was strolling, hands in his pockets, eyes down on the pavement. I hastily put the mop and bucket away and called out that I was heading home. Without waiting for an answer, I rushed to the street and hustled to catch up to him.

"Hello!" he said, turning to the sound of my quick feet.

"Hello," I said. I was suddenly mortified having chased after him. Papa would be furious. I didn't care.

"I just finished at the park," he said.

"Yes, we just closed up too."

"Are you free then?" he asked.

I nodded.

"Would you like to see a movie?"

I nodded again. Papa would be livid if he found out. But he wouldn't find out.

"Is there a back door?" I asked.

Ellis laughed. "Why?"

"Well, that is my father's shop," I said, pointing, "and he is still in there..." I trailed off, embarrassed to mention the event at the wedding that had triggered my father's anger.

"He can't see us go in?"

"He wouldn't like it."

Ellis considered this. "Let's walk around the block, the long way. There is a side entrance. Perhaps it will be open tonight."

We strolled and he was charming. He pulled candy out of his pocket and offered me one. I unwrapped the taffy, pulling the paper wrapper from the sticky sweet with some difficulty. Thin sugary strands along the edges fought back, separating into threads.

"They're the newest thing. They are called Mary Janes. Have you ever had one?" Ellis asked.

After taking a bite, the candy instantly embedded itself in my teeth. I shook my head no, unable to reply.

Once our mouths were ungummed, he said, "They are good, aren't they?"

I nodded. A subtle peanut flavor filled my palate as the stickiness slowly dissolved. I crumpled the wrapper and stuck it in the pocket of my skirt.

I looked periodically over my shoulder, certain that Papa was right on our heels.

"Everything all right?" Ellis asked.

"Papa is fairly strict, and he saw us... um... together, in the foyer, at my sister's wedding. He is still angry."

He nodded and grinned, but said no more about the kiss. Instead, he asked me more about Ivy and Oliver. I told him how it was hard to shine in Ivy's shadow, and how much I adored Oliver.

"How about your family?" I asked. "Are they still out in California?"

"They'll be there forever. Ma and Pa are miserable people, stuck in a life they both hate. Pa has a bad shoulder, and so it is hard for him to keep a job. They never really got along, my parents, always bickering and griping at each other. They are both the kind of people who constantly complain but never actually do anything to improve their situation. I'm their only child, and they were always involving me in their disputes, asking me to take sides. I spent my childhood dreaming of the places I could go, other cities I could live in, away from them. I never understood how they could stay together, hating their lives as they did. I got out as soon as I could."

"You talk about wanting to go back to California, though."

"California itself is great. I don't ever want to slow down, though, stay in one place like my parents did. They are mired in unhappiness, miserably rooted to one spot." He shuddered at the thought. "I won't even be here in Willow Grove much longer."

"I beg your pardon?" I thought maybe I hadn't heard him correctly.

"The park season is almost over, and I won't have a job once it closes. It will be time to move on, try somewhere new."

He shrugged. It was casual, infuriating. Our footsteps echoed in my ears. He was leaving so soon? I could taste the disappointment thickening at the back of my throat, sharp and metallic. What about all that he had said about perhaps going West together? My cheeks boiled with embarrassment. Why had I chased after him? If caught with Ellis, surely Papa would tighten his reins on me, and for what? Why did I jeopardize any chance at all to earn my father's trust for a man who was busy planning his next destination on the map without me? Why did Ellis even invite me to the movies? Perhaps I was just another girl in another town, someone to have a little fun with and then leave behind.

We walked the rest of the way around the block without speaking. The theater marquee was surrounded by white bulbs. *A Fool There Was starring Theda Bara and Edward José* was spelled out above the ticket booth. I felt like a fool myself. Inside, I shuffled my feet and avoided any conversation starters that Ellis sent my way. I considered leaving, but didn't want to risk Papa to see me walking out. I'd stay for the first twenty minutes of the show. By then, Papa would be on his walk home.

I was grateful for the dark theater where Ellis wouldn't be able to see me. We sat next to each other as I slowly built a wall between us. Suddenly, his hand snaked out toward me. He opened his fist and in his palm was another Mary Jane. I shook my head, declining the candy and any further kindness from him, focusing intently on the screen.

Virginia was sitting a few rows ahead of us, carelessly flicking popcorn into her mouth, gazing around the theater, completely ignoring a boy I didn't recognize seated next to her. As she scanned the crowd, she spotted me and waved with enthusiasm. I waved back with a simple shake of my wrist, wishing to be invisible. I could feel the mortification on my face and was sure that everyone could see it too. Virginia squinted to see who I was with. Ellis gave her a smart wave, as if to confirm that I was there with him. A bit flustered, she smiled and turned around to face front quickly.

The lights in the theater lowered and the black and white images danced silently across the screen, punctuated by the sound effects made in the balcony. It was hard for me to concentrate, my thoughts so focused on my own impulsive foolishness. Ellis looked at me from time to time, and though I could feel him wanting me to look back at him, I stared straight ahead.

The ominous music echoed my mood, but I was soon thankfully lost in the magic of the film. When the movie was over, we rode the crowd out of the theater, cascading as a group onto the sidewalk. I could hear the high voice of Virginia calling out to us. Ellis found my hand and held it tightly in his, pulling me out of the crush. I wanted to take my hand away but couldn't deny how wonderful his hand felt cradling mine and so allowed it until we were alone further down the road.

"Are you all right?" Ellis asked.

"Yes, I'm fine."

"You became very quiet all of a sudden."

"I was watching the movie. Isn't that what we were meant to be doing?"

"But before that too. And we were meant to be enjoying it together."

"Why? You are leaving in a few weeks. What is the point of us even getting to know each other? Why did you even ask me to the movies?"

"I wanted to spend some time with you."

"Is this what you do? Meet a girl in each new town, be charming, give her candy, make her interested in you, and then leave? On to the next?" My volume and word speed were increasing as I nearly spit at him.

"No, Tish. I really do like you. There have been other girls in other towns, yes, but I have never met anyone like you. You're smarter than most girls, though, funnily enough, you can't even comprehend how interesting you truly are. Most girls I meet want a house and family. You talk about art and travel and experiencing new things. Those are things we both want."

"Yes, but the difference is that you will get to do it all. I'll be stuck here, only dreaming about it." My fate washed over me. Everything was as it had been before I met him. It was as if he never existed. I deflated and my anger was gone. "Maybe I should just go home."

"If that is what you want."

He took my hand again, gently, but held it secure, and made as if to walk me home. My nerves crackled like kindling on fire, but I knew I needed to douse the flames.

"Goodbye, Ellis," I said, removing my hand from his. "It was very nice getting to know you. I wish you the best of luck wherever you are headed next."

"Tish, wait."

I didn't. I couldn't. Yes, he was handsome and exciting, but none of that mattered because he was leaving town. I felt abandoned as well as jealous of his ability to simply up and go. I turned quickly away from him and hurried alone up the hill toward my house, closing the door on us.

Inside, Papa and Mama were in the sitting room. They both flew to their feet when I came through the door.

"Tish, where ever have you been? You left the shop hours ago! We were worried sick!" Mama said.

"I'm sorry, Mama. I ran into Virginia and we went to the movies." It wasn't exactly a lie, and it rolled off my tongue easily. The truth didn't matter. Ellis wouldn't be in town long enough to anger my father further. "I should have sent word, but I just got wrapped up in the film."

"Well," Mama sighed. "We are glad you are all right. Time for bed. We need to be at the shop early tomorrow to make a new batch of Perfection Salad. We had quite a run on it today."

I nodded and apologized again before heading upstairs. As I dressed for bed, I removed my hair pins and emptied the pockets of my dress. My fingers stuck to a yellow candy wrapper. I pulled it out, remembering the sweetness of the taffy. I crumpled the paper and tossed it away, trying to forget the man who gave it to me.

• • •

The next morning, Virginia stopped into the shop for a visit, full of curiosity and gossip. Mama asked her how the movie was and I held my breath for Virginia's answer. She made no mention of Ellis to Mama.

"Why don't you girls go into the back," Mama suggested, "and count the cans of anchovies that we have left. Let me know if it is less than thirty."

Once on our own, Virginia's curiosity boiled over. "You disappeared so quickly that I didn't even get to meet the boy you were with. Not really a boy, though, was he? Is he older than we are? Tell me *all* about him. I'm simply dying to know!"

"Shh, keep your voice down. He's nobody, Virginia. He works at the park but is leaving town as soon as the park closes."

"Well, that's unfortunate. He's very handsome, in a dark sort of way."

"Oh, do we have to talk about him? It was silly for me to even spend time with him last night. I went home right after the movie." Desperate to change the subject and stop thinking about Ellis, I asked, "Who were you there with?"

"That was Michael Wyatt, but who cares? I told you, I don't care about any of those boys. I have bigger things in mind."

"Richer men, you mean?"

"Well, yes. Mr. Malcolm was in the barber shop yesterday and I could see his eye twitch when I asked Mama if I could go to the movies with Michael!"

"Virginia, how wicked!"

"How else will I get his attention?!"

"But why would you want to? If you don't like anyone in this town, why not travel a bit—we could go together—and maybe you'll meet someone elsewhere. If you marry Mr. Malcolm, you'll be stuck here in this town with him forever."

"Yes, but in a such beautiful house! And I would never have to sweep up dirty old hair clippings again! He lives so close to you, we could see each other every day! You and I could be great friends forever."

"We will be great friends forever, but, you know, you won't be able to visit every day. I'm not staying here. I'm going West."

"Yes, yes. You're very progressive, Tish. But how are you going to make it happen? Your father doesn't seem the type to just let you off on your own. He wouldn't even let you go to the park without my mother as chaperone. I can't believe he let you out with a man by yourself last night!"

"He didn't. I snuck out. I told them I was at the movie with you. But, Virginia, it was such a mistake." I covered my face. I could barely go on. "He is leaving town, just like that. How easy it is for him. I feel so tiny, like a mouse. Papa never understands me, and for a minute, it was like Ellis truly did." I sighed. "Well, no sense in dwelling on it anymore. There won't be anything between us now. Let's talk about something else."

• • •

A few weeks later, Ivy invited me to luncheon at her new home. I reluctantly went, after deciding that feeling inadequate at Ivy's was a change from feeling clumsy in the shop, and spent the trolley ride to Chestnut Hill bolstering myself for the afternoon with my sister.

Tucked on a quiet block of West Moreland Street, Ivy's house was tall and narrow with gables and dormers, dark stone and scalloped shingles. With an ample porch and decorative cast iron finials on the yard gate, it had a distinct air of good taste.

Ivy sauntered around inside, drink in hand, perfectly at home here. I doubted that she had lifted a finger since she had arrived. Her cheeks were rosy and her grin lit up her face. She spent our time together telling me how she had everything she had ever dreamed of: a handsome husband, a beautiful home, a life of leisure. Her contentment made me reel with jealousy, a feeling painfully familiar in regard to Ivy, but now heightened by my static life. I gritted my teeth, barely listening to her prattle on, as we sipped the iced tea her housekeeper brought to us on the slate area out back. When William came home from the office, he drove me back to Willow Grove.

It was evening by the time we arrived there and Mama, Papa, and Oliver were at the table eating dinner. William didn't stay, but I sat down and joined them.

"How was Ivy's?" Mama asked.

"It was beautiful. They really have a lovely home." I helped myself to the roast beef and potatoes that sat on the table.

"I'm glad you were able to spend time together," Mama said, passing me the bread. "We had an interesting day, didn't we?" Mama continued, looking at Papa. A grimace appeared on his face.

"Mr. Howerth came in again," Mama said.

"That man!" Papa said. "It's ridiculous. He came in just to stir up trouble. And at our busiest time, too, so that all of our customers could hear." Papa began jabbing his fork into his meal.

"Oh, how awful. What happened?" I asked.

Mama took a deep breath to begin the story. I expected her to be as angry as Papa, but there was a twinkle in her eye that I didn't understand. "So, yes, it was just about lunchtime and the rush had begun, though I suppose Mr. Howerth wasn't particularly busy at his barber shop at the time. Anyway, he came in to the delicatessen and started pointing out, rather loudly, all the products that might be German. He struck up a conversation with another customer about the filthy Huns and the conflict in Europe, and just went on and on."

I could feel anger radiating off Papa in hot waves.

"It was terrible," Mama continued. "Papa was trying to help the customers, but he was getting angrier and angrier..."

"That son of a...," Papa interjected and then trailed off.

"Son of a what?" Oliver asked.

Mama shot them both a sharp look but continued with the story. "Papa couldn't say anything, couldn't get into a fight with Mr. Howerth there and then. I tried to smooth it over, but Mr. Howerth kept going." She paused and smiled. "Then one of the customers started defending us. He stood up for Papa, saying that, despite his heritage, it sounded like Papa wasn't siding with his war-hungry ancestral home."

"I had already said as much, but Howerth wouldn't listen," Papa grumbled.

"No, he wouldn't, but the man just kept on arguing with Mr. Howerth, quite boldly in fact, and Mr. Howerth eventually stormed out of the shop!"

"Well. I am glad to hear that at least we have one loyal customer," I said.

"Actually, this was a new customer," Mama said. There was that twinkle again. "It was your friend. That man who was a server at Ivy's wedding."

I was stunned. Ellis was still in town? He had gone into the shop? And defended Papa? Had he been looking for me? A silly grin crept up my cheeks and I couldn't keep it down. I looked at my plate, feeling my face get hot.

"Ellis?" I asked, trying not to be too hopeful.

Mama grinned. "I suppose so. After Mr. Howerth left, he asked after you. Seemed rather disappointed that you weren't there. He left, but came back with a letter for you. I'll get it," Mama said.

I looked at Papa, sure I would see disapproval. He just kept eating, his fork jabbing at his plate in a blatant attempt to ignore my gaze.

Mama returned from the foyer, letter in hand, and I ripped open the note.

> *Dear Tish,*
>
> *I was in town today to pick up a paycheck, but stopped in to the delicatessen in hopes of seeing you. I have secured a job at the shipyard in Philadelphia, and am rooming near there for the next few months. I feel terribly about how we left things and I would truly like to spend some more time with you. If you would like that as well, please write back.*
>
> *Ellis*

Oliver was curious and climbed into my lap, crinkling the paper. He peered at it and I let him hold it. "What does it say, Tish?"

"It says he'd like to spend some more time with me," I said, snuggling Oliver close, gleeful. But would Papa allow it? I peeked at him around Oliver's curls. "Papa, may I?"

He grunted and waved me away with his hand. A thrill ran through me. I supposed that was a yes.

• • •

I sent a note to Ellis the next day and then waited to hear from him. Each moment before I heard back was spent in self-doubt. Had he changed his mind?

These thoughts were unavoidable and infuriating. I had always scoffed at Ivy for her focus on William, and hated how I was now behaving similarly. I tried to remain calm, think of other things, read my book, help Mama, paint, but time and time again my thoughts returned to Ellis.

He sent a quick note asking to take me to Kemble's Oyster House here in Willow Grove on Saturday evening. He planned to take the trolley into town and pick me up at seven-thirty.

When he arrived, we walked downtown. The street lamps were beginning to flicker on. A warm breeze did little to cool the air. Soon, I could feel sweat run down my back.

"Is it hot like this in California?" I asked.

"It's hot, but not as humid. It is almost wet here; the air is so heavy. In California, there is almost always a breeze by the ocean. And sometimes a green flash."

"A green flash?" I asked.

"Yes, at sunset, just at the moment when the sun disappears behind the ocean, there is sometimes, not every day, but sometimes the top tip of the sun turns green and hovers. If you blink, you'll miss it."

"Sounds amazing. Have you seen it?"

"Once or twice. It helps to look for it every day," he ventured. I could hear unease in his voice, and I was glad to know that I wasn't the only one who felt at risk.

"I'd like that," I said, earning a grin. He took my hand in his and we continued into town.

When we arrived at Kemble's, he opened the front door for me and I stepped inside. Small and simply decorated, it smelled of the wax candles standing dripping in old wine bottles on each table. There were a few other couples there. Some had their heads tucked over their plates. Others were relaxing, leaning back in their chairs with a glass in hand. I had never been to a restaurant as fancy as this. I let Ellis usher us over to a table by the window, and sat when he pulled out my seat. A voluptuous waitress approached with paper menus and greeted Ellis by name.

I raised an eyebrow at him, wondering how he knew her, but not daring to ask. Instead I held my menu up in front of my face to see what they offered. He chuckled and looked at his menu.

"Ellis!" A voice boomed and a swinging door banged. A robust man came out of the kitchen wearing a filthy apron which he used to wipe his hands. He clapped Ellis on the back. His hair was dark and wet, slicked off to the side. He smelled like the ocean.

"Hey there, Marty. Great to see you! Is your pop back there too?" Ellis asked.

"Nah, it's just me today. Pop's gone down the shore to haggle with the supplier. Want some oysters? You know we only serve the best."

"Yeah, great. Why not have Betty bring us a dozen?"

"Will do. It's great to see you, Ellis," Marty said. Then, nodding at me, added, "Miss."

When Marty returned to the kitchen, Ellis explained, "I used to shuck oysters with Marty in Cape May. He and I heard about the park together a few years ago, and when he told his dad, they decided to open up the restaurant."

I nodded, keeping my eye on Betty as she sauntered over in her tight skirt and sleek black hair. High above her head, she held a silver tray of opened oysters nestled on a bed of ice. She lowered it to our table and asked if we wanted anything to drink.

"Do you have any champagne back there?"

A low whistle emitted from her pursed red lips. "Sure, Ellis. We got some, but it ain't cheap."

"That's all right, Betty. We'll take it," Ellis said. She slowly walked back toward the kitchen, hips swaying like a sleek eel. I couldn't take my eyes off her. I heard Ellis chuckle again. "That's Marty's wife," he said. Then lower, "She's a piece of work. She's not particularly bright, but Marty looks at her like you are now, with your eyes popping out of your head. You should see them fight, though! It's a sight to behold! Have you ever had oysters before?"

I looked at the tray laden with purple and white shells. The watery gray globs within were anything but appetizing. I had eaten oyster fritters before, but those oysters were chopped fine, battered in flour, and fried golden in oil. These seemed naked, without anything to hide their true selves.

"I have never eaten them raw," I admitted.

"You'll love them. Just pour one into your mouth, chew just a moment, and then swallow."

I picked up an oyster, holding the oblong shell to my lips. I could smell the brine. I tipped the oyster between my parted lips and was suddenly awash with slick salt and sea. It was wonderful, fresh and dazzling as the sun's glitter on the water. Ellis seemed pleased and tucked into the oysters as well. Betty arrived with the champagne, opening the bottle with a loud pop and gush of foam, but I kept my eyes on Ellis, who grinned back at me.

It was my first sip of champagne, too. Papa never permitted alcohol, and I felt a rush of independence as I brought the glass to my lips. The bubbles tickled my nose and the liquid exploded and fizzed in my mouth like the park's fireworks. In that moment, I knew that I wanted to be with Ellis for as long or as little as we could. I craved the new experiences that Ellis offered. Being with him was like standing before the sunrise after the dark night. I loved the way he looked at me as if I were the only one in the room. I loved the way he didn't make me feel juvenile for never having had a raw oyster. Rather, he seemed eager to share something new with me. I began to understand that his deep stare wasn't predatory, it was focused, and I reveled in being his focal point. He seemed to enjoy exposing me to new things, as if somehow I was worthy of it. We fit together, me eager to learn, he eager to teach.

We talked about his job at the shipyard, and I told him about the days in the shop. I opened up about my painting. We talked and talked. He took a long gulp of the champagne and, with a wink in my direction, signaled for more oysters.

CHAPTER SEVEN

Molly

Despite my good intentions, I couldn't put Hayden down long enough to cook. The meat turned brown in the fridge, the produce rotted to fruit fly ridden mush. My days began to run together—mixed up and broken down into shattered two-hour increments based on Hayden's feeding schedules. I felt like an old sponge, dry and smelly and only useful for cleaning up messes. On the few occasions that Corey had shown interest in the bedroom, I was too tired and too grimy, constantly covered in some sort of baby discharge.

It mattered little, though, as most of the time Corey didn't seem to notice. Any free time he had away from the office, he wanted to dedicate to Hayden. Corey came home from work, grease stained take-out bag in hand, gave me a brief platonic kiss, and then focused on Hayden. With the baby securely in his arms, he chatted with him as if he were one of his college buddies. In a soft voice, he sang old fraternity songs with ghastly inappropriate lyrics. Corey seemed very happy.

I tried to push away my feelings of being ignored. It was hard to admit that I was jealous of my baby and the attention that my husband was paying to him instead of me, but there it was.

Feeling barely visible, I settled in for another night on the couch next to my boys, taking my seat in the same spot where I sat most of the day. While Corey seemed content to relax at home, away from the rigors of the office, I desperately wanted to go out. I wanted to do something that adults do, maybe see a movie, or grab dinner, a gin and tonic, or maybe a glass of wine. Anything to break up the repetitive boredom of feed, wipe, repeat. My skin itched for night life.

"Corey, let's go out next Friday," I said.

"Ugg, I'm so tired on Fridays. All I want to do is come home, relax, and be with you guys."

He listlessly flipped through the channels on the television. I held onto the edge of my emotions, hovering over something dark, a scream sitting just under the surface. Would Corey even react if I let it loose? It was like I wasn't here at all. I had disappeared, lost in the wilds of the baby's needs. It no longer mattered if I needed to use the bathroom, or brush the mats out of my hair. The baby's needs came first. And the baby seemed to always need something.

I desperately wanted to feel like more than the baby's nurse. I needed Corey to appreciate me for me, rather than the lady who kept his kid's bottom clean.

Some women seemed to revel in motherhood. Every moment is a blessing and their baby an angel. I didn't seem to be cut from that motherhood shroud. Shouldn't I look at my baby's face and think that all the sleepless nights and scream-filled days were worth it? I was outmaneuvered by a tiny child and needed a break.

"Please, Corey. I could really use it."

"Who will we get to babysit? Jocelyn and Hank just took Colten to another tournament in Cooperstown."

"I'll ask Liz across the street if she knows anyone. It will just be a few hours."

"Liz? You hardly know Liz, let alone some girl she recommends."

"Liz's kids are alive—whoever she recommends will be fine."

"Okay, but we meet the sitter first, and then just a quick dinner. Two hours, tops."

I nodded, taking the small victory and trying to ignore the feeling that he didn't want to spend more than two hours alone with me.

Liz had plenty of recommendations, and together she and I decided on Betsy, a girl who was reliable and available.

The next Friday afternoon, I carefully picked out an outfit, tearing apart still unpacked boxes to find pants, shirts, dresses. I decided on a dress that highlighted my ample nursing bosom and hid the extra girth lingering around my waistline. The dress was a flowing crimson and I paired it with a soft black cardigan sweater. With Hayden in one arm, I rummaged through my jewelry box with my free hand and found some dangle earrings. I carefully bent down and fished some high heels out of the dark corners of my closet. The shoes seemed tighter than before, but dates required high heels and so I resolved to wear them anyway. With my outfit planned, I spent time daydreaming about having my arms free, with Corey's full focus on me, our conversation ranging from current events to how much he loved me.

An hour or so before it was time to go, I positioned Hayden's swing chair next to the shower and strapped him in. As soon as I was out of sight behind the shower curtain, he began fussing. Hoping to soothe him, I opened the curtain partially and sang to him. I quickly shaved my legs, nicking my ankles a few times, and used extra conditioner in my hair in hopes it would help retroactively. I could have stayed in there for hours, the cascade of warmth running down my back, if not for the escalating screaming. Reluctantly I shut off the water, dried myself quickly, and rescued Hayden from the seat. He nestled in but continued his tirade. With soaking wet hair, I sat on our bed and nursed him until he was snoozing. I lowered him onto the center of our bed and finished getting ready. Like a schoolgirl who has just been asked out by her first crush, I became jittery with anticipation of the night.

This morning, Corey had said he would be home at seven, so I had arranged for Betsy to come a little earlier to show her where things were and what Hayden needed. Though scant feelings of guilt about leaving the baby were starting to creep into my mind, I reasoned that he would cry all evening for me anyway; it didn't matter much if he cried with someone else. As long as he was alive and safe by the time we arrived home, I would be happy. His snooze didn't last so

I dressed him in his footed pajamas and changed his diaper. I left two pumped bottles of milk out for Betsy to give him later.

When I heard the doorbell ring, I checked the mirror one last time and was fairly pleased with what I saw. My hair looked nice, smooth and sleek, and the makeup that had sat unused for months did wonders for the dark circles under my eyes. Though my body shape had definitely changed, my big contour underwear squeezed my midsection into something that was fairly acceptable.

With Hayden on the playmat, I welcomed Betsy in and showed her the evening routine.

"Hello, family," Corey said when he came in from work. "You look pretty tonight, Molly."

Pleasure rippled through me.

"And there's my handsome boy!" he continued, "Did you have a good day, bud?"

I didn't want Corey to get comfortable, lest he change his mind about going out, so I quickly picked up Hayden off the playmat and said, "Say hello, and goodbye, to Daddy, buddy!" I began to turn Hayden around to face Corey and felt a warm splash on my face. A sweet and sour smell was in my nose. Hayden had vomited all over me. It was in my hair, covering my neck, and spilling down my shoulder, arm, and front of my dress.

"Oh, Mrs. Hess, here, let me take Hayden for you," Betsy said, rushing to help. "I'll clean him up. There are new pajamas in his drawer, right?" She whisked him away and I just stood there, utterly defeated, arms out, frozen by vomit. I spit something chunky out of my mouth.

"Oh geez. Do you still want to go?" Corey asked. I knew he was looking for an excuse to stay in, loosening his tie and fumbling to remove his shoes.

"Stop! Yes! We are still going. Don't take your shoes off. I'll be right back down."

I raced upstairs to the bathroom. My face and neck were sticky and washing off the vomit smeared my makeup. My hair was matted and wet in spots and I wiped at it with a wet wash cloth. I ran a brush through it the best I could, hiding the soiled strands behind cleaner hair. Back in my room, I searched for another outfit to wear. Settling on a brown sweater and jeans because they were clean and nearby, I checked the mirror. With a sigh, I headed downstairs.

• • •

Though I searched for topics for discussion, we rode to the restaurant in silence. I refused to talk about the baby and struggled to find another subject. I supposed Corey did too, since he sat quietly beside me, focusing intently on the road. It wasn't a long drive, but each moment that spread out in front of us made me more uncomfortable. We used to share companionable silences, peppered by a glance and smile every so often, but this was different. We were in a dearth of things to discuss. Where had I gone? I used to be fairly interesting.

"Do you think that Hayden will be all right?" Corey asked.

"Yes, Corey. He'll be fine. Tell me about your day."

"But, how long has Betsy been babysitting?"

"I don't know exactly. A few years for Liz's kids, I suppose."

"Does she know where the emergency numbers are?"

"Yes."

"And she knows not to let anyone inside?"

"I'm sure she does." My voice was shrill and I stopped myself. This wasn't how this was supposed to go. "We get so little time to ourselves," I said more calmly. "When is the last time it was just you and me?" I took his hand closest to me and tried to save the evening with a pasted-on smile.

Corey sighed. "You're right. Let's try to have fun tonight. How was your day?"

"Fine, I guess. Hayden was pretty grouchy. He always is though."

"At least you get to spend time with him," Corey said and began talking about work and his colleagues. I looked out the window at our town. We were stopped by the train crossing and waited while the train passed. Through the blaring whistle, Corey was telling a story about some hilarious thing that happened to him and his officemates at lunch. We pulled into the restaurant parking lot and I laughed at the peak of the story just as I was supposed to.

"I think you are really going to like this place. Anne says it's wonderful," Corey continued.

"Who's Anne?"

"I just told you that whole story about her and Jim... Molly, weren't you listening? She's the payroll manager."

"Oh right, of course," I quickly covered. "Sorry. What did she say about this restaurant?"

"She said it was great. Awesome oysters."

"Well, great."

We were seated and I drank the gin and tonic I had ordered a little too quickly, loving the way it rang all the way through to my fingertips. Corey and I used to go out drinking often. I'd work until the restaurant closed, and then we'd go to our favorite bar, staying until the bartender declared last call. Back in our apartment, we'd crank up the music and dance, nightcap in hand, before falling into bed tangled up in each other.

Now, I slurped up the ice-cold dregs of my gin and tonic. It tasted like home. With our meal we switched to wine, the tannic liquid staining our lips. Finally, Corey and I had things to talk about. The more I drank, the more I wanted to chat. I went on and on as if I hadn't actually talked to another human in years.

"So I found this black book of recipes when I was packing up the bookshelves," I said.

"Oh, yeah?" Corey asked, dipping his fork into our tuna tartar appetizer.

"Umm hmm," I said, taking a bite of it myself. It was cool and luscious, with just a hint of citrus. "The book is full of old menus and recipes from Hess's Delicatessen. Some are really strange."

Corey furrowed his eyebrows at me. I had made the mistake of insulting Aunt Tish.

"Well, maybe not strange, just old-fashioned," I back peddled. "When did they open the place?"

"It was her parents' before her, so maybe the Twenties? When I was a kid, it was deli sandwiches and take-out potato salad, that kind of thing."

"Maybe I'll try to make one or two of the older recipes, see how they taste."

"Sounds good. I miss your cooking. And I loved Aunt Tish's."

Of course he did.

Our salads arrived dressed perfectly, balanced with elements of crunch, acid, and sweetness. Next, Corey had a steak spiked with peppercorns and I savored a creamy green pea risotto. It was wonderful to be out, wonderful to be served food that I didn't have to cook, wonderful to have the wine poured for me every time my glass dipped below a certain level.

I wanted to stay for another drink at the bar, but Corey was anxious to get home. I knew that when we left the restaurant, the shiny mood would burst. We would be back inside our lives again, in charge of an unhappy baby who I wanted so desperately to love me, and within hours, Corey would find a reason to be back at work. I reluctantly accepted my coat from the check station and walked to the car.

"You okay to drive?" I asked Corey as we crossed the parking lot.

He laughed. "You drank most of the wine!"

"Yum. It just tasted so good! I have three extra pumped bottles at home, so don't worry, Hayden won't get any of it."

"You're a good mom."

I said nothing.

"You know that, right?" Corey asked, stopping before we reached the car, turning my body so that I was looking straight at him.

I shrugged, looking down at the macadam.

"You are. I know I am busier at work than you would like, and I'm sorry that you are doing it mostly on your own. I'm really glad you are there with Hayden, and I know he is too, even if he doesn't act like it. You'll get used to being home with him."

I nodded, but wondered. Would I get used to it? Did I want to? The wine commingled my emotions and I fought off tears. I just nodded, not able to say anything, and turned toward the car. I heard my door unlock and I climbed into the passenger seat, buckling my seat belt. My chest prickled with the tell-tale signal of milk letdown and I felt my breasts leak, wet spots spreading through my sweater. We drove through the streets, still unfamiliar to me, and back to the house. It was a pretty house. I could admit that now.

I stumbled up the stairs, using my jacket to cover the wet circles on my chest. Corey paid Betsy. I vaguely heard her tell him that Hayden was a little fussy at bedtime, but pretty happy overall. I changed into my pajamas thinking, well, of course the baby was happy, he only hates me. I didn't dare pop my head into the nursery to check on him. I crashed into bed and, with the wine's help, slept.

• • •

It was still dark when Hayden roused me, his wails rising in urgency and volume as I felt my way through the hallway to his room. A quick diaper change and I carried him back to our bed. Corey still slept soundly within, his arm thrown over his head and mouth parted slightly. I propped the pillows up on my side of the bed and latched Hayden on to eat. The clock read 4:47 a.m., and though it was still earlier than Corey's alarm was set to go off, I was pleased that Hayden slept this late.

As he nursed, I leaned my head back against the headboard and watched the sunrise out the window. Pink at first, then blazing orange, the light filled our bedroom. I had slept for five straight hours for the first time in months, and even that little extra sleep made a difference in my mood. I had a twinge of a headache from the wine, so settled back down into the covers after Hayden fell off my breast, partially sated and partially back asleep. His head dipping startled him into waking, so I sat up, switched him to the other side and nursed some more. Quiet again, I continued to watch the sunrise, enjoying the rare moment of peace, the edges of which were tinged with the beginnings of a feeling of gratefulness. Corey rolled over and woke slightly. His arms found us as he nuzzled his whole body close.

"Good morning, family," he said in a deep, sleepy voice muffled and buried in my hip.

I smiled down at him and Hayden, noting the similar slope to their noses and the dimples in each of their cheeks.

"Your son slept through the night," I said, softly so that I wouldn't jinx it or wake Corey if he had drifted back off to sleep.

"Hmmm, oh yeah?" came the half-asleep murmur.

"Yup, and I feel like a new person. I slept five hours. In a row."

"Big stuff," he mused.

"I know!"

Corey was awake now and sat up. He leaned over and lightly kissed me on the lips, and then smoothed Hayden's hair and kissed his forehead. "So, what do you two have planned for today while I pop into the office?" he asked, rubbing his eyes.

"More unpacking, maybe, and a walk around the neighborhood. Other than that..." I trailed off, not confident that even these small things would happen. "I really liked that risotto last night; maybe I'll try to recreate it. Or try one of the recipes from Aunt Tish's book." The details of our conversation last night were hazy because of the wine. "Did you say she took over the deli from her parents?" I asked.

Corey shrugged. "I actually don't know the exact details, come to think of it. I know she lived here in this house her whole life, never married, obviously, just stuck around and helped raise my dad. I think I asked her once why she didn't have a family of her own—you know, in that way children have of being brutally curious. I don't really remember what she said exactly, maybe simply that we were her family. She always seemed happy when we visited, my prying questions notwithstanding. We used to spend a lot of time here. She had the space for us all, and always welcomed us on Sundays and holidays. I think my dad used to feel obligated to visit, you know, since she was alone, but I always had a great time here.

"My mom was always moaning about how difficult I was as a baby, and even as a kid. 'Why can't you just behave like Hank?' she was always saying. So I was here a lot, all summer some years. Aunt Tish never seemed to mind that I was a little rowdy."

He got up and started to get dressed but he kept his voice low. "I remember she had this candy jar, full of lots of different penny candy. Hank and I would always raid it. He liked the green and white peppermints, but I always dug around until I found the Mary Janes. Do you remember those candies?"

I nodded.

"I loved those," he said. "They are hard to find now, too old fashioned I guess. Back then, Hank and I thought we were being sly, hiding the wrappers in our pockets to throw away when we got home so no one knew we were snacking. Over and over we would sneak to the candy jar. One day, Aunt Tish caught us. We thought we were going to be in so much trouble. Hank immediately swallowed his peppermint, the whole thing, but I couldn't hide the Mary Jane. It was too sticky and my mouth was all gummed up. In her sternest voice, she asked us if we had been eating candy before dinner. Hank said no. She knew he was lying. Even though he had a clear mouth, his lips were all green." Corey chuckled at the memory of it. "I confessed and told her I was sorry the best I could with my mouth all gummed up like that. She got this funny look on her face when I pulled the crumpled Mary Jane wrappers from my pocket. Instead of yelling at me like I expected, she laughed and pulled me into a tight hug. When she let go, I could see she had been crying a little, but she was smiling. From then on, those candies kind of became our thing. She set aside Mary Janes for me each time we visited, and then when I got older, I gave them to her for Christmas or Easter."

"You've never told me that. What a sweet story," I said.

"Yup, I was her favorite, the kid she never had maybe. Looking back, she was kind of a spinster, I guess. She worked in the deli and painted a lot of the paintings hanging around here, but never married or had a family. Just me. Hank too, but her and my relationship was different. Stronger."

I nodded. "And she was the mother you never had."

"I guess so, yeah," he said, buttoning his shirt.

I knew now in the pit of my stomach that it would be a fight to get those dark still lifes and landscapes off the walls. They weren't my style—our style, Corey's and mine—but it seemed like childhood nostalgia trumped my decorating tastes. This place might never be my own. I shifted Hayden down flat on the bed and shimmied out to the bathroom. I found the Advil and took two with a big glass of water, trying to knock out the headache before it roared in further.

Even though it was Saturday, Corey left for work and the long, boring day loomed before me. Placing Hayden in his swing, I padded to the kitchen. In my fog, I stubbed my toe on an unopened box in the walkway and cursed loudly. Hobbling to the fridge, I found it full of half-eaten take-out containers. I picked at a few, standing right there with the door open. Still hungry, I rummaged through the cabinet and found the iced oatmeal cookies I had bought at the grocery store.

I opened the plastic packaging and was hit in the face with the sweet and spicy scent of the days spent with my mom before she died. The cancer had dulled her appetite, but she still hankered for these. I had trouble recalling her face these days, but the taste of these cookies brought her memory into focus.

I put one in my mouth and crunched a piece off. They were crisp, with a familiar sharp cinnamon tang and a muted honeyed raisin sweetness. I wished that my mom was here now to eat them with me. I imagined us sitting together, fussing and cooing over a happy Hayden, sharing cookies while she doled out advice, maybe on how to get him to sleep longer, or nurse on a better schedule. She would help me unpack all our boxes, and find a way to ease Corey in to erasing some of Aunt Tish's overwhelming influence to make this house our own. She would encourage me to be the best mother I could be, be the best woman I could be.

"You can do more," she had said. But I wasn't sure that I could even do this. I felt hollow.

I ate three more cookies in rapid succession, shoving them in my mouth and nearly choking, unwilling to let her memory slip away when I swallowed. With tears streaming down my face, her companionship was present in each bite. But it wasn't enough. Gasping for air, I spewed hard crumbs out of my mouth, ran to the tiny bathroom, and vomited. Last night's wine burned my throat and reminded me how much things had changed.

• • •

Breathing slowly, I washed up and checked on Hayden. He had thankfully fallen asleep in the swing. Seizing the precious moments of solitude, I grabbed Aunt Tish's black recipe book and flipped through. Hastily, I chose one of the first recipes: Stewed Chicken. It was intriguingly odd. The recipe instructed to boil a whole chicken, three strips of bacon, a teaspoon of nutmeg, and a half teaspoon of pepper in a full pot of water. It seemed simple enough to restart my culinary career.

I rummaged around and happily found that I was already armed with all the ingredients. Quickly, knowing my time was limited, I plunked the bird into the pot and covered it with water. I sliced some bacon and dropped it in, looking on as it floated and bobbed. I sprinkled the nutmeg into the water and let it fan out across the surface. Pepper floated for a moment and then sunk to the bottom. I turned on the burner, covered the pot for its one-and-a-half-hour boil and began to prep the sauce as the recipe described. I juiced a lemon and mixed it with two tablespoons of currant jelly, and left it while I went to check on Hayden.

The swing made its rhythmic click clack, and I collapsed on the couch next to it. My eyes fought to stay open, but then snatched sleep like a starving wolf.

It felt like only a moment later when Hayden's cries pulled me up from a dream. I awoke furious, still voraciously hungry for rest. I felt worse for having napped, more tired than I had been before I fell asleep. My eyes were dry and my eyelids were sticky. I could smell the chicken in the pot and wondered what time it was. How long had we slept? As I stretched, the anger dissipated a bit, morphing into a deep disappointment that I couldn't rest longer. I stood and picked Hayden out of the swing, nestling him to my chest, bouncing and cooing to soothe him. We walked together into the kitchen to check on my meal.

A lift of the lid revealed a yellow foam on the surface and bacon bits rising and falling as if they were in a lava lamp. It needed more time, so I spent the next hour or so bouncing, cooing, and making stuffed animals dance to entertain Hayden. Then I rechecked the bird. It was tender, so I put Hayden back into the swing and hoisted the chicken out of the pot. The skin had fallen off and the meat was pulling away from the bone. I laid it dripping in a bowl, sneaking a taste. It was soft and supple.

I sliced some Brussels sprouts in half and tossed them in a roasting pan with olive oil, salt and pepper. I started a second pot of water to boil and pulled a package of farro from the cabinet. Once cooked, I would toss the farro with the Brussels sprouts. The sprouts' charred and nutty flavor would go well with the farro, and be a simple side dish to serve with the chicken. I hummed to myself and sang songs to Hayden while I worked. I was practically dancing, feeling like myself again, creating something wonderful for the people I loved.

Too soon, though, Hayden's back began to arch and he called out to be let out of the swing. Begging silently for more time, I quickened my pace. The lemon juice and currant jelly that I had mixed earlier still needed to boil and reduce. Then Aunt Tish's book said to combine that mixture with a cup of stock from the cooking pot and thicken it. With Hayden's swelling protests banging in my ears, I made a quick roux of butter and flour and mixed it in. The sauce became lumpy; in my rush, I didn't take time to temper it. Cursing and sweating, my hands whisked furiously at the lumps, and I called out to Hayden in tones that became less and less soothing. He was wailing at full force, his face red and arms in the air. I continued to work, sick to my stomach with the guilt of ignoring him, but also angry that I couldn't easily finish this one task.

I dropped the dirty whisk in the sink and took a deep breath to ensure that I hoisted Hayden out of the chair with a gentler touch than I felt inside. In my arms, he reeled his head back fiercely, nearly throwing himself to the ground in his anger. I started bouncing him and my tears fell to the kitchen floor. I looked around the room. It was a complete mess. I tasted the sauce. It was sharp with the tang of nutmeg and lemon and tart currants, simply awful. A few fixes popped into my head, but I couldn't do any of them now. Corey would be home soon and Hayden needed to be fed. I left the mess behind and went up to Hayden's nursery in search of distraction.

I had failed at dinner. I hadn't worked fast enough. Hayden hadn't given me enough time. The food I made was terrible. I was so tired. Why couldn't I do anything anymore? Where had I gone? Quiet tears of failure began falling as though they would never stop. I sat to nurse him, my nipples raw but my nerves more raw still, and as he ate, I chewed at my thumbnail until I could see the nail bed below.

"Hello, I'm home," I heard Corey call a little while later from downstairs. Then, "Molly? Are you here? Is something burning?"

Oh no! I never turned the burner under the farro off! I stood quickly, unlatching Hayden. His wail immediately gained siren strength. I raced downstairs to the kitchen, the baby still sideways and my breast flapping as I ran.

The pot smoked on the stove. All I could do was look at it. I stood there, breast exposed and dripping, a screaming baby in my arms.

Corey met me in there and shut off the burner. "Molly! You could have burned the house down. You need to be more careful. You're a chef, for crying out loud."

He was right that I could have set fire to the house, wrong about my being a chef. My bottom lip quivered, but there was nothing left. The tears did indeed stop. I had dried up. I was nothing. I was a feed bag, an endless slave to a tiny, relentless master. I turned my back on Corey and took up residency in my worn divot in the couch. I tucked in my one breast, only to pull out the other and offer it to Hayden, my eyes unfocused, too tired to feel anything but the furious pull of his little mouth as he sucked everything out of me. I listened to Corey clank things around in the kitchen. He entered the family room and I just stared at him.

"What were you making for dinner?" His voice was soft, approaching me like he would a frightened child.

I said nothing. He waited and then asked again.

"Chicken," I answered, "but the sauce is terrible. Brussels sprouts are in the oven. And that mess I burned was farro."

"I could cook more farro. Not in the pot that you killed, but in different one." He tried a smile.

"I just want to go to bed," I said, hearing the quake in my voice. "I can't do this. I'm so tired." I handed the baby to Corey and without another word, I climbed the steps and into bed.

• • •

I woke when Corey came eventually to bed, and before I could roll over and get comfortable again, Hayden was awake and crying.

There was no end. Hayden was up for hours that night, restless, wailing, wanting neither food nor a diaper change. He wasn't feverish, he had burped, he was dry, he didn't have a hair wrapped around his fingers or toes. I had tried everything to soothe him, but all that worked was holding him. Despite my exhaustion, I danced around the room, patting his back. Eventually, Hayden fell asleep. I tried to put him in his crib, my gummy legs begging for a break. Without my arms encasing him, though, he instantly woke up enraged, his back arching and his face beet red, needing to be soothed all over again.

And so, we continued to dance. After countless attempts, Corey stumbled into the nursery and took over, but Hayden just screamed louder.

"Don't worry, Mommy. Hayden and I are going to go work this out downstairs, dance around down there, maybe watch a few highlights from tonight's game..." Corey used the calm, cooing timbre that he used to talk to Hayden, and his voice trailed off as he padded down the steps.

I tried to settle into bed. Tossing and turning to get comfortable, I tried to drown out the hiccupping wails from downstairs. Even with my eyes closed, I could feel Hayden's need vibrating through my body, the blood in my temples thrumming with each scream. The longer I laid there and listened, the more keyed up I became. After a few moments, I gave up my attempt to sleep. It was impossible while he was crying. Like a prizefighter knocked so hard that he doesn't know he should stay down, I raged with adrenaline, swung my legs out of bed, and stormed downstairs.

"Just give him to me," I demanded. It was dark, but in the illumination of the television, I could see the startled look on Corey's face. I held my arms out in insistence. I glared at Corey and spat, "I can't sleep when he is screaming anyway, so I might as well just be up with him."

"I'll sit with you, Molly. We can do this together," Corey tried.

"No, just go upstairs. Get some sleep. There is no reason for both of us be awake. I'll try and feed him again." I sighed, loud and angry. Hayden belted in full fury, his bare gums visible in his open-mouthed rage while I flopped on the couch, grabbing the remote and deftly changing the channel.

Corey went back upstairs. I hiked up the hem of my shirt, unhooked my nursing bra, and positioned Hayden. He latched and quieted. The low canned laughter from the television was punctuated by Hayden's tender gulps and sighs. He fell asleep and fell off my breast. I adjusted him to my shoulder, flipped off the television, and walked up stairs, burping him along the way.

Ever so slowly, I lowered him into his crib and tip-toed away. Once out the door, exhaustion took over and I crept to our room where I found Corey fast asleep.

Bed. Finally. Its pillows and warm comforter welcomed me, the sheets rumpled and soft. I nestled in, closed my eyes, and took a deep breath, promising myself I'd be a better Mommy tomorrow.

Hayden started to cry again.

I sat straight up and let out a scream, guttural and beyond anger. "Why won't that kid sleep?" I was reaching full volume now and this—not Hayden's cries—woke Corey.

"I'll go get him," he murmured, his elbow propped up on the pillow, eyes half closed.

"No, it won't do any good. He just cries and cries. No matter what. I can't stand it anymore. I just can't stand it!" The tears were streaming down my cheeks and all my muscles were tight. I pounded the bed beside me in staccato to my words. "I can't do this. I have no idea what to do. I can't get him to sleep and I am so tired." I continued to rage, raunchy language from my days in the Aubergine kitchen burbling out of me. I was a beast, furious and helplessly cornered, nearly unhinged. Corey's eyes were fully open now, frozen on me, just watching without saying a word.

I gave him an exaggerated aggravated sigh and I went into Hayden's room and picked him up, shame and regret at my outburst following me there. Scared of myself and wondering if Corey was scared of me too, I took Hayden downstairs and latched him on. Again.

By then, a dim orange light was peeking in through the windows and nothing was on television but infomercials. I settled on the one where three pulses on a bullet-shaped machine got you salsa and some overly impressed friends. As slow as the dawn, tears continued rolling down my cheeks, droplets falling on Hayden's pajamas and neck. Eventually, at long last, Hayden and I both slept.

The early morning sunshine blazed through the windows and I woke on the couch with a quiet baby, his belly and cheek nuzzled to my chest and under my chin.

As the night filtered through my memory, I felt my guilt sour my stomach. I stroked Hayden's back, savoring his sleep. With my nose up against his head, I inhaled forcefully, taking in his baby scent. With each breath, I hoped his smell would kick-start any motherly instincts buried deep within me, providing inspiration on how to handle motherhood with grace. If anything changed, it was imperceptible. My self-loathing stuck in my throat and the day still loomed ahead of me, with nothing but Hayden's cries and my own inadequacies to keep me company.

Mired in self-pity and shame, I looked around at our new home and its walls that now confined me. The house was still full of boxes, pushed up against the edges of the room, half full and splayed open like surgical patients. Our framed art and wedding portraits still sat in layers on the floor, just leaning on the walls. In the morning light, I noticed that Corey had left last night's dinner dishes on the coffee table. Chicken bones sat dry on a plate with withered Brussels sprout leaves.

I could hear Corey bumping around upstairs, and I remembered with a sickness that he had another golf outing. It could have been a Sunday together, full of promise and sunshine, but dark edges began to cloud my vision. I was facing it alone. Corey seemed to still be going, even after the night we'd had, and the betrayal burned inside me. I closed my eyes and took deep breaths, trying to tamp down the scream that threatened and would surely wake the baby. Early birdsongs came from outside the window. A robin, perhaps with a full nest of hungry chicks, found reason to sing. The cheerful song mocked me.

I carried Hayden upstairs and settled him in the middle of our bed. Corey puttered around, looking for his gloves, his spikes, his tees, rummaging in his closet with his back turned to me.

"I'm going to grab a quick shower before you leave, while Hayden is asleep," I whispered.

He turned, looking put out. "Molly, I have to go. Right now. I'm going to be late. You slept in too late."

"I'll be really quick," I promised. "I haven't showered since Friday and my hair is so greasy it hurts. Please, Corey, it'll just take five minutes." I made my move toward the bathroom.

He caught my arm, tenderly, but with a firmness. "Seriously, Molly. The guys are waiting for me. Just take a shower during Hayden's next nap."

I took a deep breath, nervous that the fire forming at the pit of my stomach was going to blaze out of my mouth. Slowly, very slowly, I turned and looked at Corey. "Please, Corey. Five minutes of this whole day to myself before you spend the entire day out playing golf."

"I have to go," he said, brushing my cheek with the briefest of obligatory kisses and running out the bedroom door. The air in my lungs was sucked out of the room behind him. "Bye, buddy," he called to the baby when he was halfway down the stairs. And then he was gone.

His SUV engine roared in the driveway and made its signature ticking sound as he backed out into the street. The day promised so much, but denied me everything. I sat on the edge of the bed, unwilling to look at my child, so sweet in his sleep, so helpless, and so unfortunate to be stuck with me as his mother. I wanted to be patient and gracious about his incessant crying, knew I should be, knew losing my temper only made things worse. I expected more of myself and felt deep shame at my inadequacy. How could I yell like that about a baby crying? I was a terrible mother. A terrible human being. Even my husband couldn't wait to get away from me. Hayden didn't deserve this. He deserved a mother who was understanding and kind. I had screamed at the top of my lungs. Because of my baby. I was a monster.

As slowly as possible, without jiggling the mattress and waking Hayden, I laid down next to him. My limbs felt like rocks, immovable, heavy with exhaustion. I watched him sleep. His smooth cheeks and nose held the perfection of all babies as gazed upon by their mothers. I yearned to touch him, stroke his cheek, but held back for fear of waking him. He was beautiful in sleep. He was quiet and easy to love.

His eyelids fluttered and my stomach plummeted. I wasn't ready for him to wake up yet and froze like a deer startled in the woods. Just a few more minutes of silence, I pleaded over and over in my head. He grimaced, and then his face smoothed again. I let my eyes close and rested, hoping some sleep would be enough to fizzle the fire that raced through all my nerve endings, hoping that I would be enough for Hayden as a mother.

CHAPTER EIGHT

Tish, 1917

My courtship with Ellis continued, and we spent most of our time together. We talked about our future and where we would travel, but I was still only seventeen. So, for the summer, Ellis continued his work at the park and then found odd jobs when the season ended. He took a small room at the boarding house in Willow Grove, and we fell into a happy routine of life together. On his days off, I would leave the shop early and we would spend our time roaming the park or huddled as close as we dared in my parlor under the watchful eyes of Mama and Papa. He made me feel noticed and important and I loved how he listened intensely to my every word. Interruptions were frequent, though, as Oliver traipsed in and out, pretending to be a war plane or a chugging steam engine, with no shortage of little boy energy or chatter.

Outside of Willow Grove, frightening events continued to occur in Europe, brought to our doorstep daily in foreboding newspaper headlines. I read over Papa's shoulder about the Germans conquering Romania, hoping that Mr. Wilson would indeed continue to keep us out of the conflict. By March, the headlines broiled with the tragic sinking of the Lusitania and United States merchant ships by German submarines.

By now, it was well-known around town that Papa was a German. Even if Mr. Howerth hadn't been doing his nasty part to spread word, Papa's accent and formality glinted like the reflection off a U-boat periscope. In the shop, he did all he could to ensure everyone would know he was now an American and a peaceful man, despite his warring ancestral countrymen. He stopped making sausages and stressed American isolationism to everyone in town who would listen.

At the dinner table, Papa and Ellis debated back and forth, Ellis insisting that the United States step in to stop German aggression and Papa repeating his economic ideas behind our neutrality. The war consumed Ellis, and these discussions frequently went on for hours. Often I waited, coat on, hat in hand, to be escorted out for the evening, while the two of them stayed deep in discussion. Leaning in toward each other, their arguments rose in vehemence while I sighed loudly in a vain attempt to remind Ellis of his reason for being at our house.

Mama would eventually come in, having been the only one to notice my aggravation, and gently shake the men out of their exchange. With her hand on Papa's shoulder, she waited for a pause and then casually asked what time the movie began or when we were meant to be at dinner. Ellis would blink, look up, startled by his surroundings as if awakened on a train at a stop past his destination, and then see me standing and waiting. Reluctantly it seemed, Ellis left Papa at home. Ellis would fume all the way into town. And I knew Papa was surely continuing his diatribe at Mama's back as she worked at the sink.

When the newspaper published the telegram written by a German foreign secretary suggesting that Mexico attack and conquer the southwestern United States, Papa threw his hands up and marched down to the draft office. He was fed up with the way Germany was behaving, and disappointed when he was turned away for being too old to serve.

Ellis followed suit. Because was young and able, he was eagerly welcomed as one of the first to sign up. Our area required three hundred forty-four men to enlist, and once he passed the medical exam, Ellis' name appeared in the local newspaper as one of the brave to volunteer.

Despite the rationing, grand parties were thrown in honor of the volunteers, attended by the most important men in town. The boys were served fine food, including fresh corn from local farms, and encouraged to eat their fill. Upon return from one of these parties, Ellis regaled me with the story of the host who insisted that to be a real man, each soldier needed to eat ten ears of the corn. Patriotism was high around town, and strangers on the street would often stop Ellis to give him a hearty handshake or clap on the back.

There were a rash of weddings in town. The men going off to battle were eager to secure their sweethearts. Frank Leeds got married to a local girl, and Mr. Malcolm proposed to Virginia. Papa preempted any possible proposal from Ellis, insisting to him that not marrying me would give him more incentive to come home safely to secure my hand.

As a new recruit, Ellis swelled with pride and sense of duty, and on the surface, I was proud to be with him. A threatening fear hovered below, though, and seeped in during quiet moments when I had time to think. Though I was able to outwardly show my support for Ellis' decision, when I was alone, everything took on a brutal, bruised quality. The blossoms on the rhododendrons that stood in front of our porch burst forth, reminding me of wounds on a soldier's uniform, and Sousa's patriotic songs air-lifting over from Willow Grove Park blasted like a betrayal.

The night before Ellis left, he received permission from the commanding officer to visit me. Thankfully, Mama and Papa understood our need for privacy. When Ellis arrived at the house, he and I sat in the parlor and Mama closed the pocket door separating us from them in the dining room. The fear in her eyes was equal to the pride in Papa's. They slowly retreated to allow us to say our goodbyes.

Ellis was dapper in his uniform. We sat quietly together, my hand in his, our eyes downcast. It seemed as if there was so much to say, but nothing important enough to warrant words. On the eve of his departure, I certainly wasn't going to waste time talking about the stain I couldn't get out of Oliver's shirt, or the chicken salad that needed to be prepared at the shop tomorrow.

"How are you feeling? Are you nervous?" I finally asked, desperate to simply hear his voice, needing to hear it so that I could remember its sound and cadence in the coming months.

"Yes. A little," he said. "I will miss you very much."

"I will miss you too. But I'll write, as often as possible, and look forward to receiving every letter you get a chance to write me."

"I'm sorry to leave you, Tish, but I know this is the right thing to do. Those Huns won't stand a chance now that we are involved."

I tried to echo his confidence and patriotism, but without leave, tears began to snake their way down my cheeks. I felt Ellis' gentle hands on my face and was fearful that this would be the last time he would touch me.

"Please try to be brave," Ellis said, my chin in his palm. When I looked up, his face was so close to mine that I could see every long eyelash, every root of his thick eyebrows. His features became muddled by my tears and I blinked them away, desperately trying to memorize his details. "Once we kick those Germans back to Berlin, I'll be home and we'll make our way West. The mountains will be gorgeous on your canvas."

I nodded, snuffling and composing myself. He kissed me then, putting into it all of the time that we would be apart.

• • •

At eight the next morning, I stood on the platform at the Willow Grove train station, crowded with soldiers' families. Together we waited in front of the steaming engine that would lead them to training and onto war. Parading footsteps echoed in the cool morning air, and our boys were now suddenly disciplined men. In their crisp uniforms, they were led onto the platform by Boy Scouts bearing the American flag. I stood on my toes searching for Ellis, peering over the jostling crowd. Though I knew his gait and features by heart, the men melded into reproductions of each other and I was panicked that I wouldn't find him. My eyes skittered across the marching rows until we finally made eye contact. A grin marked his handsome face; he was searching for me as well. I swerved and shoved my way through the crush, shouldering my way to be closer to him.

The formation stayed still in the hushed air until the men were given permission to mingle with the crowd. The platform swelled with conversation and embraces as mothers clutched their sons, fathers draped protective arms around shoulders, and sweethearts embraced. Ellis reached out his hand to me and I rushed forward to grab it. Burdened by a large sack on one shoulder, he pulled me to his free side.

I looked up at his face, his hair peeking out from under his triangular overseas cap, and saw with a sinking ache that Ellis was afraid. Without any of the bravado I had seen in him last night, I feared that now that he was marching under the command of an officer with his worldly possessions in the bag slung across his back, he began to realize that going off to war was more than just patriotic rhetoric.

"I love you. And I am so proud of you," I whispered, lightly kissing his cheek.

I wanted to reassure him further, but I trusted myself with no other words. With my free hand, I ran my fingers over his chest and fiddled with the buttons on his jacket. His Adam's apple bounced off the uniform's high collar as he swallowed deeply and straightened his back. Mustering strength for each other, we stood on the platform, hands firmly entrenched, my head tucked under his chin, letting the surrounding noise fall away.

Too soon, the call was given to board the train, and when I stepped out from under his care, I was relieved to see his courage was mustered and he was ready. The grin was back and the moment of fear had subsided. He gently removed his hand from mine and cupped my cheek. We kissed then, briefly, and said our goodbyes. I watched him turn, disappearing into the mass of brown uniforms ascending the stairs of the southbound train.

I searched the line of train windows, fighting the reflection of the station, hoping to see him within, but I never did. Perhaps his seat was on the other side of the train car, or perhaps he needed the time we shared on the platform to be our goodbye. I stood alone, though surrounded by people waiving handkerchiefs and calling out farewells, as the train chugged out of the station.

● ● ●

The next day, I returned to the shop. I completed each task in a haze. I watched my hands work as if they were someone else's. I could not shake the fear that had descended upon me with Ellis' departure. It sat heavy in my stomach.

With all the fanfare of the men leaving, patriotism in town was in a fervor. While we felt it too, the simple fact that our last name was Hess seemed to project otherwise.

About a week after Ellis left, we came in to find the word *HUN* written in capital letters across the window with soap. Papa grabbed the bucket and immediately wiped it away with hot water. His hands shook slightly for the rest of the day. His jaw remained clenched and ready for a fight every time the bell on the door rang to announce a customer's entry.

Over the next few months, business was slow, and though I hoped that it was just because the park was no longer in season and the weather had turned cold, I feared otherwise.

To expand our customer base, Papa decided to start selling toasted cheese sandwiches. They were inexpensive to make and we had the bread on hand to sell anyway. It seemed an American offering, as Mr. Kraft hailed from Illinois, so we hung a sign up in the window and hoped that a few people would order them.

Papa asked me to make some to test them out, so I sliced bread and cheese and put each sandwich in a cast iron skillet in the oven. I turned the oven on high and waited for the cheese to melt and the toast to brown.

I passed the time watching the icicles drip and harden out the front window. They held colors inside of them—reds and blues—if I turned this way or that. The world outside was white and shiny and I supposed I would miss the snow a little when Ellis and I went West. I was envisioning the snowcapped mountains of Colorado and Utah when an acrid smell filled my nose. I heard Papa yelling and ran to see what was the matter. Smoke was pouring out of the oven and filling the shop. I had forgotten about the cheese sandwiches.

Papa threw open the oven door and was hit in the face with a black plume of smoke. He pulled the skillets out, their charred contents now unrecognizable, and clattered them into the sink and under the cold running water. I turned the oven off and desperately tried to fan away the smoke. I coughed and moved away. Unable to face Papa, I went to the front door to open it and let in some fresh air.

The winter breeze sliced into my face and I accepted its bite as punishment. Why couldn't I manage to succeed here?

I propped the door open, crossed my arms against the cold and Papa's anger, and went to the back to help him clean up.

"Papa, I..." I began.

He continued to scrub the pans and wouldn't look at me.

"I'm sorry, Papa. I just wasn't paying attention."

"It's always something, Tish, isn't it?" he said through gritted teeth.

"Papa, maybe it's time to admit that I'm just not cut out for this..."

"Oh, hogwash," Papa yelled. "You don't want to be here. You don't care about our business."

"It's your business, Papa. I have never wanted to be part of it," I yelled right back.

"Oh, I know. Painting and travel and all such nonsense. There's a war on, Tish. Our family livelihood is failing, and you can't get away fast enough." His anger suddenly left him and he walked away from the steaming pans.

I sighed and followed. I hated to disappoint him, especially since I knew he was right. "I'm sorry about the sandwiches, Papa. Truly, I am. I know this is important to you. I will try harder in the shop from now on." I walked over to him and took his hand. "But please try to accept that I do, honestly, want to paint and travel. When Ellis gets back, we will go West."

He shook his hand out of my grasp and left me in the back to clean up.

• • •

We spent a cold winter huddled inside while the snow piled up in the streets. Letters came from Ellis about once a month, telling vaguely of the shelling and the gassing, but they all ended upbeat and with confirmation that he was without injury.

Our holidays were subdued. Wheat, eggs, and meat were rationed, so we celebrated Christmas with a simple meal of brown onion soup. Mama baked a potato bread, using less flour than called for in her usual recipe, and together we baked a buckwheat spice cake for dessert. Papa was able to get a few Tinker Toys for Oliver, but we exchanged little else.

Weeks would pass without a letter from Ellis and I would startle awake from dreams in which I heard his voice, muffled by something and calling my name. I huddled deeper into my blankets, alone in my room, fearful he would never return.

When the weather warmed, we planted a garden and added hens to our existing clutch. I was in the garden one afternoon when Virginia barreled through the back gate with the latest on her wedding plans.

"Oh, Tish, everything is coming together!" she said, settling down next to me in the newly turned dirt. "Ken has been so helpful with the Phoenix Hotel, and they have assured him that there will be plenty of food for all of our guests. I was just so worried when the ration cards came out that we wouldn't be able to have a nice reception, but it's amazing what Ken's money can do! Isn't it wonderful?"

I continued to place and cover the roots of the tomato seedlings while she tittered. The plants were large enough now to move outside, their green leaves reaching for the sun and outgrowing the small pots we had begun inside the house a few weeks earlier. "That's lovely, Virginia. I'm very happy for you."

She frowned. "You are not." She placed her hand on mine. "I know that Daddy has been saying the most awful things. I can't stand it! I have asked him to stop; he knows I adore you! He's just gotten so fearful of anything German. I told him that you would be a bridesmaid and that's that. So cheer up—I'm getting married!"

I missed Ellis with a pain that was physical, more so with every word that Virginia said about her happy life.

Mistaking my silence to be about her, she asked, "Do you think marrying Ken is a terrible idea?"

"It isn't a terrible idea if you love him."

"Well, I do. I also happen to love his house and the life he offers me. Is that so wrong?"

I turned to her, made a motion to touch her arm but reconsidered, fearing that my dirt-caked hands would soil her dress. "No, it's not so wrong," I said. "I'm sure your marriage to Mr. Malcolm will be as grand and wonderful as his house."

"Ken. Please do start calling him Ken," she pouted. "Perhaps Ken is an odd choice, but don't forget that he is a kind man."

"And a family? Do you want to start a family with him?" I involuntarily shuddered at the thought, thinking of his lanky frame and sharp nose. I hoped Virginia didn't notice.

"Yes, of course. I'd rather have a family with him, living comfortably, than scraping by with some boy, even if we are madly in love. My parents married for love. Oh, I know it's not easy to tell now, and that's the problem. They loved each other once, and what did it get them? At the end of the day, not much more than a few dollars and a dirty pile of hair clippings."

"Happiness, Virginia. They once got happiness from being together."

"Not for long. A year or two maybe, until worries over money started eroding everything. Becoming Mrs. Malcolm will make me happy. We won't have the arguments that my parents have, concerned all the time about paying the bills and who in town respects us. What good is marrying a man that you love just to hate him a few years later because living is so difficult? Ken has everything established already. We won't want for anything. Without that to worry about, being happy will be easy."

"Yes, I am sure it will," I said, turning to tend the summer squash.

There would be no changing her mind. Surely money and status didn't guarantee marital happiness. I knew making a marriage work took effort, even if a couple had financial stability.

Conversely, Mama and Papa worked tirelessly when Papa was starting out and they were still very happy together. I wondered how Ellis and I would fare, scraping by for the first years of our life together. Would we be able to survive those tough times? Ellis and I would take odd jobs as we hopscotched the country, vagabonds together, two mouths to feed. But we would be together—surely that was the important part—off on our grand transcontinental adventures.

"Want to stay and help me with this?" I asked Virginia as I pointed to the rest of our garden.

"Oh, no. Take a quick break, I want to show you the invitations Mama bought in Philadelphia. They are beautiful."

She coaxed me toward our back door. In the kitchen, I washed the dirt from my hands and wiped them on a clean towel. Virginia pulled a crisp white card out of her satchel. The date was set for her to become Mrs. Malcolm.

• • •

With summer came the rash of renters in the neighborhood. New faces populated the streets, and we got to know a few families who were spending the summer away from the city. The crowds streamed down to the park. Despite the war, there were still two concerts each day, and fireworks each night. I took Oliver a few times and we ate popcorn and drank *Orangeuce*. I rode the Mountain Scenic Railway with him clutching my arm and squealing with delight. I screamed along with him and felt a momentary release. When the cars clattered into the housing station, the weight seemed to crush again.

It was published in the newspaper that Frank Leeds had been killed in France. His passing brought me to my knees. We had only spent a few moments together at that dance at the park, but he was the first person I knew who was killed over there, and his death brought it home. That summer, many other names appeared in the *Public Spirit* newspaper. The sad news of heroic casualties lined the front-page columns each week, bracketed by strong urgings to *Buy Liberty Bonds!* and the names of more men who had enlisted.

We ate fresh vegetables from our garden and used honey instead of sugar. We followed the instructions in the women's section of the paper to make our own cider vinegar with ripe apples and a yeast cake, freeing up acetic acid for the country's production of airplane wings. We began using the patriotic prose "reed birds" instead of frankfurters and this new moniker graced the menus of the restaurants in town. Papa never drove the car on Sundays, adhering to the Gasless Sunday ban.

For months, the slush of falling letters and the postman's departing footfalls brought nothing but bills for Papa and letters for Mama. No matter how many times I shuffled and read the envelopes, there was often nothing from Ellis. In the terrible moments following the mail's arrival devoid of a letter, I was wracked with worry.

I was out on the porch one afternoon escaping the heat of the house and rocking slowly in the wooden chair. There were no clouds to cool the sky. I spotted the mailman as he turned onto Berrell Road, sweating in his short pants and carrying a heavy pack. I watched as he sauntered up our porch stairs, a bunch of letters in his hand.

"Afternoon, Miss," he said, touching the brim of his cap.

"Good afternoon," I said.

He handed me the day's delivery. My eyes fell on the air mail stamp and I rose to my feet. There were two letters from Ellis, a happy bundle proving he still lived. Relief swelled within me and I let out a whoop, startling the postman as he reached the sidewalk. One letter told of a firefight where he sustained a few scratches and lost his uniform jacket. The other described how he had been gassed but had kept his mask on long enough to avoid ill effects. I read them over and over, crinkling them against my body with an ache that no paper could soothe.

• • •

After weeks of blistering heat, the summer ended suddenly, emptying the town of tourists with the close of Willow Grove Park's twenty-third season. John Philip Sousa concerts had roared patriotism to ten thousand listeners that weekend, the last before the gates of the park were shut tight. Mr. Sousa announced that he was reporting back to the Naval Reserve Force; the end of his governmental leave had come. When the trumpets quieted in his last orchestral movement, he, too, left Willow Grove for war.

Time passed slowly as the days cooled. The park season had brought us customers again, and soon Oliver would start back at school. Through the windows of my bedroom, shut tight now against the crisp air, I watched the hills paint themselves in autumn. Bright reds, burning oranges, and brilliant yellows contrasted against the enduring green of our pine trees. The sycamores out in front of the house shed their brown leaves, raining them to the ground in great numbers, giving the yard and street a snapping crunch. The days got shorter and I waited for the war to end. Though the sun set earlier each evening, the daily waiting seemed just as long.

Autumn was normally a quiet time in our town, a time when locals reemerged and reacquainted themselves with neighbors without the rash of strangers, but this year, new faces from the city began appearing. It was not warm weather that drove them out of the crowded city, but Spanish Influenza. This strange illness was advancing, nearly as dangerously as the Kaiser.

Every week, the paper brought news of death. The flu and the front competed for ink and victims. The Health Department declared all churches, hotels, and even Oliver's school to close. Signs were hung in town stating fines for spitting and instructing people to use handkerchiefs when sneezing or coughing. With the flu so rampant, Papa reluctantly closed the shop. We stayed home, cooped up, always together and underfoot, making and remaking messes we had just cleaned up.

Mama canceled most of her social obligations, but I could not keep Virginia from visiting. Her wedding had been beautiful and I had been honored to stand by her side, despite her father's distain. Now home from her honeymoon, the new Mrs. Malcolm came over and broke up our monotonous days.

"Did you hear Abington Hospital isn't accepting any more patients?" she asked over tea in our sitting room. "Ken read me the article from the paper this morning. They are at full capacity and the nurses have all gotten sick and there are only volunteers left to help. Isn't it awful?"

"It is. The soldiers are getting sick too."

"Yes, Ken said that this morning also. Such sad news, but I must say, it is divine being in that house as a new bride. He has a wonderful cook, you know. She brings us breakfast and I can just relax in my robe. I am so happy, Tish."

I took her hand in mine. "I'm glad, Virginia," I said, though honestly what I mostly felt was jealousy. While her life was continuing, mine had so much waiting and uncertainty.

• • •

In November, the war finally ended. The buzz started around town and when the newspaper confirmed the news, joy raced through me. Ellis would come home, Papa's business would rebound, and my life could begin to move forward again. It was all over, and though I was still waiting, this had a different feeling, a hopefulness tucked into it. A letter arrived from Ellis sharing news of the armistice. He and some Germans had swapped cigarettes for chocolate like old friends. Relief lifted the cloud of dark times; Ellis had survived the war and was coming home.

Thanksgiving came and went without him, though. I set a place at the table for him, despite hearing no word of his estimated return. During the meal I was lonely, gazing across at the empty chair, but I gave thanks that the war was over and that he would be home with us soon.

Ivy and William joined us for the meal. Mama and I were secretly hoping Ivy would arrive with good news and a round belly, but she was just as slim as ever, and, I believe, for the first time in her life, disappointed for it. William seemed very self-conscious, mentioning his flat feet more than once whenever table talk turned to the war.

"How's business going, Dad?" William asked between bites of mashed potatoes.

Papa sighed. I wondered how he would answer. Would he tell William the truth? Would he say how many nights he had spent tweaking the precious recipes written in his black book, looking for ways to cut costs but still offer a quality product to his dwindling clientele?

"It's been difficult," Papa said.

"Did you ever consider changing the name of the shop? There is so much anti-German sentiment—unfounded in your case, of course—but a name like Hess is sure to draw the wrong kind of attention."

From my seat next to Papa, I saw the muscle in his jaw flex into a tight rope. He swallowed his current bite and answered slowly, "I will not change it. Hess is our name. It is our family business."

"Hear me out, though," William plowed on, apparently taking no notice of Papa's distaste for this kind of suggestion. "You wouldn't have to change anything else inside, just the name to get them in the door. And you could keep it in the family. What's the last name of the boy who Tish is involved with? They will surely get married when he returns. Give the shop his name. They very well may take it over eventually anyway."

My stomach dropped. "But we aren't going to stay here and take over the business," I rushed to say, the words shooting out of my mouth like knives.

Papa's eyes were dark and he jabbed his meat with his fork.

"More peas, anyone?" Mama said, perhaps a little too loudly. We finished our meal, but I knew the discussion was far from over.

• • •

Ellis still wasn't home at Christmas. His letters said that even though he wouldn't be part of the Occupation Army in Germany, there was some holdup and he remained stationed in France awaiting his return orders. I lovingly packed up some cigars and mailed them to him in Europe. In early December, a beautiful little painting of a town called Domremy arrived from him. A tiny church was painted in the far background of the landscape. I brushed my fingers over the heavy swaths of paint and grain of wood on the frame, so happy to hold a piece of art that Ellis had once held as well. The note that came with it read:

> *Darling,*
>
> *All I do is sit here and think of you. We have recently been on the move and have found accommodations in an old barn in this town of Domremy. It is cold and damp, nothing but rain here and strong biting winds. It is making the men are quite foul tempered. No one agrees on anything and there are often fistfights. This seems worse than war. At least then, we were fighting an enemy instead of each other. We have been told that we are sailing home soon, but we have heard that before. I remain hopeful. I dedicated years of my life to this war and am eager to be done with it. My thoughts remain with you and the adventures we will have together.*
>
> *All my love,*
> *Ellis*

I missed him terribly. There was an ache, a longing, that consumed me, hovered in the background, all the time. And, worst of all, I was beginning to forget his face. I knew he had dark hair, deep eyes, thick brows, but I couldn't put those pieces together in my mind. Now that the war was over, it was nothing but a waiting game for both of us.

CHAPTER NINE

Molly

Waking nights and endless days ran into each other and I longed for a fast forward button. One morning, the crick in my neck woke me up. As I slowly rotated my head, feeling the sore spots in my neck work themselves out with resounding cracks, I attempted to locate myself in my surroundings. I was sitting up, Hayden's head lolled on my arm, his mouth wide open, his tummy bulbous and sated. I could hear the shower running, and I assumed Corey must be getting ready for work. What day of the week was it? My shirt lay open, my chest chilled and exposed. How long had we been here?

As sleep fell away, I realized I had fallen asleep in the rocker. I stood up with the temerity of my former self and instantly regretted it. My legs were still asleep and they buckled under me. Clutching the baby tight against my body, I threw my free hand out and just caught us both before we collided with the carpet.

Our jarring tumble woke Hayden and he began to wail. I soothed him while sitting on the floor, swaying him in my arms and wiggling my toes in an attempt to get the feeling back. Corey appeared in the doorway with a towel around his waist. His hair was still dripping and steam rose off his back.

"What are you doing on the floor?" he asked.

"Just hanging out. We like it down here," I spat at him.

"Hayden doesn't seem to like it."

I sighed. "Hayden doesn't like anything. Here, take him for a second so I can go to the bathroom. It may be my only chance all day."

Corey lifted Hayden out of my arms and our son calmed almost immediately. It was hard not to take that personally. With a heave, I hoisted myself off the ground, buttoned up my shirt, and shuffled to the bathroom.

Yesterday I had taken Hayden to the pediatrician for a check-up. They looked him over thoroughly and answered all my questions. I was relieved to hear that he was healthy and thriving, but remained dissatisfied by the simple diagnosis of "colic" and the doctor's assurances that his constant crying would pass.

In the bathroom, I stood in front of the mirror wondering how much longer the colic could last. Three weeks? Three months?

I looked terrible. There were dark circles under my eyes and my cheeks were baggy. My lips were so pale they blended into the rest of my face, and there was some sort of crust just under my chin. My hair stood on end in strange spots, with wisps flying upward out of my greasy ponytail. The saggy shirt I was wearing was dappled and discolored with spit-up Rorschach's along my shoulders, which sagged with exhaustion.

Though I knew I felt terrible, I still wasn't prepared for the mirror's harsh reality. Like Frankenstein, I tore myself away from my reflection with a groan and went into our room to find the boys. Corey was getting dressed, so I flopped down next to Hayden, who was settled in the middle of the bed. I watched him punch the air and kick out with his legs.

"Want to get a shower, Molly? I have a few more minutes before I have to leave."

"I'm too tired." I closed my eyes, enjoying a rest, even momentarily, next to my happy baby.

"You're kind of a mess this morning... Did you sleep in the rocker all night?"

I said nothing, though fury burned my face. Rage empowered me, giving me the strength to stand up. Without a word, I returned to the bathroom and closed the door.

A mess? Of course I was a mess. I didn't need him to point that out to me. What husband in the history of the world ever benefited from telling his wife that she didn't look good? Of course I looked awful. I was exhausted and outmatched by a tiny baby who hated me. And why shouldn't he? I just nearly dropped him and crushed him by landing on top of him. Corey couldn't understand because for the thirty minutes each day he spent with our son, Hayden was an angel. The other twenty-three hours and thirty minutes, the kid was eternally irritated. Well, fine. Let him have his thirty minutes. I would take a shower. And a long one. I'd shave my legs. I'd wash my hair, rinse. And as it suggested on the bottle, I'd repeat.

• • •

My skin was red apple red when I finally turned off the hot water. I had let it rain down on me, nearly choking on the steam. It didn't lift my spirits as much as I had hoped. Instead, melancholy seemed to leak into my steamed-open pores. How was I completely failing at this? Did other new mothers feel this way? Most of my life, I was easily good at things. Before I left college, I didn't have to work particularly hard to get by. If I hustled in the kitchen, I could keep up with the guys. But my baby, my own baby, was a mystery. If motherhood were any other job, I would be fired by now. Corey seemed content to keep me in the position, despite giving performance reviews that focused mostly on my inadequacies.

I toweled off and steadied myself against the day. I took a few deep breaths while looking in the mirror. I looked marginally better. Resolving to take it one hour at a time, I went into the bedroom, found some yoga pants, a nursing bra, and a button-up shirt. It was quiet downstairs when I found Corey and Hayden. Corey was eating breakfast and reading the paper while Hayden was bouncing in a seat set in the middle of the dining table.

"You look better," Corey said.

I let it slide and went into the kitchen to scrounge up my own breakfast. While pouring my cereal, I heard Corey call to me. I poked my head in the dining room.

"Hummm?" I asked, popping a few bits of dry cereal into my mouth.

"This isn't so hard. He's perfectly happy."

"Uh-huh. He does certainly seem to be happy now," I said. My teeth ground the cereal into dust.

"Okay, family. I'm off," Corey said as he stood, his sign he was getting ready to leave me for the day. "I'll be home around eight. Have a great day!"

Corey kissed Hayden on the forehead and I walked with him to the front door.

"Have a good day, Molly. I hope he stays happy like this all morning."

As if on cue, Hayden began wailing. Left alone in the dining room, his cries began gaining strength. Corey gave me a sympathetic look and closed the door. What would we do for the next ten hours?

Luckily, Liz stopped by around ten. She knocked briskly on the door and marched in with her usual bravado. I was getting used to it, and I liked her confidence.

"What are you up to today?" she asked.

I shrugged. "You're looking at it."

"Want to go to the mall? Walk around a little? Get out of this dark house? Forget about unpacking for a while? I need a new dress, and I bet you could use some retail therapy."

I nodded and started the long process of packing up everything we needed to leave the house—the diapers, the wipes, the extra bottle, the binkie, the change of clothes, my wallet, my cell phone. Liz waited patiently and we drove over to the mall together.

She led the way through the three-story cavernous place, pointing out various stores. We stood waiting for the elevator and when it arrived, I wheeled the stroller in. On the wall of the elevator was an enlarged old and grainy photograph of people at an amusement park. They were dressed in old-fashioned clothing standing at a refreshment stand offering *Orangeuce*, a large roller coaster looming in the background. On the bottom, white letters read *Willow Grove Park Midway, 1918.*

"What is this? What is a midway?" I asked Liz.

"Oh, before this was a mall, it was a huge amusement park. The midway is where all the games and concession stands are. My kids would have loved it if it was still here. It had rides and concerts too. There are old photographs like this all over the mall."

"Huh. I wonder if Aunt Tish ever went there."

"Probably," Liz said with a shrug. "The whole town was built up around Willow Grove Park. They tore it down in the late seventies, though."

I peered closer at the figures in the photograph. Might one of them be Aunt Tish? The elevator door opened and I bumped the stroller out. We walked into a store that Liz liked and I steered Hayden's stroller around the racks while Liz picked out a few things. When she found something, I parked the stroller outside the dressing room and sat on the couch provided for waiting husbands. I rolled the stroller back and forth, knowing I was on borrowed time before Hayden got fussy.

From behind the partition door, Liz called, "Have you signed up for one of those baby classes?"

"Not yet," I called back.

She stepped out in a light blue shift dress that gathered at the side. She looked great, but she wrinkled her nose at the mirror. She turned from side to side. "You should sign up. You're sure to meet a few new moms there that you'll like." She faced me and continued, "I hate this dress."

She went back inside the changing stall, still chattering. "Of course, there's always some moms there that seem to have it all together. They don't, though. Everyone is crazy for the first few months. Let your crazy flag fly a little, see who else throws theirs up. That woman will be your friend forever." She stepped out of the dressing room again. "What do you think of this one?"

Now she was wearing a white t-shirt dress.

I shook my head. "The other one is better."

"There, honesty. Thank you."

My cell phone began to ring and Liz ducked back in to change. I fished around in my bag, flinging baby stuff all over, before locating my phone. It was Corey.

"Hey babe, how's your day? How's Hayden?" he asked when I answered.

"Fine. We're out at the mall with Liz."

"Great, great. Listen, I just got scheduled to be out of town next week. Okay with you?"

Panic immediately flooded my limbs and I stood straight up.

"What? No! Corey, are you serious?"

"Yeah, completely serious."

"How long?" Dread tinged my voice.

"It's only for five days. In Houston. Before you start getting crazy, I already called my mom, but of course she can't come and help out. Maybe you could ask your dad to come or something?"

"My dad? You know my stepmonster won't let him out of her clutches long enough to visit."

"Maybe they will both come?"

"Hilarious. That's not making this any better." Blood was rushing in my ears. I picked at the cuticle on my thumb and drew a single bead of blood.

"Listen, Molly. I have to go on the trip. It's complicated. I can't really talk about it right now, but I don't have a choice about going."

"Is everything okay at work?"

He hesitated. Then, quickly said, "Yes, yes, fine. Everything is fine. I have to go on this trip, though, I just do, whether or not it is convenient."

"Then why did you even call to ask if it was okay?" I pushed the end button on my phone and tossed it into my bag. Liz stood there, back in her own clothes, watching me.

"Everything all right?" she asked.

"Nope, not remotely," I said as furious tears pricked the corners of my eyes.

• • •

Hayden soon got fussy and we called it a day. We drove home and as Liz went back to her well-manicured house, I trudged across the street and through our severely overgrown lawn. Corey hadn't had time to do any work on the outside of the house, and while I could ignore it when I was inside all day, it was painfully obvious from here on the sidewalk. I climbed the porch steps and jimmied my key for a while before the door gave way. The indefatigable must filled my nose and dust motes danced in the sunbeams. Home sweet home.

I picked up the phone and called my father. Holding my breath, hoping he'd answer instead of my stepmother, I listened to the line ring down in Florida.

"Hello?" It was him.

When he asked how I was, I wanted to tell him how difficult I was finding motherhood. I wanted to tell him how isolated I felt in this new town, away from everything I knew. I wanted to tell him, but I found myself swallowing it all, unsure if I trusted him, unsure of how he would judge my honesty. Unable to face his criticism, or worse, his indifference.

"I'm fine Dad," I said instead. "How are you?"

"Great, we had a visit from Joseph and Anne a little while back. Joseph and I played a few rounds of golf. It was nice. How's your new place?"

"It's coming together," I lied. "Corey's aunt left a lot behind, so I'm working to make it our own."

"And Hayden? Is he sleeping much for you?"

"No..." My voice cracked with the truth. I had to stop talking.

"Molly? You okay?"

I couldn't hold it in any longer. "I'm not sure, Dad. I'm so tired, and Hayden doesn't really seem to be very happy. Corey is working a lot. He's has a business trip next week, and I could really use some help."

Dad was quiet on the other end.

"Dad?"

"Yes, I'm here, Molly."

"Could you, maybe, try to come up? You could both come, see the new place, meet Hayden?"

Inside I was screaming, "I need you to come! I need help!" but I simply couldn't say it. I steeled myself for his inevitable decline of my invitation. Surely, he would have some excuse, some previous commitment. I just knew he wouldn't come.

"Okay," he said. "I'll book a flight and send you my schedule."

"Really, Dad? Thank you! That's great! I'm so excited."

And, for the first time in a while, I was.

CHAPTER TEN
Tish, 1919

It had been hot all day, but an early summer storm loomed in the distance. The clouds began collecting mid-afternoon, dark and rolling in like plumes of ash. Mama and I were in the backyard hanging clothes. The air suddenly cooled. A streak of light shot through the sky followed by a deep grumble of thunder. Wind whipped over the hill, making the pine boughs dip and dance. The ground sizzled and steamed when the first droplets fell. We yanked the clothes off the line and tossed them back into our baskets. By the time we were through the back door, the rain was pelting the roof. A second roar of thunder soon followed the first and clapped so loudly that it shook the house before settling into its low rumble.

Oliver came running to the kitchen where Mama and I stood.

"It's all right, Ollie," Mama soothed. "It's just a storm. Let's go up to your room where we can see it better and listen." She put down her wash basket and walked with him upstairs.

The windows throughout the house were open to the day's early heat, and the curtains flapped hard as cool air rushed in. I moved from room to room, closing the windows to just about an inch so that the rain wouldn't get in. When done, I stood at the front door and watched the branches of the sycamore trees out front wave through sheets of rain. Lightning flashed and backlit their shape. It was dark for midday, the sun hiding from the storm. I loved a good thunderstorm and listened, jumping a little, at each crack of thunder.

Papa would be closing up shop soon. There hadn't been enough business, even with the park now in full swing, to warrant Mama and my being there this afternoon. The lack of customers put Papa in a constant foul mood, and today would surely be worse for his having to walk home in the rain.

I continued to watch out the front door for a while. The storm seemed to go on and on, stalled above us. A touring car in the deserted river of our street caught my eye and I was surprised when it putted up to our house and parked outside. Perhaps Papa had asked someone in town for a ride.

Through the rain drops, I could see a man climb out of the backseat, hunched over, carrying a large pack, and draping a large overcoat above his head for cover. The mass moved up onto our porch and was soon standing in the shelter of its roof. The man unfurled himself from the coat and I first noticed his dark curls had been shorn close.

Ellis was home! His face, dripping wet, turned up toward mine.

I threw open the door and ran into the wind. He put down the pack and opened his arms. I tucked myself in. If he was speaking, I couldn't hear it over the pelting rain and gusting wind. But he was back!

Though it had been nearly two years, I still fit just as I had before, my head tucked just under his chin, like a perfectly snug puzzle piece. Joyful tears streamed down my face and I sucked the wind in like I was suffocating.

I was so happy that my insides were humming, but I could tell his hum was of a lower and more sullen pitch. Ellis pulled away from me and I looked at his face. There was a deep sadness in the wrinkles around his eyes. Regardless, he smiled and leaned in. His lips were gentle on mine at first, but the years apart increased our urging and the kiss turned heady quickly. Though the street now stood empty and nothing was around us but the crashing, flashing, and washing sky, I felt exposed and wanted the privacy of the house.

I led him inside and he took off his wet outer layer. I was not willing to let go of his arm, needing to stay physically connected, and we fumbled through the removal while the thunder continued to drum outside.

"Who's here?" I heard Oliver call from upstairs, his feet clomping like a horse on his scamper downstairs. "Mama, there is a man here...in his undershirt..." Oliver called up, wary of the wet stranger.

"Hello, there, Oliver. It's been a long time," Ellis said laughing, ruffling his hair with the arm I was not clenching.

"This is Ellis, remember?" I said to Oliver.

Mama descended the stairs and when she saw Ellis, her eyes lit up. "Ellis, how wonderful that you are home," she said, coming to us and squeezing his shoulder.

"Mrs. Hess, it is wonderful. And lovely to see you all."

"It's quite a storm out there. Did you walk from the station?" she asked.

"No, I got a lift from a fellow I know over on Dallas Road. We were on the train together and he drove me from the station."

"Do you have a place to stay in town?" Mama asked. As she spoke, I realized that I hadn't actually said a word to Ellis yet. There were so many that I wanted to say, but they caught in my throat. I let Mama talk as I looked up at him, both hands around his arm, never wanting to let go again.

"I haven't secured a place yet," he said. "I was hoping that I might use your telephone to call the boarding house, or maybe the Red Lion Inn to see if they have rooms."

"Of course, but visit first. Join us for dinner. Maybe afterward, the storm will let up. I know Mr. Hess would enjoy seeing you as well. Oh, Ellis, we are just so happy to have you home!" She embraced him warmly, then grasped my brother by the shoulders to stop him from the dance he had been doing around Ellis' feet. She pivoted Oliver, and led him back upstairs. "Let's go hang Ellis' shirt to dry," she chatted to him as they climbed to the second floor. "Papa will be back soon. Do you think he'll be sopping wet, too, when he gets home?"

Ellis and I were alone again and he kissed me. A small, sweet kiss, with my face in both of his strong hands. His palms were rough, just as I remembered them, and they trembled slightly.

"It sure is good to see you, Tish."

"Welcome home," I said.

We walked into the sitting room and sat on the settee. He told me about his travels home. After trekking across Europe, there was finally a ship to bring him back to the States. From New York, he took the train into 30th Street Station in Philadelphia, and then the train out to Willow Grove. He talked about his buddies from his unit and how it was hard to say goodbye, even though it was what they had been wanting and waiting to do for months. He briefly mentioned a few men who didn't come home, buried in the fields, but moved on quickly and would say no more about the fighting.

I tried to tell him about the people here, about William and Ivy, and Virginia and Mr. Malcolm, how John Philip Sousa was back at the park, playing as part of his transcontinental tour. I yammered on about the paintings I had been working on, and as I spoke, his eyes darted around the room.

"Where is that painting? The one I sent you?" he asked, jumping up and peering around the corners into the other rooms.

"It's upstairs in my room."

"Go get it. I'd like to see it."

"Ellis, no. Let's just stay down here and talk to each other."

"I don't want to hear anything more about what things are like in Willow Grove. It feels like a different place now. A place that was part of before. Maybe it is me that is different now, I don't know, but I feel like this place is already part of my past."

Not understanding, and unsure of this new, franticly pacing Ellis, I said, "And me? Am I also part of your past?"

"No, darling, no," he said, coming back to where I sat on the couch. "I love you. Let's go West together. Now. Let's start a new life, away from this tiny town. I already feel stuck here. I need to move away."

"I'd love to Ellis. You know I would, but Papa won't let me go without being married."

"Then let's just get married. Let's just go downtown tomorrow and do it." He was up again, raking his fingers back and forth across the top of his head. I could no longer hear the thunder outside, but a storm raged on Ellis' face.

"Calm down, Ellis. You just got home. You haven't even been here for an hour."

"I have been thinking about this for months! Doing nothing but sitting around in some ramshackle bombed-out barn with rain puddles for blankets, for months. And darn it all if it isn't raining here too! I'm ready to go. I can't stay here any longer. It feels false, part of who I used to be. This place doesn't belong to me anymore. Let's get married and go."

Although I longed to be married to Ellis, and cared little for a big wedding, this delirious proposal was not what I had in mind. Like a thief, he seemed anxious to flee, and I felt like the jewels being hastily shoved into a bag. He was frightening me. I had to get him to slow down.

"Come here, love," I said, hoping a soothing tone would beckon him back to the settee. "It's all right. It won't be raining here all the time. Look, it is already subsiding. And we will get married. I'd like to do this properly, though, not be rushed. Let's just take some time to plan our journey and our wedding. I understand now how you feel about it here, and I don't want you to be unhappy, but you just walked in the door, Ellis, and that was a terrible proposal." I smiled in an attempt to lighten the mood.

It took a beat longer than I hoped, but Ellis smiled back at me. "You are right," he said. "That was a terrible proposal. When your father comes home, I'll speak to him about it properly."

"You are home now. We are together. We'll be traveling soon. I can't wait to see it all, and with you." I continued my soothing tone, pleased that it seemed to be having some effect. "In the meantime, will you take me to see Sousa tomorrow if the weather clears?"

"Yes," Ellis said, calm for now. "Let's go see Sousa tomorrow."

I should have been feeling elated. He was here at my side. I should have been ready to just pack up and go, but there was something different about Ellis. There was a frantic darkness that scared me. He would be fine after a little more time at home, though, surely. As we sat together on the settee, I hoped I was right.

• • •

Papa came home from the shop, hunched and sulking like a scolded dog. Before even taking off his raincoat, Oliver rushed up to him yelling, "Tish's friend Ellis is here, Papa!"

"What's that now, son? I can barely understand you. Stop jumping."

"Ellis is home, Papa," I said as Ellis and I entered the foyer.

"Well!" Papa said. He shook Ellis' hand. "Welcome home, Ellis. When did you dock?"

"Early this morning. Took the train down from New York, and then straight here."

"Well, just look at you! Fit and strong after fighting the Huns. Showed that Kaiser who's boss, eh?"

"Yes, sir."

"Come to dinner, everyone," Mama called from the dining room.

The table boasted a fine meal. Chunks of chicken glistened in a cream sauce with mushrooms. Baked tomatoes split their skins and overflowed with stuffing and herbs. Lemon slices bobbed in the sweating pitcher of lemonade. Papa went to the kitchen and came back with two bottles of homemade beer. They hissed and bubbled up as he opened them.

"To welcome home our brave soldier," he said, handing one to Ellis. After tapping the bottles together, both men took a long drink, ending with a grin.

As we ate, Ellis shared stories from *over there*, one involving a Frenchman whom they had paid to rent his barn. At some point there was a miscommunication about a chicken which ended comically with the Frenchman nearly kicking them out.

"That man, he sure loved his chickens," Ellis chuckled, and we all laughed too. I watched him and saw his face fall immediately after his laugh ended, as if the entire cheerful story had been affected. Though he heartily complimented Mama on her cooking, he mostly pushed his food around on his plate and gulped his beer as if he were walking the desert. He was a changed man, almost a stranger it seemed, stuck inside the body of the man I loved.

We sat at the table awhile after finishing dinner, until Oliver said, "Mama, may I get up? My foot is twinkling."

"Twinkling?" Mama asked.

"Yes, like a prickly star."

Suddenly understanding, we all smiled. I looked over at Ellis and he was staring off into the distance.

"Perhaps you should be seated correctly on your bottom, rather than on your foot, and it wouldn't fall asleep," Mama said. "Stand up. Walk around a bit. It will stop feeling that way."

Papa stood too, indicating that he was headed for his cigar box on the porch. With a look at me, Ellis followed him, asking, "Sir, may I join you? I'd like to discuss something."

I stacked the plates and carried them into the kitchen. Oliver was stomping around the house trying to wake up his foot, and Mama was at the sink.

"Do you think he is different, Mama?" I asked.

"Perhaps. War is a difficult thing to manage."

"He acts happy, but he doesn't actually seem happy. He seems anxious and restless. He wants to get married right away and head West."

"Hmm, I was wondering what the discussions were about on the front porch. Now I understand. I know that is what you want—have wanted, Tish—but don't rush into anything. He needs some time to adjust to being back in the country. He'll be just fine soon, back to his normal self. You'll see."

I nodded and went back to the dining room to collect the remainder of the dishes. As I shuttled between the rooms, stacking the bowls and plates next to the sink, my uneasiness grew along with the pile. We were nearly done washing up when we heard the front door close and the men's voices back inside.

"Go, dear," Mama said. "I'll finish the rest."

I put down my dish rag and went to find Ellis. On my way past Papa in the library, he patted my shoulder and smiled at me but said nothing and continued into the kitchen. I found Ellis in the sitting room. He was using the telephone. I sat down and waited, watching him and searching for something about him I recognized.

"Well," he said, replacing the earpiece, "Neither the Red Lion Inn nor the boarding house have any rooms tonight. I guess I should have called earlier. That Sousa really draws a crowd," Ellis said.

Mama and Papa had joined us, hearing the tail end of this.

"Perhaps I'll call over to the McGuires on Krewson Terrace, or my friend on Dallas, to see if they will put me up for the night."

"Nonsense, Ellis. I'll make up a bed for you here," Mama said, getting a sharp look from Papa. She put her hand on his forearm and fixed a look at him. He acquiesced quickly under her touch and did not protest. "It's getting late anyway. Tish, fetch some blankets and we'll make up the davenport. Oliver! Time for bed, my sweet."

There was a groan and the scampering of feet as Oliver tried to outrun bedtime. The door separating the dining room and the library squeaked and I knew where he had taken up a hiding spot. I went to the dining room and flung the door shut, exposing the space behind it, filled with my crouching, giggling little brother.

"Come on, Oliver. Let's go upstairs. If you get dressed quickly, I'm sure Mama will let you come downstairs to say goodnight to Ellis," I said.

"He's staying?" Oliver's eyes were as wide as the full moon. He followed me, then pushed past me to win an undeclared race and change into his night clothes. I collected sheets and an extra pillow from the closet for Ellis. The house usually cooled at night, and the storm had washed away most of the day's heat, so I grabbed a light blanket as well.

With Ellis on the couch, the rest of us retired upstairs and I continued up the winding circular stairway to my room. As I undressed, I could see the lights from town hazy and spread by the rain. My thoughts were just as hazy.

He was home, and back after so long. I wanted things to be the same as they were before the war, but they couldn't possibly be. I worried about our relationship; were we too different now? I knew I still loved him. One look at his face and I knew it. But he was so changed. How could things between us truly ever be the same?

Was I foolish for insisting that we go to the park tomorrow? I wanted to be somewhere with him that had once belonged to us. We had met at the park, and I was hopeful we would have an easier time reconnecting there. I stopped myself from these dizzying thoughts with a firm head shake and dressed in my night clothes.

Of course things would be fine; he was here, and that was what mattered. More importantly, he wanted us to run away together, as soon as possible. I filled the empty room with laughter at the sheer pleasure of being so desperately wanted and being so close fulfilling the dream that I so desperately wanted.

I climbed into bed and pulled the sheet up to my chin. My eyes wouldn't shut, though, and I tossed and turned in my small bed. There was a sound on the steps, a creaking on the landing. In the shadows stood Ellis. I sat up quickly. He came to my bedside.

"Ellis," I whispered in a rush, "you can't be up here!" I pushed him away and pulled the covers up across my chest.

"I was very quiet past your parents' room. And nonsense. We will be married soon."

"Not if Papa finds you up here!"

"He is very fond of me, said so just this evening on the porch, when I asked him for your hand."

He had asked Papa! My body warmed with pleasure all the way down to my feet. It had always been a shining future... when we knew each other better, when we were older, when the war was over, when, when, when. And here we were. We had arrived at now. Now he had asked for my hand. Now he spoke to my father. Now we would be married. Now I would see the country with my love at my side.

"What did he say?" I asked, hopeful, so hopeful that Papa would support this.

"I told him that I loved you very much and had waited long enough through the war and wanted you to be my bride. He said that he and your mother were very fond of me and that he would be pleased if I became your husband."

"Did you mention leaving town?"

"That part pleased him less, I'm afraid. He said he couldn't stop us from living our lives wherever we saw fit, but asked that we announce our engagement and get married here in town. He said that there was no reason to rush, insisted upon waiting until I found proper employment, in fact. But he did give me permission to ask you to marry me. And I couldn't wait a moment longer to do it. So here I am. But, tell your father that I waited until tomorrow at the park."

I laughed and agreed. He pulled at my sheets and swung my legs around so that they hung off the bed and I faced him. He was already kneeling, but he took my hands in his.

"Tish, I love you so much. Will you marry me?"

"I will." I moved toward him and kissed him. Many of my doubts washed away in that moment, and I was light and full of air. My heart began to beat faster when Ellis held my kiss. He stood, our lips still together, and moved himself into the bed. My whole body felt the surprise and glorious weight of him as he pressed his body to mine. I broke the kiss and looked into his expectant eyes. I truly wanted to continue, but was frightened that we would be discovered.

"Tish, we are going to be married," he said in answer to my unspoken worries and then quieted all protests with his lips on my mouth.

I felt my body rise to meet his and ignored my schoolgirl propriety. This is what I wanted too. And we were to be married. I closed my eyes, stopped thinking, and just enjoyed his soft caresses.

Our limbs entwined, an urgency began to take over in Ellis. He moved faster and more insistently. His desperation seemed to grow. Pain and pleasure mingled inside me, and the small sounds escaping my throat were muffled by his mouth hard on mine. I sought out his eyes again, but they were vacant. When we finished, he buried his head in my shoulder and I could feel his chest heaving.

• • •

In the morning, the bird songs woke me. I was alone in my small bed, but as I opened my eyes, I was joined by the memory of last night. I sat up, my body tender and my mind bruised. It hadn't been what I expected. Perhaps our coupling had been what Ellis needed to shake off the horrors of the war, but it had felt strange, like it needn't have been me at all. I loved Ellis, at least the Ellis I knew before the war. Resolving to bring that Ellis back, I said a silent word of thanks that we had met, he survived the war, and now was going to be my husband. He was back with me now, and his mind would come back too, given enough time. Mama was right: War was hard and ugly, and once he could be reminded that he was safe and loved here, he would calm down and settle back into his usual self. Papa had insisted that we wait a bit, and for the first time I was grateful for the delay.

I dressed for the day at the park, checking the mirror to see if I was somehow changed. Did I look different now that Ellis had been in my bed? I was a bit flushed, perhaps, and still somewhat bewildered by the act itself, but otherwise I seemed quite the same. I went downstairs. I could smell the heady scent of bacon in the pan and found Ellis folding up the sheets that he had used on the davenport for at least part of the night.

"Good morning," he said, his eyes mischievous to match his grin. I expected him to lick his lips like a carnivorous beast. I blushed when he grabbed me and nuzzled my neck.

I recognized his touch, pre-war and comforting, instead of vacuous and feral like last night. Unable to stop my grin even as I pushed him away, I said, "Stop. Papa will see you!"

"Ah, let 'im!" Ellis said. "I'm going to be your husband soon. If he gives me any guff, I'll just steal you away and marry you tomorrow."

"Ellis," I chided, nervous our behavior would give away what had occurred upstairs overnight. I could hear Papa hustling down the stairs. I grabbed a sheet and began folding, unfolding myself from Ellis.

"Good morning," Papa called, moving aside the front door curtain and gazing toward the street. "Newspaper here yet?"

He went outside to search and Mama called us all to the table. There we found a haystack of bacon slices alongside hardboiled eggs and toast. There was coffee, too, hot and fragrant, and I helped myself to a cup. Ellis loaded his plate. I was glad to see that his appetite had returned. Papa read behind his paper, having found it on the front steps, and throughout breakfast only made murmurs and crunches from behind the black and white print. Oliver bounced around, begging to come to the park with us, but Mama put an end to that, thankfully. After breakfast, I offered to help clean up, but Mama handed us a packed picnic lunch of bread, cheese, and summer sausage and shooed us out of the house.

Puddles still lay in the street from last night's rain, but the air was warm. Ellis and I had walked this direction before, down the same streets into town. I thought about the day we first met, about how Ivy and William had walked this way, arm in arm, tightly together.

Now, Ellis walked next to me, close but not touching. I reached out and took his hand. He flinched as if he hadn't remembered I was there.

"Are you all right?" I asked.

He quickly softened and entwined his fingers in mine.

"Yes, I was just thinking, that's all. It's been awhile since I have been here, and to the park."

"Are you looking forward to seeing it again?"

He shrugged. "I suppose so."

"Well, the Sousa concert should be wonderful," I said.

He gave me an unconvincing smile.

When we arrived at the park, we were immediately immersed in the sounds of the midway games and thrilled shouts of the riders aboard the amusements. Ellis hunched his shoulders, lowered his head, and walked resolutely through the crowd while I rushed to keep up. I could tell he wasn't enjoying it. The crack of a ball against milk bottles made Ellis rear up, his features heavy with old fear. I touched his shoulder. He was shaking.

"Let's go," I said as quietly as I could and still be heard over the bustle. He took my hand and we walked back toward home.

• • •

When we arrived there, if Mama was surprised to see us, she didn't act so. It was a relief. I didn't want to explain our early return to her, and I was sure Ellis didn't, either. She simply said, "I telephoned Ivy and William while you were out and they have agreed to come to dinner tonight. They'd like to celebrate your homecoming, Ellis. I do hope you can stay."

"Yes, thank you, Mrs. Hess. That will be lovely. I do need to make arrangements for long-term accommodations, though. May I use your telephone?"

"Of course, Ellis. Any time."

His hands trembled at his sides as he turned away. I joined Mama in the kitchen while she mused out loud about the dinner menu. Once she had decided on Stewed Chicken, I began helping her while I waited for Ellis to finish on the telephone.

Ellis walked into the kitchen, rubbing the back of his neck as if he had been working all day. His voice was husky and dry.

"Well, they have space again at the Wagamon Boarding House. I bet it hasn't changed since the day I left two years ago. I'll go on down there now and get settled in. What time shall I return for dinner, Mrs. Hess?"

"Oh, I'd say about seven o'clock. If you're hungry, take the picnic lunch with you. You can bring the basket back this evening."

"Thank you."

"My pleasure. We're glad to have you back, Ellis." Mama wiped her hands on a towel. She walked over to Ellis and placed her hands on his forearms. "What you did over there was brave and strong. We are very proud of you." She squeezed his arms. Turning to me she said, "Tish, why don't you walk him out?"

"Yes, Mama."

On the porch, Ellis and I both started to talk at the same time. I laughed and he smiled. It was nice to see his face like that again. I stayed quiet and let him speak.

"I'm sorry about the park. Are you terribly disappointed to miss the Sousa concert?"

"No, it's fine. With the windows open, we can usually hear it from here. I just wanted to be out in the world with you." I paused, uneasy about asking. "Ellis, what happened?"

"It was just all too much. I'm not who I was before the war, and I don't want to try to be that person again. Being here, trying to do the same things... It's all so loud and everything grates on me now. I have a terrible headache. I'm going to get down to the Wagamon and try to rest. I'll see you this evening." He hoisted his pack and the picnic basket, and after a brief kiss, he was on his way.

• • •

I was making the sauce for the chicken when Ivy and William arrived. I had strained the cooking liquid and added lemon juice and currant jelly, and was now making a dark roux of butter and flour to thicken it. This was my third attempt after burning the first two. I simply couldn't focus on the bubbling butter and flour mixture.

Mama left me to my thoughts and greeted Ivy and William at the door. William's friendly booming voice carried through the house, and Ivy's clicking high heels announced her approach. Well-coiffed and impeccably dressed in a sharp suit, she appeared in the kitchen as beautiful and slim as ever. More so, I thought. I imagined what I looked like, sweating from cooking, flour on my fingers and splatters on my apron.

"Hello, Tish," she said. Her haughty voice was tempered with something soft, sadness perhaps. Despite growing up with her and listening to her voice until I wanted to scream, it sounded unfamiliar to me now, different somehow.

"Hello, Ivy," I said. "How are you?"

"Still barren, it seems," she spat bluntly.

I didn't know how to respond. I could see the pain in her eyes, but I was wary that, like a wounded cat, she might strike at anyone trying to help her.

"Now Ivy," Mama said, billowing in and saving me from coming up with something, "give it time. Have you spoken to the doctor?"

"Yes, Mama, of course I have. Even William has, though he'd be humiliated if he knew I told you. They can determine nothing wrong. According to my mother-in-law, though, I am just being selfish. If I really wanted a baby, she says, we would have one. She says that she agrees with Teddy Roosevelt. That I am 'shrinking from the primary duties of life for my own love of ease.' I think she is going to embroider a pillow with his quote about 'willful sterility' on it."

"I'm so sorry, Ivy," I said, moving toward her.

"What do you know of it, Tish?" Ivy said, her claws suddenly unsheathed. The sadness was gone and the hiss was back. She left the kitchen, joining William, Papa, and Oliver in the sitting room. I didn't dare say that I knew more about being a woman than she thought, after last night, but I did feel sadness for her. Her body, ever her reason for being proud and imperious, was failing her in its most basic way. It must have been heartbreaking. I wondered about William. Was he taking it well, being supportive, or was he judging her inability as she was?

Soon the doorbell rang. I let Ellis in and we all sat down for dinner. Over the meal, we talked about William's business, and Papa's business, and soon, the men asked Ellis what his plans were.

"Well, I just secured a room at the Wagamon, and so I suppose I'll be looking for a job here. Eventually, we'll be heading West."

"I'd be happy to have your help down at the shop," Papa said. "Business should be picking up now that the summer season is here, but I should have time to train you up a bit."

My stomach clenched. I knew what Papa was doing. He was trying to get us to stay in town.

"No, thank you, Mr. Hess. You'd be better off finding someone more permanent. We aren't planning on staying around long enough," Ellis said, and relief washed over me.

"Nonsense," Papa said, sternness entering his voice. "You'll be here for a few months at least. Why not come down Monday with Tish and I'll show you around."

The muscles in Ellis' cheeks began to flex and his jaw locked into place. A low rumble, almost a growl, began in this throat. "No," he said.

The table was silent, and I was sure that Papa was furious to be spoken to in this manner.

Suddenly, William chimed in, overly boisterous and obviously so. "We are doggone glad to have you back home, Ellis."

"Doggone glad," Oliver repeated, grinning, earning him and William a stern look from Mama.

"Sorry, Mama Hess, but we are glad," William said. "I am just so disappointed that I wasn't able to join you over there. These old flat feet," he guffawed.

"Don't be sorry," Ellis said flatly, focused on his plate.

"But, truly, I am. Not being able to do my duty was hard for me to face, actually," William admitted.

Like the first firework on the fourth of July, Ellis unexpectedly exploded. His fork clattered to his plate as he shouted at William, bits of spittle flaying the table. "Hard for you to face? Over there, we faced death every second, watched good men fall flat on their faces in the mud with a bullet through their brain.

Those beastly Huns, the gas, the barbed wire... William, you had better kiss those flat feet of yours in thanks for not having to go over there. Hard to face? You don't know what that even means."

When he was finished, William sat silent. My eyes were wide and Ivy looked away as if something very interesting was transpiring in the growing dusk outside. Oliver sat still for perhaps the first and last time at the dinner table, just staring at Ellis. Papa was focused on his meal, and cleared his throat loudly. It was Mama whose voice broke the dead air.

"We are all very grateful for your service to our country, Ellis. As I have said before, and will say to anyone who will listen, we couldn't be more proud of you. I am sure you saw unimaginable things, but you are home now, in the presence of people who love you and hope to call you family. Now, let's lower our voices and continue our meal. I have made an Orange Feather Cake to welcome you home." She got up from the table and brought it in, a small mound bedecked with fresh blackberries from the yard. She began cutting it and passing it on plates even though most of our dinner plates were still full.

CHAPTER ELEVEN
Molly

Though I had been putting off signing up for a baby class because I dreaded the drive there—and, admittedly, I enjoyed refusing any of Jocelyn's suggestions on principle—the idea wouldn't go away, and gained appeal with Liz's suggestion. I picked a time that wouldn't interfere with the naptime schedule I was trying to establish and packed Hayden in the car. He hollered the whole way, as if the car seat were on fire. I reached back to flick the toys attached to the bar of his car seat in vain. Finally, I gave up and just sang to him, hoping the sound of my voice would reach him through his cries.

My nerves were frazzled by the time I arrived, and if it hadn't meant facing an immediate drive back with him screaming, I would have bailed on the class altogether. I unlatched the car seat and heaved him into the building. Once he could see me, he calmed down a little but still wailed as we entered and I checked in.

"Please take off your shoes," the lady at the desk said, "We don't allow outside shoes in the play area. Do you have socks?"

159

I was wearing sandals, but I had read online that socks were necessary so I fished them out of my bag and waved them at the lady. See, I was prepared, my smile said. I can do it all!

"Wonderful," she said and showed me where the class would begin in just a few minutes.

The other babies in the waiting room were quiet and happy, their mothers already in their socks, diaper bags neatly stowed in small foot lockers, waiting to go into the play area.

When it was time for class to begin, we all filed in. Primary colors abounded, red slides, blue mats, yellow oversized foam blocks. It was like a padded room for insane babies.

The instructor began singing a welcome song, and I followed the other mommies over to the center mat area. We sat in a circle. Some of the moms sang along with the instructor, their babies lying on their back in front of them, looking at the ceiling, which was the plainest thing in the room. I laid Hayden down, being sure to do what the others did, when the others did.

There were a few more songs, and a puppet, and then the perky instructor called out, "Okay, mommies, time for today's discussion question! Let's go around in a circle and say what we like to listen to in the car with baby."

Luckily, she started at the other end of the circle, as I almost laughed out loud at the question. As if I listened to anything but Hayden's screaming.

"We like a lullaby CD," one mother said.

"I just put on the news and she conks right out," another said.

"Madison likes jazz," a mommy added.

"I can listen to anything I'd like. The car lulls Joey to sleep," said the next in line.

Soon it would be my turn. How was I going to be honest? This was like being in a room full of Jocelyns. All of these mothers seemed to be loving motherhood, loving their easy babies, all smiles and sunshine. Their ease made my struggles seem worse.

I felt awful. Maybe I should just pretend to have a happy baby. He was content right now; perhaps it would be believable.

The woman next to me answered, "I can't listen to anything in the car. Delaney is a total jerk when she gets into the car seat."

Gasps and tongue clicks from the other mothers filled the room. The instructor laughed awkwardly, trying to smooth things over. I perked up, a burst of laughter exploding before I could hold it back. I looked at this lady next to me and thought, *she gets it.*

"Why are you all so appalled?" she said. "I love her, but she acts like a total jerk in the car."

The other mothers looked away, not bothering to hide their disdain. The woman who made this declaration seemed unaffected. Her blond hair hung thick in an angled bob, and she ruffled the back to give it more volume, a gesture that somehow showed off her confidence.

The instructor was uneasy and ready to move on, and so focused on me. "Ok. Well. Next is a new couple, baby Hayden and Mommy Molly. Molly, what do you and Hayden like to listen to in the car?"

"Actually, we don't listen to anything in the car either. He screams the whole time and the radio just adds to the noise. I guess you could say that Hayden is a jerk in the car too."

More gasps and haughty tongue clicks came from the rest of the group. I looked at the woman with the bob next to me and smiled. She smiled back.

We broke away for free play at the instructor's request and the other mothers moved their babies away from us quickly, scooping their infants up like protective chimpanzees. I sat still, not knowing how my infant would play on any of these play structures. The woman next to me stayed too.

"Hi, I'm Christy," she said. "This is Delaney."

"I'm Molly and this is Hayden, my jerk."

She grinned. "Is he a fussy baby?"

"Unbelievably fussy. Delaney too?"

"Yup, most of the time. It's hard, isn't it? Draining, and not what you expected it to be like when you had a baby. These other ladies just don't seem to get it. They are all cheery with their jazz and news. What baby likes jazz?"

I chuckled. "Madison is very sophisticated, I guess. Mature beyond her years."

As we laughed together, I was immensely comforted by being understood. We chatted about our husbands and families, getting to know each other. I told her about Aunt Tish's house and she seemed interested in hearing more about it.

Did I dare be completely honest?

"It's a mess, actually," I said. Christy raised her eyebrows and I continued, "I think it was beautiful once, but it's full of my husband's aunt's old things and he won't let me get rid of any of it. Most of our stuff is still in boxes."

"Man. Is her stuff nice at least? When you say aunt with an old house, I start thinking about antiques and fine art."

"Oh, there's art, all right. Old still life paintings and European townscapes. It's not my style. And I didn't think it was Corey's either. Honestly, it's like living in someone else's skin. My husband has never been happier, though. It's the home of his childhood. When we moved, he told me it was this great old house, lots of charm. But when we got up here, it was... well... it wasn't as nice as he said it was."

"Could you change a few things?" Christy ventured.

"I'm beginning to think that I can't," I said with a sigh.

We talked a little more about our lives before and after baby and then Delaney started to cry, grabbing Christy's attention. Like dominoes, the other babies' moods' fell one by one and soon the room was loud with crying babies and fretting mommies. Everyone packed up to leave. The instructor waved her hands in the air and with a forced smile called out, "Come to our open gym time when your baby isn't fussy!" before retreating from the cacophony into a back room.

I soothed Hayden with a smile on my face. Welcome to my world, *ubermoms.*

• • •

Dad made arrangements to fly in the night before Corey left, and Corey planned to pick him up from the airport. Hayden had been up repeatedly through the night, and when the sun came up, I was awake to watch it. I fumbled with the ridiculously long wrapping of the baby sling, positioned it over my spit-up soaked pajamas, tucked Hayden in, and went downstairs.

Corey eventually came down and settled at the dining room table to read the newspaper.

"Morning, family," he said. "Okay, so I'll pick your dad up around seven tonight and we'll come here. Do you want to go out for dinner or shall we pick up some take-out on the way home?"

"Take-out. He may be tired from his trip, and I'm always tired."

"Take-out it is, then."

"I'll call Han Palace so it will be ready for pick-up when you get there."

"Sounds good. See you later tonight," Corey said. He kissed the top of Hayden's head and left for work.

I spent the day tidying up as best as I could and putting the sheets on the guest bed. I was excited to see my dad, but wary too. We hadn't seen each other in a while. I reminded myself to be grateful that he was coming to see me now.

I didn't have time to think on it much further as no amount of feeding, soothing, or snuggling would calm Hayden that day. I walked him back and forth, trying everything I could to make him happy and counting the minutes until Corey arrived back home. A little after six o'clock, I fell to the couch and latched Hayden on. He quieted and nursed and I started to nod off myself.

The door slamming woke me up.

"Molly? Molly? Did you order the food?" Corey called from the foyer.

"What..." I said, looking around. The room was dark now and I wondered what time it was. I must have ordered; the smell of greasy wok found my nose. The lights flicked on, bright and accusing. I rubbed my eyes.

"Did you order the food? Your dad and I went to Han Palace and they said they didn't have an order for us. We waited forty minutes. I've been calling you."

"Oh, sorry." I said, standing up and tucking myself back into my shirt. I saw my father standing silently in the doorway. "Hi, Dad." I said, moving toward him and greeting him with an embrace.

From afar, I could feel Corey's anger, the stiffness in his posture, frustration at me radiating in waves.

"Sorry about the food," I said. "I must have fallen asleep. Welcome to Willow Grove, Dad. Come on in. Would you like to hold him?"

Dad sat down and took off his windbreaker. I gently placed Hayden in his arms and watched him smile at his grandson.

"I'll go get some plates," I said, grabbing the food and going to the kitchen. Corey followed me.

"What's going on, Molly?" he hissed. "You're not even dressed. You had one job today and that was to order the food. I'm starving."

"Keep your voice down. You're embarrassing me. I said I was sorry about the food. I actually had two jobs today, by the way. The first was taking care of your son. I've been up since four a.m., and I fell asleep. I had a hard day. I said I'm sorry."

"I had a hard day too." Corey ran his fingers through his hair and sighed. "Let's just eat." He took the plates from the cabinet and huffed into the dining room.

We started dinner in silence, helping ourselves to the food. There was estranged awkwardness from one side of me, overblown anger from the other.

"The house is really beautiful," Dad ventured into the tense air. "I love its old charm."

"Yeah, thanks," Corey said, now in happy territory. "I have loved this house my whole life. We celebrated every holiday here, and sometimes my parents would even ship me off to Aunt Tish for the summer. I'm so glad we have it and can give Hayden the same type of childhood."

I busied myself chewing.

"And, Molly? How about you? Settling in okay?" Dad asked.

I nodded, swallowing hard and using the time to think of an answer that wouldn't start another argument with Corey. "Yes. I don't really get out much yet."

"Well, tomorrow, we're going out," Dad said. "On the drive in, I saw a, how do you say it, P-H-O, restaurant. What the heck is that? I think I want to try it. My treat."

I smiled. "It's Vietnamese, Dad. It's pronounced *fah* and you'll like it. I haven't been to this one, but I'm sure it's good."

"Sounds like you have a nice day planned," Corey said. "Thanks for coming, Rich."

Corey kissed the baby but tersely brushed by me before walking up to bed.

• • •

Corey slept through the night, snoring softly when I woke with Hayden. His alarm sounded early, but I chose to snooze through. He was gone, flying to Houston, by the time I fully woke. Dad and I puttered around until lunch.

"Hayden hates the car, Dad. Just warning you," I said as I lugged the car seat down the front steps. It had taken me most of the morning to gather the things that I would need for our short outing to the Vietnamese restaurant. Dad hauled it all in my overstuffed diaper bag behind me down the stairs.

"It's a short trip. We'll be okay. If it will help, I'll sit in the back with him."

"How do you know so much about babies?" I asked.

"Well, you were a baby once. And we have had lots of visits from Nicholas, Joseph, and Michael when their kids were babies."

I kept silent. Nicholas, Joseph, and Michael. Of course he had spent time with them and their children. Despite my dad being right in front of me, I could taste my loneliness for him. I watched him, like I would a stranger on the street, cooing and chatting to Hayden. By the time I was settled in my seat, Hayden was quiet, mesmerized by my dad.

At the restaurant, they offered us a high chair, turning it over to show me how it held the car seat. It was wobbly, though, and in the end, I opted to put the seat on the chair closest to the wall. Hayden was asleep.

"Let's order quick. This might not last!" I said, pulling off my jacket and opening the menu.

After ordering, Dad looked at me and asked, "So, how are you, really?" I was surprised by his sudden intimacy. As if he had earned it.

"Dad, come on. I'm fine." I wasn't sure I wanted to discuss it. I didn't want to cry in this restaurant.

"Molly. I flew all the way up here, left your stepmother alone to shop and spend god knows how much. Please don't lie to me."

I fiddled with my chopsticks. And then the answer flooded out of me. "I don't know, Dad. This is harder than I thought. I thought Hayden would arrive and—poof!—I'd just know what to do, he would be happy, and I would love him instantly. And I do *love* him, it's just that, sometimes, well, sometimes, it's really hard to *like* being a mom. He is always crying. I feel like such a failure, and I am so exhausted that I'm not even myself. And the house is terrible. It isn't my own and I'm afraid it never will be." A tear slid down my face and onto the tablecloth, making a dark wet circle.

"And things with Corey?"

"Aww, Dad, you saw how it was last night. It's not good. I can't even focus on our relationship. Everything is about keeping this little being alive and happy, and there isn't room for anything else. Corey works really hard but doesn't seem to see how hard I am working just to stay afloat." I took a sip of water and continued. "It's hard living in Aunt Tish's shadow. I have never even met her but I feel like I am supposed to just fit right into her life, be as caring and perfect as she was. That's what Corey wants. He's never home, though. I am stuck in the house that only he loves, without him. My only company is Hayden, and he screams at me all day."

I looked up at Dad and couldn't read his face. Maybe I had gone too far. He fidgeted uncomfortably in his seat.

"I'm sorry, Dad. I shouldn't be unleashing this all on you. I'm fine, really. I'm just adjusting."

"Molly, don't do that. I don't know what to do about Corey, but I do know that being a new mom is hard. Your mom thought so too. I didn't help much. I was working, I guess. It was just the way of things."

"Did I ever tell you what Mom told me before she died? She said that I should do more than be a wife and mother."

"Is that what you want? Are you thinking about going back to work?"

"I would like to eventually, I think. What I'd really like is to fix up the house. Make it more my own. That may make me feel better. What do you think Mom would say about all of this? I miss her so much."

"Me too." I knew he was telling the truth. "She would say you should do what makes you happy."

"I think that she would have been a big help with Hayden," I said. "I think I could have called her and asked her questions and advice. Without her, I feel like I have to be strong and figure it out on my own. I'm afraid I'm not doing a very good job."

Dad reached across the table and took my hand.

"Look at that kid," he said, gesturing toward Hayden, whose mouth was moving in a slumbering suckle. "You're doing a better job than you think, Molly. I'm proud of you, and Mom would be too," he said.

"Thanks, Dad."

The tablecloth began to be polka dotted with my tears, but I felt better than I had in days. The waiter arrived with bowls of exotic broth. My sadness curled up with the steam rising from the soup and dissipated somewhat. I was grateful that my father had come to visit, and told him so. We tucked into our meal.

• • •

I woke up the next morning excited about what Dad and I would do together with Hayden that day. Where would we go? Maybe a walk? Maybe the park? Maybe he would want to try another restaurant? There was a baby class on our schedule, but we could skip it. Or maybe Dad would want to tag along? With our renewed closeness, I was ready to face the day.

I found my father downstairs, dressed, suitcase by the door. Confused, I asked, "Dad? What's going on?"

He ran his fingers through his hair and looked at the floor.

"Your stepmother called last night. I need to get back."

My mouth was suddenly dry. "What? You just got here. Corey is still out of town. Your flight isn't scheduled for two more days."

"I know, it's just, well... last night when she and I talked, she said that there is a crisis with Michael. She doesn't really want me to talk about it. She rescheduled my flight for eleven this morning. A shuttle is coming."

My heart was seizing in my chest. What was happening? Was he really leaving? After everything I had confided in him yesterday?

Dad leaned in to kiss my cheek and I stood stock still. He went to hold Hayden and I pivoted away from him.

"No, Dad," I said. "I can't believe you are leaving now."

"I'm sorry, Molly. Your stepmother needs me."

"I need you too, Dad! Weren't you listening? I am drowning here. Look around you—we have been here for months and we are still living out of boxes. These bags under my eyes may never go away. Corey isn't coming back for three more days!"

"I am sorry, sweetie, but my flight has been changed already." He took me by the shoulders. "You can do this. The shuttle is here. I have to go."

"Fine, go," I said, knowing that I would not be able to make him stay. I felt like a child on the first day of school, watching my parent walk away, full of fear and uncertainty at what lay ahead.

He tucked his head and left. Fury rose up at the two men who had abandoned me and I slammed the door behind him. A pane of glass fell out of the ancient door and shattered at my feet.

Through the empty space in the door, I watched my dad ride away.

Hayden reared his head back and began to wail.

CHAPTER TWELVE
Tish, 1920

December's early darkness had come and the daylight, highlighted with reds and golds of a lingering autumn, fell quickly. I was nearly finished with the night's dinner of roast beef and Lyonnaise potatoes. The onions were popping in the browning butter. Drips from the meat sizzled in the oven as they hit the tray beneath.

I finished slicing the potatoes and began to turn on the house lights. Oliver played with his trains on the rug in the front room, periodically sounding a loud whistle and station announcement.

Papa and Mama arrived home from town, shivering and windblown. Now that it was certain that I was leaving town, Mama had been helping Papa at the shop for the past few weeks. While she reacquainted herself with the tasks there, she had put me in charge of Ollie and dinners at home.

Ellis still refused to work at Hess's Delicatessen and took a job again at the shipyard. He continued to have dark days that scared me, but on those days he either left my company or simply stayed away, explaining later. The worry that lived at the pit of my stomach for the entire war had now morphed and taken up permanent residence. Ellis wasn't getting any better.

And neither was Papa's business. They had made some changes, but still customers were scarce. We were planning my wedding, which should have been a happy time, but worries clouded everyone's enthusiasm.

Mama entered the kitchen, bringing cold air with her.

"It's snowing," she said.

Turning from the stove to the window, I watched for a moment as the magical fairy dust collected on the pine boughs. Soon the branches would be heavy and drooping. Like a kitten on soft feet, the downy fat flakes tamped out all sound, creating a universal hush as it blanketed the yard.

As with every first snow of the season, a certain nostalgia crept over me. My entire life I had been planning on leaving, going somewhere it never snowed, and now, watching it from the window, I was sure I would miss it.

I felt a searing pain in my finger. I looked down and the potatoes were turning red. I had cut myself with the paring knife. I howled, squeezed it, and began to get lightheaded as the blood seeped through my clutched fingers.

Mama rushed to my side. She produced a towel, pried my hand off my wound, and wrapped it tightly. Soon the pain subsided a bit, though I could feel my heartbeat in that finger.

"Tish," Mama shook her head. "You really must pay attention. That is an awful cut, and now we have to throw away all these potatoes."

"I'm sorry, Mama," I said. "I'm so terrible at food preparation. At least I didn't do this at the shop."

She nodded. "I wish you hadn't done it at all, actually."

"Did you have many customers today?" I asked.

"Not as many as we would have liked. If we can get through the winter, we will be all right. Things have actually picked up since the war ended and people don't seem to think ill of your father any more. But with you leaving, I'll have to work there for a while. There simply isn't any money to hire someone else to help Papa. He's talking about getting a loan to cover some of the expenses and hold us over for a bit, but I'm not sure there is anyone in town who will give him one..." Her brow furrowed in a look of worry that she had come to share with

Papa. She trailed off, perhaps thinking she said too much. "Don't you worry about it, though, Tish. Let's focus on the holidays and your wedding. Papa and I will manage just fine. Were you planning on getting together with Ellis this evening?"

"Well, I was, but perhaps not now with the snow. He planned on coming over around eight o'clock, but I'll ring him now and suggest that he just stay in."

"Yes, that might be wise. Tonight we can finalize the wedding plans, just us," Mama said. Hearing me sigh, she held her hand up and continued, "I know. You don't want anything lavish like Ivy, but there are still decisions to be made."

Decisions. Indeed. Though the ones that Mama was talking about—the flowers, the cake—were ones that I didn't spend much time on. The decision to marry Ellis, the man he currently was, hung heavy on my heart during his bad days. And now, with what Mama had confided about the shop, a distinct worry about abandoning Mama and Papa and the family business began to creep in.

I was firmly set on my desired path, though, quite close to achieving exactly what I wanted. It was hard to admit that the golden luster around my dream had faded a bit with the reality of it. I feared I would regret stopping its forward motion, but there was also much to fear in staying the course.

I put no voice to these fears, though. Not to Mama, not to Virginia, and certainly not to Ellis. Under the electric lights that burned bright that evening, Mama and I sat together in the sitting room with the radio churning out "The First Noel" and "Adeste Fideles" as we discussed the menu for the wedding luncheon and strung cranberries for the Christmas tree.

Later that week, Ellis happily reported that William had given him a contact at the Standard Oil Company. They needed workers in California, and so he was going to New York to meet with a few men there to see what was available. For days, he floated on this news. It seemed as if, finally, the darkness had been put behind him. There was joy in his voice as he planned his trip. The adventurer that I had known in him had returned, and I saw more and more of the old Ellis in the days approaching the interview. With the possibility of an exciting future within our grasp, my fears began to subside. Maybe this was just what he needed to permanently heal.

He planned to leave the following Monday morning, taking the commuter train to Philadelphia, and then another train from 30th Street Station to New

York's Penn Station. He had found a boarding house ten blocks away from the Standard Oil office where the meetings were to be held.

Papa even offered Ellis money to pay the fares. When he declined, Papa insisted. I knew this might be a sacrifice for Papa, but I hoped that he was offering because he was able.

"Son, you are going to be family soon." He shoved the cash into Ellis' breast pocket and would not hear otherwise. I squeezed Papa's forearm in thanks, knowing he understood that this job would mean our departure.

I packed all of my hope inside Ellis' bag and hugged him hard the Sunday night before he left. I would see him when he returned from New York, surely with good news of a job in California. The promise of our tomorrow lay just a few train rides away.

• • •

My feet touched cold on the wood floor when I climbed out of bed the next morning. Dressing quickly in the dark, I walked to the window. More snow had fallen overnight and then hardened into a crystal crust over the lawn. The tops of the tree branches were gently iced like glittering sugar cakes. Christmas was just two weeks away, and there would be much to celebrate. Ellis would be back from New York in a week or two, hopefully with good news about a job in California. His darkness would fade. We would be married and on our way.

I went downstairs, finding Mama in the kitchen making breakfast. The oatmeal on the stove bubbled up steam in popping puffs.

"Good morning, Tish," she said as she bustled about. "Breakfast is almost ready. Could you please pour a pitcher of milk and place it on the table? I'll go rouse Ollie. Papa should be down soon. He is giving me a ride to the station today. My train leaves just before eight o'clock. Could you please stop at Rothwell's Drug Store and pick up some nice paper for wrapping gifts?"

"You are going downtown?" I asked.

"Yes, to pick up some of the loan documents your father has been discussing with a few banks. Papa wanted to go himself, but in the end, he decided he had better stay at the shop."

"I could go, Mama," I offered.

She waved me off. "It's all set. Papa phoned ahead and each bank is expecting me. I want to stop at the confectioners for chocolate for Ollie for Christmas, too. Can you walk him to and from school?" I nodded in agreement. "And don't forget to get the wrapping paper I need from Rothwell's."

Papa came to the table, followed by a sullen Ollie. Papa's bow tie was straight and tight, and Ollie's sat askew on his chest. Ollie's hair looked tousled and disobedient, and his face was a pout. He flopped his body into the chair with reluctance, without turning his legs under the way Papa expected of us at the table. Papa lifted his eyes from his oatmeal and looked across the table at his son.

"Oliver, sit properly," he said.

"Come on, Oliver, perk up," I said, settling into the chair next to him. "This is the last week of school before Christmas break. Christmas Eve will be here before you know it. Maybe you'll get some of those cream-filled chocolates you like," I cajoled. Coming into the dining room and settling at the table, Mama threw me a smile. I received only a grunt in response from Oliver.

We ate our breakfast in a quiet rush. When the clock chimed its heavy single tone of seven-thirty, Mama hustled us all up from the table and toward the foyer for our coats. I helped Oliver into his heavy wool jacket, cap, and mittens, and found his school books, securing them into his strap. After buttoning up my coat, Mama handed me Oliver's lunch pail. She secured her favorite maroon hat upon her head, smoothing the pheasant feather that embellished it, and hurried Papa out the door.

A bitter wind muscled its way into the house as we opened it to the morning, and our bodies constricted in the stinging air. We all huddled into our outerwear, our necks shrinking into our shoulders, backs hunched and chests braced against the wind. Our farewells were brief, Mama and Papa seeking the still air inside the touring car, and Oliver and I quickening our pace toward the school house.

It was about a mile's distance, and the winter air sliced my cheeks with each howl of the wind. Ollie and I passed the time mostly in silence, too chilled, or perhaps, in his case, still too sleepy, to speak. Our thirty-minute walk took us through the center of town, along Davisville Road, and up the steps into the schoolhouse. I stopped in a moment to greet his teacher, Mrs. Ely, lingering a bit to warm my hands, and then was on my way back to town.

The air was still biting, but the wind had stilled. Three crows swooped and hopped from tree to tree along my way. They called out, scratchy and loud, in short bursts of staccato competition as they swooped against the gray sky.

When I reached Rothwell's, I pulled open the heavy door and was welcomed by a tinkling bell and a rush of warm air. The pharmacy was crowded this morning. I made my way to the counter to request the wrapping paper Mama wanted.

"Good morning, Miss Hess. Cold today, isn't it?" Mr. Rothwell smiled warmly.

"Yes, it certainly is, Mr. Rothwell. Christmas will be here soon. I was wondering if perhaps you had any wrapping paper in stock," I said.

"I do. I have two different kinds this year. A beautiful red with holly leaves and one that is green with cherubs. I'll get them both so you can decide."

While I waited, I fiddled in my satchel for my change purse, my fingers thick and without dexterity inside my gloves. Behind me, the hushed tones of the customers, gathered in groups, rose in volume as more joined the conversation. Though I was trying to mind my own business, my attention was turned to the door as someone rushed in, desperate to join the gossip. Two separate groups had formed into one, pulsing with whatever small-town news was juicy enough to discuss this morning. They were too far away for me to hear, save for a few high-pitched gasps that rose from their huddles.

Mr. Rothwell returned, rolls of paper in hand, and placed them on the counter for my inspection. They were fine paper. Mama would be pleased with either one.

"Terrible for those people who were in the train crash this morning..." Mr. Rothwell said.

My head snapped up. "Train crash? What train crash?"

"Yes, haven't you heard? Seems as if a commuter train heading into the city collided with a commuter train on the way out. Don't know why they were on the same track. The trains are stacked atop one another. Hot coals poured out and there is a terrible fire. Those cars are wood, you know. The ambulances are rushing people to Abington Hospital, though a man who stopped in here on the way back from the crash site said there aren't many survivors."

My chest constricted and there was a thrumming in my ears. Mama. Please let it have been another train. Not the one she was on. Please. I felt ill.

"Are you all right, Tish?" Mr. Rothwell asked.

"Um, yes, thank you," I forced the words out, abandoning the paper on the counter and rushing for the door.

I ran straight across traffic and into our shop. I was breathless and light-headed opening the door. I burst past the customer Papa was helping and raced behind the counter. Papa turned to face me, affronted.

"Tish, how terribly rude of you..." Papa began.

I cut him off. "Papa, did you put Mama on the train this morning?"

"Yes. Nearly missed it, though I'm glad she didn't have to wait on that cold platform for long. Terrible wind this morning. Why are you so upset?" He handed the customer some wrapped cheese and then we were alone in the shop. My throat felt thick and I could feel the blood pulsing in my temples. My eyes were watering from fear and the cold.

"Papa. Haven't you heard? A train on the way into the city crashed this morning. I just heard about it over at Rothwell's. Do you think Mama could have been on that train?"

I watched as his face fell and his pallor become white. He swayed and his back hit heavy against the counter.

"I'll... I'll..." he stammered. "I'll make some calls."

There was an ache at the pit of my stomach, as if I had eaten a brick and it was slowly sinking, pulling my insides apart.

Papa picked up the telephone and rang the hospital switchboard. Silently, I reassured myself while he waited to be connected. No sense in panicking yet, Mama would say. Just wait and see.

Maybe she hadn't been hurt. Maybe she had only some minor injury, like a cut or bump on the head. I imagined her retelling the tale to us when we all got home. I watched Papa's face, willing it to have been the train before or after Mama's, willing Mr. Rothwell to have been mistaken, willing her to be all right.

I could only hear Papa's side of the conversation, but his reactions heightened the worry I had been fighting off. When he hung up the phone, he took a moment to settle himself before telling me what he had learned.

That moment stretched out long and harsh. I didn't dare demand the information. Once I heard it, it would be real, and the stillness of now would erupt. And so I waited, watching Papa's face for any sign of hope, but the longer it took for him to speak, the more I understood the truth.

"Mama was on the train, and she is in the hospital now. She has been hurt. Badly. They have been calling the house. They say we should come as soon as possible." Papa's voice was low and serious.

Suddenly frantic, I yelled, "Let's go to the hospital then. Now!"

"Yes. I... I... need to put all of these things away, close up the shop..." Papa trailed off, infuriatingly slow and dazed.

"Papa, leave it. We need to be with Mama now. Get your coat. I'll call Ivy."

As Papa turned away from me, staggering out from behind the counter and fumbling with the coat rack, I grabbed the telephone and rang the switchboard, asking to be connected to Ivy's home in Chestnut Hill.

It buzzed endlessly and my foot bounced on the tile floor, involuntarily and impatient. Every moment seemed critical. I couldn't stay still.

Finally, my sister's cheery voice was on the line. I hated to tell her, drag her out of what might have been a wonderful day, but I shared the details we knew, and told her we were going to the hospital. She said she would come as soon as could and made me promise to get in touch as we heard more.

Papa was still fumbling to put on his coat. He seemed suddenly old. Frail and confused, his feet shuffled and his shoulders were hunched. I walked around behind him, hoisted the coat to his shoulders, hurried him out, and locked the delicatessen door behind us.

"What about Oliver?" he asked.

Ollie. With a sharp intake of breath, I realized how hard this would be for him. I didn't know if word had reached the schoolhouse, or if he had been awake enough this morning to pay attention to Mama's plans for the day. I hated the thought of him worrying all day, but I wasn't sure what state Mama would be in when we arrived. If she was badly burned, maybe delirious, perhaps it was better if he didn't see her that way. But what if this was our last chance to be with her? Could I deny him the opportunity to say goodbye? I looked at Papa, searching his face for an answer to how to handle this horrific situation. His face was blank, crestfallen and unhelpful.

"We'll stop by the schoolhouse and fetch him," I decided aloud and we walked out into the cold to Papa's touring car.

Though utterly despondent, Papa drove very authoritatively up Davisville Road and stopped outside the school. He remained still in his seat, and I took this to mean that I was to go in after Ollie. I told him I would be right back and shut the car door.

Mama rode in this passenger seat just hours ago. Her hand touched the cold metal of the handle, and I wished I could feel the warmth it had briefly left there. Had I kissed her goodbye this morning? I thought back. No, we had rushed away from each other in the raw weather.

My presence in the classroom, only an hour into the day, surprised Mrs. Ely, and her face flashed anger at the interruption.

"I'm sorry to bother the class, ma'am, but there has been an accident, and I'm here to pick up Oliver."

Mrs. Ely's face smoothed and she showed concern. "Yes, of course. Oliver, you may collect your things."

Oliver grabbed his books and slid out from behind his desk. His dark eyes filled but held, and he looked up at me. "Tish?"

"Come on, Ollie. We need to go," I said, my arm around his shoulder. And with that, we left the classroom and joined Papa in the running car. Papa had the wherewithal while we were inside to turn it around so that we were headed back toward the center of town and could continue on to the hospital. Ollie and I clambered in and settled in our seats.

"Papa? Tish? What happened? Where's Mama?" Oliver asked from the backseat.

Papa stayed silent, his stone face fixed on the road ahead. It was up to me to tell Oliver. I shifted in my seat so that I could look back at him.

"There was a train crash this morning, and Mama was on the train. She is at the hospital now and we are going to see her. We don't know how she is feeling, or if she will be awake when we get there."

"Is Mama going to be all right?"

"I don't know. Let's get to her and see."

The tears that had threatened in the classroom spilled over onto Oliver's cheeks. I snaked my hand back to hold his. He let out a low moan that sounded like, "Mama." I looked over at Papa for help and saw tears shining on his cheeks too.

• • •

The hospital was crowded when we arrived. A loud and demanding group huddled around a single nurse, begging for scraps of information, mouths open like baby birds. We maneuvered though the press and entered the ward.

Though he still hadn't said a word, now that we were here, Papa's motion had determination. I gripped Oliver's hand, as much for my comfort as for his, and we hustled to keep pace with Papa. Cots were pushed up against the walls and people lay in them, gruesome in the blazing ceiling lights. Charred clothing hung off bodies, patches of flaming red skin beneath. Small puddles of blood pooled on the floor. An acrid stench consumed the air, weakening my knees and propelling me forward, away from the carnage. As we passed, I hugged Oliver to me, and put my hand up near his outer eye, like a horse blinder, hoping to shield him from this memory.

Some cots stood unattended, the inhabitant suffering alone, staring at the ceiling, while others were surrounded by crying women or shouting doctors. We careened through the center of them, jostling left and right as needed. In our haste, Ollie and I collided with a cot that was being moved by a team of nurses. We gave way and waited before trotting to catch up with Papa. Ahead, he paused to check the numbers on the rooms, then suddenly barreled into an open doorway, disappearing from the hallway. Inside, we found him crouched over Mama's silent form.

The roar of the hallway didn't carry in to her room, and the bright lights passed away when we crossed the threshold. Dim and quiet, and now seemingly far from the chaos, we could hear Papa's low keening. He rocked on his bent knees, chest heaving, head bent over the bed, firmly clasping Mama's hand.

I stared at her other hand—charred and sooty—and had trouble recognizing it. Mama's hands were fine and well kept. This hand was a muddle of red welts, branding, and raw skin dappling darkness beneath. The fingernails were broken and blackened.

With bravery I wasn't sure I possessed, I looked at her face. Mama's eyes were closed, and a wild gash of red wet the thick bandages wrapped around her head.

"Mama?" Ollie whispered. Then, to me, "Is she..."

He and I stepped closer, still clutching each other, and stood at the foot of her bed. Oliver released me and moved to Mama's side. Grasping the foot of the bed frame with both hands, I stared hard in the dim light at her chest, searching and waiting for a rise in the bedsheets. It came. Slowly and without much of a crest, but she was breathing.

A man in a white coat appeared behind me. "Are you the Hess family?"

"Yes," I said. "This is my mother."

The doctor looked at Oliver and then addressed my father.

"Sir, may we have a word outside? I'd like to update you on your wife's condition."

"No! I am not leaving her," Papa growled, not turning from her, tightening his grip on Mama's blood-drained hand.

I touched Papa's shoulder and said, "I'll go." I followed the doctor back out into the thundering hallway.

"As you know, your mother was in the train wreck this morning," he began. "She arrived here with a severe head injury; must have hit it hard on something during the collision. We did all we could to alleviate the pressure in her brain, but I am afraid it may not be enough. Most of her body is badly burned, and she has suffered significant damage to her lungs from the smoke. I'm very sorry, but it is likely she will not make it through the night. Now is a good time for goodbyes."

A nurse jogged up to the doctor, requiring his immediate assistance. He excused himself and hustled off. I nodded, a moment too late for him to have seen it as any kind of response, my mind slow and muddled in the absorption of his words.

Head injury. Severe burns. Likely won't make it through the night. Mama.

My nose prickled and my eyes needled with tears. A sob boiled up out of my mouth and I clamped it down for fear that Oliver would hear. In the doorjamb, with my back against the frame, I laid my head back and shuddered. My one shoulder stuck out into the trauma melee that filled the hallway, the other shoulder hung softly inside Mama's muted room. I stood on the edge of both scenes, alone in the knowledge of Mama's condition, not yet ready to tip into the ringing chaos of losing her.

So much pain filled this hospital. It echoed in the corridor and seized my chest as it bounced from tragedy to tragedy. Was Mama in pain? If there had been fear or pain on that train, her face showed no sign of it now. Her beautiful features held all of our comfort and security, soothed us when we were hurt, reassured us when we were frightened, and corrected us when we went astray. Her face was how we grew and learned. It was present in every moment of our becoming. Surely she would open her eyes and tell us that we could all go home together now.

Digging around in my satchel, I found my handkerchief and wiped my dripping nose. I inhaled deeply over and over until I felt calm enough to face the next few moments.

I left the doorjamb and went back to Mama's side. My steps were heavy, full and frightened. I stood with Oliver and Papa around Mama. Papa looked up at me and I shook my head, unable to say the words aloud. His frame collapsed and, seeing this, Oliver knew as well. He flung his body on top of Mama's with a wail. I stood aside, afraid to touch her, to cause her any pain, though perhaps she was beyond that. And in the end, it might pain her to be without my touch. I tentatively reached out and touched her leg to secure a connection, but lightly enough so I could barely feel the shape of her ankle.

Our silent vigil was broken by Ivy's breathless arrival.

"Papa! What is going on? There are hundreds of people out there! It took me forever to find someone who could help me find you!" Her words flooded the hush, but she suddenly stopped when her eyes stilled enough to take in our tears, Mama's injuries. "Papa..." she whispered.

"It is good that we are all here. She would have wanted it this way," Papa replied.

Ivy joined our muted circle, and we let the frantic tragedy rush by outside the doorway. In the center of us, Mama's chest slowly lifted the crisp white sheets, and then not at all.

• • •

After Mama's funeral, Ivy and William joined us at the house. We climbed the front porch stairs and entered through the heavy wooden front door as a family group, smaller and diminished greatly by the absence of just one. I collected the newspapers that littered the porch. Leaving them folded, I set them aside in the parlor.

The house was quiet. No one had remembered to wind the clock. The kitchen stood empty, without the enticing smells of a lunch being prepared. Mama's absence felt like a heavy blanket draped over us all, tamping our forward motion, confusing us in its darkness. We stood in the foyer together, eyes cast downward, all lost without Mama.

It was Papa who moved first. He tugged at his tie, placed his hat on the rack and, without a word, walked up the stairs. Ivy and I watched him go, Oliver tucked at my side fiddling one shoe with the other.

"Shall we stay for an early supper? I could help you set it up," Ivy said, removing her coat and tugging at William's from over his broad shoulders.

"Yes, thank you," I replied.

I turned to Oliver, kneeling to look at him. His eyes were liquid and on the edge of overflowing. I stroked his cheek and gave him a cocked half smile. His face stayed immobile, but he let me help him out of his coat and then turned and shuffled away. Finding his blocks, he silently began building. William followed him into the sitting room and collapsed onto the couch. Ivy and I left them there and went to the kitchen.

As Ivy laid out turkey, cheese, pickles, and mustard on a large platter, I sliced the bread.

"What now?" I asked, as much to Ivy as to myself.

"Well. Now, Papa will need a lot of help. Mama did all the laundry, cooking, shopping, cleaning. Everything. She did everything. And Oliver, well, he'll need help with everything too. I'm too far away to help with the day-to-day tasks. Those will fall to you."

She only lived seven miles away, but her implications were clear. She and William would stay and help for the next few hours, but soon they would be leaving, resuming their own lives in Chestnut Hill. I was in charge here now. Ivy was not planning to take over Mama's responsibilities with Oliver, Papa, or this house. I was infuriated by her lack of devotion to us, but so utterly exhausted that I didn't have the energy to fight her on it.

"Papa has the shop to run," she continued, "and he'll need help there too. But mostly he'll need help here. Can you picture him washing a shirt? Or mopping the kitchen floor?"

I thought about it. I had seen him mop countless times at the shop, but never here. He was utterly reliant on Mama for all household tasks. How long would his grief prevent him from managing without her?

"Last I heard, Ellis' job wouldn't start until June. Possibly by then Papa could..." I trailed off, hopeful but without real hope. I continued, "I can talk to Ellis. We will know more details of his job when he gets back from New York."

"Yes, a summer departure could be feasible," Ivy said, her voice cheering now that the situation was closer to settled. "Oliver will be finished with the school year by then too, and Papa won't have to worry so much about him in the summer. Maybe by then he'll even have found a new wife."

Shocked, I turned, eyes wide, and stared at Ivy. "How can you say that? Mama's funeral was just today. How can you even think about Papa remarrying?"

"Oh come now, Tish. Think practically. I thought you, above everyone else, would understand that is a good solution. I miss Mama just as much as you do, but Papa simply is the kind of man who needs a wife. Now, grab the tea please. Let's get this out on the table. There's plenty for me to do at my own home before William starts the work week tomorrow."

• • •

We called the men to the table, and while Ivy settled Oliver and William, I ventured upstairs to tell Papa supper was served. At the top of the stairs, I found his door shut tight. I knocked softly. When I heard nothing, I wondered if he had decided to take a nap.

Slowly, I turned the knob and peered in. He was still in his suit, sitting on his chair, legs splayed listlessly in front of him. He gripped his black recipe book tightly in his hands. His eyes looked straight ahead, focused on nothing, his mustache set in a straight, firm line.

"Papa," I ventured, "supper is on the table."

He said nothing. I could feel the tears pricking my eyes, the heavy sadness settling on me like an overcoat.

"Please, Papa. It will do you good to eat something. This is a terrible day. Let's all try to bear it together."

His eyes shifted slightly then, and he looked at Mama's side of the bed. Silently, almost imperceptibly, he said, "She's gone. Because of me. Because of this business."

His arms fell heavy and the black recipe book hit the floor splayed open and face down. I bent to pick it up. When I tried to hand it back to him, my hand hung in the air, ignored. Papa buried his head in his hands. He braced his elbows on his knees. His breath rasped, long and slow.

"Papa?" I ventured. "Where can I put your book?"

No response.

"Papa? Please. I know how important this is to you. Let me put it somewhere safe."

He remained still. I wasn't even there. I lowered the book.

"Papa, maybe we should consider closing the store for a while. People would understand. You could use the time to hire some part-time help..."

Getting no reply, I lowered my head. The leather of the book was soft. I flicked the tattered edge. What would happen to the business now that Mama was gone and Papa blamed himself? When I looked back up, Papa had raised his eyes. They met mine. It was if I had never seen them before. Gone was the strong man who set the rules and expected absolute obedience. These eyes were lost and pleading.

Neither of us were able to comfort each other. We needed Mama. She was always the one who was best at that, the one for whom we longed when sad or scared or hurt. Tragically, she was the only one who could take away the pain caused by her absence.

Tears began running down my face, the deep ache in Papa's heart increasing the loss and worry in mine. As I walked to the doorway, he remained in his chair, both of us breaking at the loss of Mama. I carried his book downstairs and tucked it on the shelf for the day he forgave himself.

• • •

After lunch, Ivy and William climbed into their touring car. They hustled through farewell kisses and drove away. Papa remained shut in his room, and so Oliver and I stood outside by ourselves, bundled up to watch them go. My arms were draped over Oliver's shoulders, my hands clasped together at his chest. We lingered a bit in the crisp air. I wondered how long we could stand there, watching the now-empty street. I dreaded facing the house without Mama inside and the pile of dishes that Ivy neglected. I was disgusted by her callousness.

"Do you miss Mama?" Oliver asked craning his neck to look up at me.

"Yes, Ollie, I do. Very much."

"Do you think Ivy misses Mama?"

"I'm sure she does, in her own way. I'm sure Ivy would rather stay with us, but she has responsibilities at her house now. Remember when Ivy got married and moved to Chestnut Hill with William? Well, she started her own life there and needs to get back to it."

"Are you going to leave too, Tish?" Oliver asked, clenching my wrists as they lay still on his chest. I could feel his tiny heart thumping beneath my fingertips, his desperate tight clasp of our arms entwined. I clung to him as he clung to me, and I knew I had to do all that I could to help him through this. I leaned down and kissed him on the top of his shiny blonde head, and the crack that had been threatening since I had heard the news of Mama finally split me in two. I suddenly knew I was mourning the loss of my independence as well as the loss of my mother.

"No, Ollie," I said. "I'll stay right here."

• • •

We heard nothing from Papa for the remainder of the evening, and the tray of food I left outside his door lay untouched. When darkness fell, early on that winter evening, I shuffled Oliver upstairs. Dressed in his nightclothes, I settled him into his small bed and stroked his drowsy head.

"Mama always sings to me, Tish. Can you sing to me?"

"Of course, Ollie."

Mama sang Brahms' "Lullaby" every night when Ivy and I were small. She had sung it every night to Ollie still. Sometimes she used the German words, the way Papa learned it, but most often we heard it in English. Our eyelids would get heavy and our bodies would relax, knowing that we were safe and warm and loved. Though I had long grown out of this bedtime ritual, I ached to hear her voice sing the song again, for me and for Ollie, whose childhood now lacked her reassuring presence.

My rendition would have to do, and so I began, "Lullaby and goodnight, with roses bedight, with lilies o'er spread, is baby's wee bed. Lay thee down now and rest. May thy slumber be blessed."

When I had finished, Oliver asked again, "You aren't going to leave, right, Tish?"

"No, Ollie. I'm staying."

"Can you stay with me now? Just for a little while?" His eyes were closed and the words came out slowly.

"Yes, Ollie. I'll be right here."

I lay down next to him, squeezing so that I fit in his small bed. His breathing became heavy and regular and I closed my eyes.

I must have drifted off. An insistent knocking at the front door startled me awake. Moving slowly out of Oliver's bed so that I didn't wake him, I made my way downstairs in the dark. I passed Papa's closed door and grasped the railing down the stairs.

No one had turned on the lights against the darkness, so I fumbled for the switch when I reached the foyer. Disoriented and unsure of the time, I glanced at the clock, but it still stood hushed, the pendulum straight and motionless.

The knocking continued. I found the outside switch, flooding the front porch with light, and saw Ellis standing at the door. I smoothed my hair and opened the door to greet him. He rushed in, taking me in his arms and holding me tight.

We stood there for a long moment, the warmth of his embrace mingling with the cold air falling off his coat. I breathed him in, his frost-filled scent cooling my nose like menthol and pulling me up out of my sleepy sorrow. He held me until I let go, and even then, his arms stayed around me for a beat longer. He took my shoulders in his hands and looked straight at my face.

"I came as soon as I could. I tried to get an earlier train, but with the holiday rush, I wasn't able to change my ticket. I came straight here from the station."

"It's all right, Ellis. I am glad you are here now. Come in. I'll put the kettle on for tea and get you warmed up."

While he settled in the sitting room, I brought in the tea and sat next to him on the settee. "The services were nice and well attended," I said. "I think Mama would have been pleased."

"Tish, I feel terrible that I wasn't there. I wanted to be with you so very badly, help you through this. How is everyone holding up?"

"Ivy is back in Chestnut Hill, and Papa has been in his room all day. Ollie is quiet and sad, afraid of being alone."

"And, how are you?"

"Miserable. It was so sudden, none of us had the chance to say goodbye." I fiddled with my tea cup, rattling it slightly against the saucer as it sat on the table. "The morning of the train crash, we were all rushing out the door. She was our everything. She held this family together and did everything for us. Without her..." I couldn't go on without breaking.

We sat in silence for a while, my eyes downcast, my thoughts swirling. "How did it go in New York?"

"Tish, we don't have to talk about that now..."

I was grateful to be allowed to let go of social graces, exhausted from keeping them up for the past few days. Inside I was screaming while on the outside, I had plastered on a bearing-up smile.

Like a marionette whose strings had just been cut, my shoulders slumped, head drooped, and my back molded into the front of Ellis. The dam broke and the tears came. He held me for a long time, as the sobs hiccupped out of me, hitching my breath. Finally allowed to feel the loss myself, I let it overtake me. There was nothing but his arms and my sadness. There was relief in finally being able to cry safely in Ellis' shelter.

Ellis began to speak, soothing things, calming words. I couldn't focus on them; the entire room had a fuzzy, muted quality. Ellis continued to talk and I murmured assent, dragging in deep breaths that caught in my throat on the way in. The tears did end, and eventually my chest stopped heaving, leaving me more exhausted than before.

"Shhh, my darling," Ellis continued, stroking my hair. "Soon we will be in California. Away from this pain. Shhh. In the midst of all this sorrow, I have some wonderful news. My meetings with the Standard Oil Company went very well. Apparently, they are booming out in California and need lots of men. They have offered me a position that starts in just a few weeks."

California soon. The thought was indeed soothing. It certainly would be nice to get away from all of this ice and sadness, see some sunshine, leave behind this town with its dirty snow and trains that crash. I could pack up and be ready to go within a week. I envisioned my face as it was kissed by the warm breeze of the coast. With my easel set up in front of me, brush dabbed with color, I felt the light from the sun and there was a smile on my face. I was with Ellis, following our dream.

And then thoughts of Oliver and Papa rushed in. How could I leave them? I couldn't. Not now. Maybe not ever. Ollie had asked and I had as much as promised to stay. I thought of their sad faces as they stood at the gravesite earlier today. I thought of the future dark, quiet nights together, just the two of them in this house. How could I leave them? How would they get by? Ivy had made it clear that she wasn't going to help. Oliver couldn't fall sleep alone, and Papa had never done laundry, or cooked, or cleaned. I thought of Papa's closed door and Oliver's tight fingers gripping my arm.

This heavy realization, immovable as a boulder, meant only one thing for me and Ellis. I pulled back from him, physically on the couch and inside as well. My sense of obligation to Ollie and Papa grew roots and attached me to the spot I had spent so much time aching to leave. California now felt selfish. Mama's death had changed everything. Slowly, like sap dripping from the maple, I began to understand that I needed to fill the space Mama had left.

"A few weeks? Did you say a few weeks?" I asked Ellis, now out of his arms and facing him. "I thought we wouldn't be leaving for six months."

"They want me to start right away. I told them yes, that I would. We'll have to be married a little sooner, but then we can leave shortly after that. This is still what you want, isn't it? California?"

"It is what I want." I paused, thinking. "It was, anyway. I just didn't realize the job began so soon. I'm… I'm… not sure I can go right now. Papa is going to need me for a while, and Ollie… Ollie might need me for longer than that."

"Tish, what are you saying?"

The words that needed to be said, once said, couldn't be taken back. So instead I hesitated before taking the big jump, asking "Maybe we could delay a bit? Until Papa and Ollie are settled?"

"I don't want to delay a bit, Tish!" Ellis shouted. He ran his fingers hard through his hair and then said more softly, "I don't know if that is possible. There may not be a job waiting for me if I don't go when they need me."

And so there it was, the need to say the words, to jump and break apart upon landing. I said, "Yes, of course. You are right. You must go. It is a wonderful opportunity. You must go."

"'*You must go?*'" he started slowly. "Tish, why are you saying, '*you?*' Shouldn't you be saying 'we?'"

"I… I can't…"

"I gave my word that I would be on the job in January." His voice was hard, final.

"And so, you must."

"Tish? We're to be married and… and I love you."

"I love you too, Ellis, but I can't leave. I won't abandon Ollie and Papa. I can't."

"Maybe you could come out to California in the summer? That would give you more time to settle things here."

"I don't know that they will ever be settled. Would you consider staying here? Living here? In Willow Grove?" I asked, though I knew the answer already.

"Aw, for goodness sake, Tish!" Ellis was on his feet now, his arms waving in the air. "Ever since we first met, all you could talk about was getting out of this town, going West, experiencing new things! I got a job. You've agreed to marry me. We are going to California!"

"Ellis, please. Keep your voice down. Please try to understand. The situation is different now. Oliver and Papa are helpless without Mama. How can I leave them?"

"They can hire someone to help out with the laundry and other household chores. Why does it fall to you?"

"It does. It just does. A maid isn't going to love them and take care of them. You should have seen them today—Papa is practically comatose, and Oliver is so needy, he wouldn't sleep without me in his bed! How can I leave them like that?"

"But it's not what we want! It's not what you want!"

"No! Of course I don't want this! I want Mama back and I want to marry you and see California!" My voice was louder and more shrill than it should have been.

Ellis sighed hard and sat next to me again, squeezing my hand in his. "Then let's. Your father is a grown man; he can fend for himself. It is his responsibility to look after Oliver. We have our own life to live now. Ivy and William understand that; why can't you? Please, Tish. I need you too. Let's get married and move to California like we planned."

I wanted to give in. With a simple nod, I could set things in motion westward and leave all of this pain behind. But I knew I would be taking guilt with me. Shirked responsibility is a heavy burden to carry. I looked at the room that surrounded me. The windows, in the evening's gloom, reflected the interior rather than allowing me to see the outside world. Ellis waited, his eyebrows raised in hope that I would finally see his point of view. I looked into his chocolate eyes and saw kindness. I held onto this moment of us sitting hand in hand, his eyes on mine, for as long as I could, waiting for the resolution to find me. When it did, I slowly shook my head.

"I'm so sorry, Ellis. I'm needed here, and if you can't stay I can't marry you..."

He stood, anger shining on his face. "You know I can't stay. Won't stay. After everything... this." He shook his head, turned, and walked out.

CHAPTER THIRTEEN
Molly

We had baby class scheduled later that morning, and after my father's unexpected departure, I found myself looking forward to it. Though Hayden was constantly at my side, I was wrapped in loneliness. I could taste the abandonment. I figured being with other people, any other people, might help.

Christy and Delaney arrived at class and I descended upon them, so happy to see them. We sat together in the circle. After the daily question and some discussion about swing safety, we were given play time on our own.

"How was your week?" I asked Christy.

"Fine, boring. My old boss called, wanting to know when I was coming back to the office. I asked for more time, but honestly, I'm never going back! I'm not sure I love being a stay-at-home mom, but I like it a whole lot better than working at that place! How was your week?"

"Not great. Corey is out of town and I asked my dad to come help out. He just bailed on me this morning, some step-family emergency. I'm on my own for the next three days."

"How awful. We should do something fun to cheer you up. Maybe we could go out to dinner when your husband gets home."

"Maybe. But then we would have to get sitters. What if I cooked and had you at our house?" As soon as I said it, I realized how desperately I wanted her to say yes. I wanted a reason to cook, wanted people to cook for.

"I thought you said your house was still full of boxes and stuff?"

"Well, it will motivate me to get the house together."

Christy agreed to come. It meant I had a lot to do, but wouldn't Corey be surprised when he came home and saw the house organized and uncluttered? The more I thought about it, the more excited I became. I was thrilled about the opportunity of getting lost in the cooking, completely in the zone, handling many dishes at once. I craved the thrill of successfully having all the food ready at once. Maybe I would invite Liz and her husband too. And perhaps even Jocelyn and Hank. The kids could all run around and I could make dinner. I'd have to call a handyman to fix the front door pane, and maybe a few other things, but I was beginning to love this idea.

Hayden fell asleep in the car on the way home from class, and I gave silent thanks for this small miracle. I carried him into the house still strapped in the infant car seat and set him down gently in the foyer. I picked up my cell phone, walked to the kitchen, hopefully out of earshot of Hayden lest I wake him. I left a message inviting Jocelyn and Hank, and then dialed Liz.

"Hey there. It's Molly," I said. "I'm thinking about having a dinner party when Corey gets home from his business trip and I'd love it if you and Joe and the kids could come."

"Oh, wow, great. We'd love to! Do you need any help getting ready?"

"No, but I do need the name of a good handyman."

I wrote down the information. While Hayden slept, I bounced around the house with sprite-like energy. I unpacked boxes and repacked Aunt Tish's knickknacks. Fussy patterned dishes and mugs went from the cabinets to the counter to the box, and our plain white plates and glasses went in the opposite direction. I had to take breaks to feed and change Hayden, but then I got right back to it.

The handyman arrived and I greeted him at the broken door.

"Think you can fix it?" I asked.

"Sure," he said, taking out his tools and a few pieces of glass he had brought along.

He worked and I worked. When he was ready to go, he found me in the kitchen.

"Any chance you could switch out these tiles tomorrow?" I asked pointing at the broken floor.

He bent down and examined it.

"Maybe. I'd have to see if I could find some that matched. If not, I can fill it. Either way, might get pretty messy." He looked at Hayden. "And loud."

Energy and motivation flowed through me for the first time in months. "No problem. Let's just get it done!"

• • •

As usual, I slept very little that night, but I rose to face the next day determined. The handy man arrived early, blocked off the kitchen, and started making quite a racket behind the plastic sheeting. In the library, I laid Hayden out on a blanket and continued to unshelve books and reshelf ours. Doing so, I found the Hess's Delicatessen book again. I picked up where I had left off. Flipping past three recipes for Boiled Dressing, I found a newspaper clipping. The yellowing page was frayed at the edges, but the dark-inked words remained bold. *More than Fifty Killed and Injured in Terrible Disaster on Newtown Railroad*, it read. *Passengers and Trainmen Mangled, Crushed, Scalded and Burned Alive.* The article included a photograph of the train, the skeletal ribs of a burned-out car left standing on the track, smoke rising ahead of it. A side panel article listed the known fatalities and a familiar name caught my eye. Hess. Our family name. Laurel Hess. Why was that familiar?

I stood and walked to the still life of onions and carrots that hung on the wall in the dining room. There it was, a signature. *Laurel Hess* in tight, neat script. Corey had said his grandmother had painted it. That must have been Aunt Tish's mother. A mother she had lost, just as I lost mine.

I returned the clipping to the folds of the back pages and flipped forward to the first menu. In fine print on the front page, so small that I had overlooked it before, read Proprietors: Julian and Laurel Hess. Flipping to later menus, I searched for her name. Instead, the menus read Proprietors: Julian Hess and Letitia Hess. "Tish" must have been short for Letitia. Later in the book, and presumably in time, the menus dropped Julian's name altogether. The delicatessen had become hers. Aunt Tish had taken her mother's place in the house and in the family business.

What did that mean for her and starting a family? Before the train crash, Laurel Hess ran the restaurant and had a family. Could Aunt Tish have done both? Could I now? An idea began to take shape. A way to do what I loved and honor the aunt that Corey loved. I could revitalize Hess's Delicatessen, putting a modern twist on some of the recipes within this book. But could it be more than an idea? How would Corey feel about daycare for Hayden? Maybe I could make some of the recipes for our dinner party, and after he tasted and liked them, broach the subject with Corey.

I didn't mention my ideas any of the times Corey called from Houston. He was terse with me and mostly just asked after the baby. I didn't tell him about the dinner party, the recipe book, or all the repair and organizational work I had been getting done. I wanted to surprise him with my capability in his absence. And I really had made good progress. Though the grass still stood tall in the yard and the siding could really use a good power wash, I was beginning to see the beauty in the place. Inside, I hauled the boxes of Aunt Tish's things to the basement. Soon, the floors were visible and I ran the vacuum over and over. The white noise even seemed to calm Hayden.

The handyman finished and the kitchen floor looked like new. It was like the cracks and chips in the tile had never been there.

I put our tablecloth over the long dining room table and filled a vase with apples for the centerpiece. I took down some of the paintings, replacing them with photographs that had hung in our DC apartment, but left the still life with onions and carrots, as a nod to the ladies of the house before me, and to soften the makeover for Corey.

The house looked more and more like mine with each change. I couldn't wait for our dinner party guests and Corey to see it.

• • •

On the day of his return, I heard Corey walk in the front door. I called to him, "Welcome home! What do you think? How does it look? I finally finished unpacking! We, my love, are throwing a dinner party! Tomorrow night. I am so excited. Christy and Mark are coming, and I have invited Liz and Joe, and Jocelyn and Hank..." I walked into the foyer and handed Hayden to Corey. "Say hello to Daddy. We missed you!"

Corey took the baby and looked around.

"Molly...stop. Just stop talking. What have you done?" he said slowly, loosening his tie with his free hand.

"Do you like it? I have unpacked all of our things. And don't worry, all of Aunt Tish's stuff is still here, as requested, just safely packed up in the basement."

He put Hayden in the Pack 'n Play and walked through the rooms like he had never seen them before.

"You took down the paintings? My Aunt Tish's paintings? And put them in the moldy basement?"

"I left the onions and carrots painting," I said, hating the panic in my voice. This wasn't going well at all.

He ignored me and walked to the kitchen. "And did you have the floor fixed? Where is my racetrack?"

"Your what?"

"*My racetrack*, Molly. Remember I told you that I raced cars in here and that huge crack was the starting line? Remember I told you I wanted to do that with Hayden when he got old enough?"

I was startled by his anger. "You could still race cars in here..."

"It's not the same," he said through gritted teeth. "You've ruined it."

"I thought I was making the house better. Fixing it up. Making it ours."

"It is ours."

"No, it's not. It's hers." My face began to burn. "This house was your Aunt Tish's through and through and I was just trying to make it feel like I lived here too. We have friends coming over and I wanted it to look nice."

"You wiped out all of my childhood memories for the sake of a stupid dinner party? That's great. Thanks a lot. Put it all back, just the way it was. You'll have to cancel your party anyway. I have to work tomorrow night; things didn't go well in Houston."

He said *party* like it was a dirty word, something shameful he had every right to cancel. The condescension hit my face like backdraft of flames, slowly at first and then all at once I was burning with it, a rushing sound filling my ears.

"You can't take off a few hours after being gone for days to do this one thing for me?" I cried.

"No, Molly, I can't. You should have asked me before planning this."

"Seriously, Corey? Maybe I should have asked you. But maybe I should have just assumed that I could *never* do anything that I wanted, *ever*, because you would be working all the time."

"Come on, don't do this. You know how much I have to work."

"Actually, no. I didn't know how much you were going to work when we moved up here. I didn't know that I would be stuck alone all day with a baby that hates me and screams no matter what I do. I didn't know that I would be forced to live in the house that time forgot, and play happy little homemaker by giving up everything that is important to me." I had risen to my feet now, looking Corey straight on.

"You agreed to quit your job and move here! Don't give me this nonsense. I didn't force you into this. We decided together, remember?"

"Right, we decided together. What else have we been doing together lately? Nothing. You barely help with the baby," I began ticking my grievances off on my fingers. "You are at work even on the weekends, and when you aren't, you are playing golf with your boss. We have been out once together once, *once*, since the baby was born. Do you know what I do around here all day? Nothing! I stare at those stupid paintings and the stupid crack in the kitchen floor. I am bored and freaked out because I am a terrible mother. You told me this place would be great and beautiful and ours, and it was a lie. It's a crumbling shrine to your aunt. I want to throw one dinner party, do *one* thing that is for me, and you crap all over it. I can't even put my own pictures up on the walls. I've disappeared here. It's like I exist only to care for Hayden."

"If you aren't happy then why don't you just..." he started.

I cut him off. "Just what? Leave? Is that what you are saying?"

"No! I was going to say *just get some help*. Where is all of this coming from? Do you want to leave?"

"No, but I do want more help from you! I want you to be present and involved and I want to feel like you think I am important again."

"You are important, Molly. You're the mother of my child."

"No! I want to be me again. Just me, important for being me. Where did *I* go? My life and the things that I want shouldn't just be erased because we have a child and you have a terrible work schedule."

"What is it that you want to do so very badly? I have provided everything for you! That's why I am working so hard!"

"I want to make this house *our* home."

He slammed his fists to his sides. "Can't you understand that I love this house just the way it is?"

I changed tacks, frustrated by this merry-go-round argument. "But I am here alone. We used to do everything together. I feel really alone in this. I feel really alone here."

"You're not alone. You have me, and Hayden. Do you know how many people have trouble having kids? There are three women in my office who can't even listen to me talk about Hayden because they are having trouble conceiving. We are so lucky and you don't even appreciate it. Sure, being a parent is hard, Hayden is tough, but where's your gratitude, Molly?" Corey's anger was ratcheting up now too, and it caught me by surprise. "If you don't start appreciating this time, you're going to miss out on everything. Hayden is growing and changing every day. He'll never again be as tiny as he is today. And that is true every day. You'll never get this time back. I don't get to have that time because I'm at the office all day, but you do get to have it, and you just want to throw it away. Just like my mom. Think about your mom and what you wouldn't give to get that time back with her..."

"Don't! Don't even bring her into this..." I warned.

"Fine, I'll talk about mine. She didn't want me around either," he said, his voice cracking. "Aunt Tish was the only one who did. So this place stays the way it was, the way she had it. Forget your stupid dinner party."

I couldn't answer. My mouth gummed up with the tears that had started, like it was full of marbles. My energy for the fight ebbed and morphed in a bottomless despair and tears rolled down my face. Corey didn't understand. He wasn't listening. Nothing would change. He would work and I would take care of his child without his help. I would fade and disappear into the existing past.

"I'm going out. I need to cool off," he said from the doorway, not looking back, and closed the door behind him.

He didn't even notice the new pane of glass. From the Pack 'n Play, I heard Hayden begin to cry.

CHAPTER FOURTEEN
Tish, 1920

To lose Mama and Ellis in one week was too much. Heartbroken seemed too simple a description. My chest ached and I struggled for breath. Tears fell freely in waves of sorrow and only stopped when I was too exhausted to continue. Every part of me was screaming to go to Ellis and be with him. But then Oliver's frightened and bewildered face, desperate about what he might lose next, appeared before me needing something: a mend in his pant leg, a haircut, a meal, and I would think of Papa's inability to carry on, function, even speak. Without me, they would have no one. My resolve flapped back and forth like a flag in the wind.

It was different before Mama's passing. Longing to get away seemed natural; my independence was just part of growing up. I felt safe being far away, as we would be tethered by letters and an occasional long-distance telephone call. I would know that life carried on in Willow Grove as it always had and things would be unchanged when I came home for a visit. Without her here to maintain the family, a move to California wasn't growing up, it was running away.

Everything about staying made me furious and frustrated, though. I was angry at the fiery train. I was angry at the rescue workers for not finding Mama sooner. I was angry at the doctors for not being able to save her. I was angry at Papa for his emotional absence. I was angry at Ivy for her lack of obligation. I was angry at Ellis for not understanding. I was so angry.

There were moments, in the following weeks, when I would forget that Mama was gone. I would be busy doing something and then turn to ask her a question. Each time, sorrow rushed in and everything darkened like storm clouds across the sky. To remind myself, I read every newspaper article about the train crash. In them lay revised lists of the dead, accounts of the trial, conviction, and sentencing of the engineers, and details of a proposed new law banning wooden train cars. I cut out the initial article, published the day after the crash and showing the ghastly burnt out train, and tucked it secretly inside of Papa's recipe book, wanting Mama to be a part of it forever.

For all of us, our mourning blanket seemed to thicken. Outside, it remained frigid and bleak, with the sun hiding behind smoky clouds. Trees with bare skeletal limbs waved in the wind's bluster and the snow that lay on the ground collected dirt and soot. The air hit my face like walking into a pine tree, needle prickles of freezing pain on any exposed skin. Inside, the silence burrowed deep into us, and although I kept our house clean, it was by rote more than anything else. No one had the strength for enthusiasm. Our loss took up space in every corner, every cupboard, every windowsill. We plodded through the rooms of this house, meant for us all, but truly a gift for her, and felt alone.

Christmas passed us by, feeling like just another mournful day. Ivy spent it with William's family, and in a way, it was a relief. We wouldn't need to put on cheerful holiday faces that lacked authenticity. Though I put a few decorations up, neither Papa, Oliver, nor I felt like celebrating. We went to bed early on Christmas Eve craving sleep's kind obliteration, with little anticipation of morning.

Oliver went back to school after the New Year. Notes were sent home pinned to his jacket from Mrs. Ely saying that he wasn't keeping up with the class, and that instead of working he was mostly staring out the window. One day, the note reported that he had shoved another boy and nearly knocked the boy into the stove. I discarded these papers after reading them and didn't discuss their contents with Papa or Oliver.

Eventually, we had to open the delicatessen again. Papa went there each day, perhaps a little later than usual. We worked in near silence next to each other and he was sullen with the customers. When he returned home, he went directly up to bed.

Ivy's phone calls went from daily to weekly. She never offered to help and never stayed on the line long, always citing some club meeting or luncheon she needed to attend.

I tried to keep up with the housework and found that the hard work kept my mind from wandering to Ellis. When I went into town to purchase the food for our meals, I kept my eyes on the ground and was thankful for the slippery icy roads that forced everyone else do the same. I wrapped my face deep in a scarf and kept my hat low on my head, hiding and unwilling to make small talk.

Back at the house, after working all day at the shop, I cleaned until my muscles felt tight and heavy like bricks and I yearned for bed. I couldn't bear the thoughts that roamed my head in the quiet moments, and found I slept better if I had the strength for nothing else. So each day I rose with the dawn, dusted every corner, expelled all the cobwebs, swept the floor and the stairs before leaving for the delicatessen. I left the clock silent. It hung on the wall, frozen at twenty-five past eight.

On days when the shop was closed, I fired up the oven and cooked meals too big for all of our diminished appetites, and our quiet trio sat at the table pushing the food around on our plates. When enough time had passed for dinner to reasonably be concluded despite the leftovers, I cleared the dishes and washed up.

My hands were white in the creases, tight and dry. The skin eventually cracked and split open, bleeding, and it felt like I could shed my skin like a snake if I splayed my fingers far enough. Maybe a new skin was what I needed. This one didn't seem strong enough to weather this winter and all the pain it contained.

Despite the stilled clock, our lives marched on. Reason told me that day by day, we would feel better, mourn less, smile more, but we didn't. Perhaps this was my fault, perhaps I was the one responsible for bringing joy back into the house.

After all, isn't that why I stayed? Isn't that why I gave up on a life of my own, to take care of them?

Ivy set our schedule with a Sunday phone call, briefly asking after Papa and Oliver, but mostly berating me about Ellis. "What have you done, Tish? Ellis loved you and wanted to make a life with you. He has a good job and I have spent a lifetime hearing nothing from you other than traveling! Men don't wait. If you're not careful, he'll marry someone else."

William was still in touch with him, and Ivy was eager to pass along updates she had heard. The news was painful each time, but I remained hungry for any information my sister had of him. "He's still in New York, you know. Staying at the Roosevelt Hotel. Why not send him a letter?" Ivy prodded.

I refused, explaining to Ivy the best I could about my obligations to Papa, and especially Oliver, hearing my own words and hoping my assured tone would finally convince me that I had made the right decision.

In our conversation one week, Ivy reported that her forewarning had finally come true. I had waited too long to change my mind. Ellis had, indeed, married a girl from New York, and they planned to live in California. I took the news like a punch in the gut, but it changed nothing.

Ivy didn't understand how my regret mingled with my obligation and love. She didn't understand how I loved them all but how these loves couldn't coexist. Fully entrenched in her own life, we hadn't seen her since the funeral, and so she never fully perceived how desperate things had become.

Papa's silence had become part of the house, palatable and ever-present. When he surfaced, I greeted him brightly, hoping to encourage any scant word spoken. He would stare for a moment or two, and then shuffle on.

The void of Papa's conversation was filled by Oliver's questions and constant need for reassurance. He had become quite nervous and questioned my every move. Would I be home when he got back from school? If not, would I be at the delicatessen? Could he meet me there?

Today had been the same. I had promised him that I would, indeed, be at home when the school day ended, and so I left Papa to fill orders himself and hustled about town to complete my errands in time. Outside, the sun welcomed me and I was buoyed by a faint breeze. The street was abuzz; a small town's intuition, something was certainly in the air. Folks whispered as I passed by, quickly turning away from me and frowning. And then, suddenly, some part of me knew it. Felt it. Felt him.

As I walked past Rothwell's, there was Ellis. He was seated in the window with two other men and a woman who was entertaining them all with a story, her hands out in enthusiastic description. One of the men with them was held in rapt attention, the other threw his head back with guffaws of laughter. They were all drinking fountain sodas. With sudden severe nausea, I knew who she must be. But who were these men? New co-workers, all on their way to California? Ellis looked out toward the street just as I was passing.

Through the glass, his eyes held mine, immediately turning sad. I slowed slightly, only my momentum carrying me past, my breath caught tight in my chest. For a split second, I expected his face to light up and for him to rise from his seat to come and greet me with a kiss. But of course, he wouldn't now. He looked straight at me and then at the woman, his new wife, before turning his attention down to his drink. I quickened my pace then, hoping to stomp down the jealousy that rose like bile in my throat.

How quickly he had moved on. It was only four weeks ago that he left for New York. Ellis' job started shortly, why was he here?

In the brief seconds it took for me to pass the window, I had taken in all the details of the woman. Lovely with soft hair the color of wheat and bright eyes; she must have been something special since they were married so quickly.

I had begun to heal in the time since he walked out my front door, but now the wound was twisted and opened again. The scab was not thick enough yet; I still longed to go with him to California, be with him as his wife.

No, I told myself, shaking off the idea. Today I needed to purchase new spring clothing for Oliver. Pants without twice-mended rips in the knees. I hurried on, each step heavier for the responsibility.

I had only gone a block when Ellis caught up with me, breathless and calling my name. I turned, needing to see him, talk to him, but afraid.

"Hello, Ellis," I said.

"Tish," he said, stating it resolutely. The sound of it gripped my chest and clenched it, forcing an involuntary and painful release of breath.

"I didn't know you were in town," I recovered.

He fiddled with the brim of his hat, which he held in his hands, soft and brown, looking down at it. "Yes, I had to settle something at the boarding house before I went West; I got out of town so quickly... well, you know. And Kathryn," he paused to look up at me sheepishly when he said her name, "well, Kathryn wanted to see Willow Grove before we left."

I nodded and bit my lip, forcefully tamping down the tears with my teeth, unable to speak. Kathryn. I felt gutted.

We stood there on the street corner as the moment stretched out silent between us. When I couldn't stand being this close yet so far away from his body one moment longer, I began to turn away. He reached for me and blurted out, "I don't love her."

The air suddenly froze and seemed to suck violently away from me.

He dropped my arm. After a few seconds, I said, "I'm certain she would be sorry to hear that. She is your wife, after all." I was unable to do anything but state facts.

"Yes. She is," he sighed. "I shouldn't have said that about her. I simply meant, well, it's not the same. I don't love her the same way... I... I don't love her like I loved you."

"Well, she looks lovely," I said, remembering the sweet face and fine clothing I glimpsed through the shop window.

Ellis reacted harshly, perhaps thinking that I had no right to this jealousy. "You turned me away. What choice did I have?"

"You? What choice did you have? What choice did I have?" I was instantly infuriated. "I want to go to California—but I can't. You know that. Oliver and Papa need me. I have to stay here. I must stay." Suddenly exhausted and sad, I continued, "We have been through this. I loved you so much, Ellis. I still do, but this life, this town, it won't make you happy..." I trailed off. There was nothing more to say.

"Will it make you happy?" Ellis asked, searching out my eyes and holding contact.

I thought about it. Minutes went by, or maybe just seconds. "I don't know. It will have to."

His mouth straightened and he swallowed hard. Unable to speak, he reached out again and his fingertips grazed my arm. He nodded, simply, finally. With a brave smile, he turned and walked the block back to his wife.

I heard that they left on the train later that afternoon, embarking on the week-long journey to California and the Standard Oil job that was waiting.

• • •

The next morning dawned bright, with much-missed sunbeams streaming onto my bed. In those split moments before I was truly awake, I basked in the warmth like a lizard. But then recollection seeped in, dark and deep, and the pain returned. My dreams had left with Mama and Ellis. My limbs were heavy, as if not my own. I got up anyway, dressed, and went downstairs.

The bright light made me see how filthy the windows were. Since the shop was closed, after breakfast I worked my way around the house wiping down the ones in the shade, trying to beat the sun. This task took most of the day, but it kept my hands and mind distracted and soon it was dinner hour. Tonight, the three of us who remained would share a meal, have a conversation, and find a way to move on, bit by bit, bite by bite if necessary.

I set the table with our fine china, ironed the napkins, and boiled a chicken. When it was cooked, I hoisted it out of the pot and shredded the meat. I added carrots, onions, and peas to the boiling water, and then returned the meat to the pot, discarding the bones. Pulling a bowl from the cabinet, I mixed together flour and eggs, salting the thick, sticky ball generously and adding drips of water until it had a gooey consistency.

I found my mother's spaetzle maker. It was a tool from my father's side of the family, a medieval-looking metal contraption with two handles, one attached to a press and the other to a cup with holes in the bottom. The handles were unnecessarily long, presumably for leverage, but the tool was unwieldy and clanked against itself as I attempted to maneuver the wet flour mixture into the cup. I held it over the pot, my arms shaking with the effort of squeezing, the handles digging into my stomach. With significant strain, a small bit of the glutinous mass extruded through the holes, but not enough to drop into the pot below. I had watched Mama do this countless times, though she didn't seem to struggle as much as I struggled now. Resting the end of the apparatus on the far edge of the pot, I took firm hold of both handles, and pressed down on the top handle with all my might.

The raw noodles slowly forced their way through the holes in the cup, tiny air bubbles popping as they went. Suddenly, the spaetzle maker shifted under the pressure of my pushing. It caught the pot, sliding it forward where it hung for a long second at the edge of the stove before toppling onto the floor. I jumped back as the dinner I had prepared splashed in thick, molten lumps onto the floor.

I stared at it and heard a low moan. For a horrible moment, it sounded like an animal. Then I realized it was me. I let the spaetzle maker clatter out of my hands to the floor.

Suddenly I was enraged. Dinner was ruined, Mama was gone, Ellis was gone, and I had thrown it all away for nothing. I was incapable of helping anyone. My hands balled into fists and I slammed them down to my sides. I was unable to help Papa and Oliver and foolish to think that I was their answer. How overly confident and ridiculous I was. I wasn't up to the task of filling Mama's shoes. Scrubbing the house until my fingers were cracked and bleeding, working at the shop, and trying to take care of the household wasn't filling them with love and carrying them through this.

With fury, I swept the bowl with the remaining dough right off the counter. A low thud resounded as the thick glass bottom of the bowl cut a deep gouge into the tile floor upon impact. The contents thickly splashed out, and the bowl shattered. I sank down, sitting right in the hot spill, and sobbed.

I ran my fingers over the divot carved in the tile. It radiated into a long crack. The divot was deep, about the size of my thumb, and crescent-shaped. Compulsively, I continued running my finger back and forth over the permanent void in the once-perfect floor. Some things couldn't be undone. The floor was forever damaged and disfigured.

The edges of the crevasse were sharp, and a thin stripe of blood appeared on my finger. I reflexively put it in my mouth. A metallic tang mingled with splashes of wasted dinner and I could taste how much I missed Mama.

After a while, the heat of the dinner soaking through my skirts began to cool and I had exhausted my tears. My finger had stopped bleeding. I wiped my face, drew a deep breath.

Oliver appeared in the doorway. "Tish?" he asked, looking around at the mess I had made.

I shrugged my shoulders. "I dropped dinner."

"It's in your hair," he said, pointing.

"Is it?" I asked. Oliver stepped closer to inspect me. Suddenly, this was all very funny. I reached up to him and wiped my messy hands on his head. "It's in your hair too."

Disbelief and a smile crept over his face. I grinned back.

"What do you think? Shall we eat this? Dinner is served!"

"Tish! We can't eat food off the floor!"

"I don't know. We might have to; it's all we have for supper! Did you make something too, just in case I threw the dinner that I cooked on the floor?" I joked.

"No! I didn't make anything!"

"Ah, well." I stood. "Toast and jam for dinner tonight then."

He touched my arm. "We'll get by," he said. I smiled at him, saw wisdom in his little eyes, and knew he was right.

I wiped the dinner from the floor, and with it, my self-pity. I would try again. And keep trying. Where the strength would come from, I did not know, but I knew that I had to keep trying. I could not fix the imperfection in the kitchen floor, but I could clean up the mess around it.

I toweled Oliver clean and climbed the stairs to change my dress. On the way, I paused at the stopped clock in the foyer. I unlatched the glass cover, picked up the key, and wound it. With a flick of my wrist, I set the pendulum going. The hands lay at eight twenty-five.

I would set the exact time later, but for now all I needed was to hear the forceful tick tock resonate through the clock's belly. I continued upstairs and, after changing, returned to the kitchen. As I descended the stairs to make the toast and jam, the clock chimed one single gong. Eight-thirty. It vibrated through the house and shook the cobwebs out of me.

CHAPTER FIFTEEN

Molly

After Corey stormed out, I didn't wait for him to come back. I hastily packed Hayden's diaper bag and we went out too. There was no way I would sit in Aunt Tish's house for one more minute.

With Hayden in the car seat, I started driving. My sorrow flipped like a June bug trapped on its back; once righted it flew into anger. What did Corey mean I wasn't grateful? He practically insinuated that I didn't love Hayden. He must think I was a monster.

Well, he was the one who made me this way. He had tricked me in to moving to Willow Grove with the promise of a beautiful house. A house and a future we could make our own. He never had any intentions of letting it be anything but hers, locked in time, exactly how he remembered it.

I wasn't Saint Aunt Tish, Savior of All Difficult Babies. And because I wasn't, Corey had walked out the door. All Corey could ever do was walk out the door. Didn't he think I needed to cool off, too? If he cared about me at all, he would have offered to take the baby for the afternoon, offered me a nap, time to get a haircut, or just go to the store by myself. But he did what he always did. He left. And that was exactly the wrong thing to do.

As I fumed, the roads went by in a blur. Aimless in my anger, the car simply arrived, and I found myself parked outside of Hayden's baby class. I checked my face in the visor mirror. My eyelids were puffed from crying and the whites of my eyes were a furious red. I looked awful. *So what*, I thought, *I'm going in anyway*. I laughed ruefully at how life had changed. The best place I could think of to find solace was open play time in the padded baby room.

I put on my socks and we stayed as long as they let us. Hayden watched the bubbles and gazed at swirling scarves during tummy time. I think he was happy. I watched him, but could not share the feeling. I dreaded going back to the house. When open gym was over, I nursed him in the car, and then drove to the Willow Grove Park Mall.

In the cool space, I found a bench near the fountain. I pushed Hayden's stroller back and forth within arm's distance. I couldn't look at the old photographs of people enjoying Willow Grove Park, feeling like one of them was surely perfect Aunt Tish. I wanted to be as far from her specter as possible. Instead, I fished inside my bag for my cell phone and called Garrett at the Aubergine bar.

"Hey, it's Molly," I said when he picked up. I could hear the clinking of glasses in the background. Desperate to be there inside my old life, I could taste my jealousy.

"Molly!" Garrett said. "How are you? How's Willow Grove? How's that baby of yours?"

"He's fine, thanks. I'm calling to see if you might have any leads on any apartments or jobs down there. I'm thinking about moving back."

"You are? That's great! We miss ya, kid. What about that great house Corey had up there?"

"It's not so great. Corey and I, well, we're not so great either." The words caught in my throat.

"Man. Sorry to hear it. I'll put my ear to the ground and see what I can come up with."

"Thanks, Garrett," I said, hanging up.

I sat for a while longer, rolling Hayden back and forth, breathing the mall's recycled air. I loved Corey, but I didn't love this life. If I were to live it alone anyway, it would be better to live it where I felt at home.

When I used up the last diaper packed in my bag, I knew I wouldn't be able to hide at the mall any longer. I loaded Hayden into the car to return to the house that wasn't mine and would never be. I knew what I had to do. I would have to walk away to find myself again. Corey wouldn't let me into the world he was stuck in, and so I had to get out. A rock sat heavy in the pit of my stomach, but I couldn't cry anymore.

Corey was sitting on the porch when we got home. Dusk had fallen. I lugged Hayden, asleep in the car seat, up the porch steps. I couldn't look at Corey. I was afraid I would lose my resolve.

"Molly. Where have you been all this time?"

I stood silently.

"Molly, please. I was beginning to worry that you weren't coming back."

"I'm not sure that I am."

He sighed and ran his fingers through his hair. I left him sitting there and went inside to pack my things.

Corey came into the bedroom and sat down on the side of the bed watching me.

"I'm not your Aunt Tish," I said. "I can't live here under those expectations."

"I know. You're right."

My head snapped up. *What?* I was wary, though. He had wooed me in to coming to Willow Grove in the first place. I couldn't let him do it again so that I would stay.

"When I was a kid," he said, "my mom made it pretty clear that she wasn't interested in being a mother. This place was the only place where I felt valued. That's not happening much these days. I haven't been able to admit it to you, but I've been working so hard because I've been trying to save my job. The Houston trip proved that I'm not good enough at work, and it doesn't seem like you think I am good enough as a husband or dad either. I guess I am just trying to hang on to this house because it is the only thing that reminds me what it's like to feel *good enough*. I wanted everything to be perfect here, just like the way I remember it. It's far from perfect, though, isn't it?"

Could it be that Corey felt like he was drowning too? Was this clutch on nostalgia the only thing keeping him afloat? I put down the sweater that I had been folding and looked at him. His eyes were sad and my heart broke for the little boy in him that needed to find solace here.

Was what he was saying enough for me to stay? Was I really ready to throw our marriage away, try to live on my own?

I started to crumble, a shard of light breaking through my resolve. I sat heavily on our bed. I fingered the bedspread next to me. Our bedspread, his and mine, overdue for a wash. The ripe, comfortable, familiar smell that our bodies had left behind filtered into my nose. It was heady with nostalgia of us.

My cell phone began to vibrate in my pocket. I pulled it out. The face of it announced Garrett calling. He had possibly found an apartment or a job in DC for me, maybe both. I let it go to voice mail.

"No, our life isn't perfect, but I'd settle for it just being ours," I said.

"Please stay," Corey said. "I promise not to let my old memories get in the way of us making new ones. I'm ready to let go, if it means you'll stay."

CHAPTER SIXTEEN
Tish

The weeks and months rolled by, as they do, however reluctantly, for the people whom death and lost love leave behind. Soon, everything seemed to be as it once was, though altered forever. Each morning, I placed my brimmed hat atop my head and wrapped my shawl around my shoulders for the walk downtown to the delicatessen.

I took my time, watching the golden pine needles slice through the air as they fell to the ground. The steady clop of my booted heels cleared my head, and slowly my overwhelming sadness lightened. By the time I arrived at the store, Papa was there, already at work, serving the customers who stood deciding their day's order.

I had brought his recipe book with me today, retrieved from the shelf and tucked inside my satchel. He didn't need the book, and maybe he didn't even want it. I remembered how he had discarded it the day of the funeral, the self-blame within. He had never asked for it back.

I lifted the partition and walked behind the counter.

Papa moved in a slow amble, taking twice as much time to fill an order. Gone was his brisk and determined pace, and I watched him, a man too young to be so old. I thought of Mama, and how she would always remain healthy and strong in my mind and never have the chance to shuffle like this, her back bent with age and her hair gleaming white.

Papa's tie hung without a knot around his neck and as soon as the customers left, I approached him and mentioned it. He grunted and turned toward the mirrored back wall. His fingers began fumbling, face contorted in aggravation.

"This darn thing!" he said through gritted teeth. Though he had been tying and untying his tie for a lifetime, now everyday things befuddled him. Before Mama passed, I knew nothing about ties, but like the other household tasks that were left for me, I had to learn. I tied Papa's tie while Papa pointed his chin to the ceiling. I could see that he had missed a few patches shaving.

Finished, I stepped away.

"How's business so far this morning?" I asked.

"It has actually been quite good," he said.

I held out the recipe book. "Have you been looking for this?" I asked.

Papa looked at his book but did not move to take it. He sighed heavily. "You keep it," he said, his voice quaking. "It's yours now. I trust you to make changes and additions as you see fit."

"But, Papa, I…" I hesitated. He had never trusted me with it before. Keeping this book, making it my own, would finalize my place here.

The bell on the door tinkled. Papa nodded towards the book, his confidence in my ability and my loyalty also in his offering. I squared my shoulders but held the book gingerly, the weight of it familiar but final. He patted my shoulder and then turned to help the customer.

And so, we were partners.

I walked to the storage room, sat down on a crate, and thumbed through the book. The tattered and spattered pages held heartache as well as fond memories. Here was the Ham Pie we ate the first days in the house when the future was wide open and the new house sparkled. I remembered the proud look on Papa's face as he watched Mama see the house for the first time, and how I marveled at the expansive view from our bedroom window.

A few pages later listed the ingredients for the Welsh rarebit we ate at Ivy's wedding. Ivy was so beautiful that day, when her life with William began in earnest, without a whisper of childless heartbreak. I remembered Mama's touch that morning, her way of letting me know that she thought I was beautiful too.

Further on in the book was the recipe for Mama's Oyster Fritters. Blanketed with dough and grease, they were so different from the chilled raw oysters that Ellis and I had slurped down with giddy abandon and chased with the pepper of champagne bubbles.

The next page held the recipe for Stewed Chicken. We ate that when Ellis came back from war, the night he spent in my bedroom and showed me how much he needed me. I flipped the pages further, suddenly desperate to find the recipe for Orange Feather Cake, the one Mama had served to quell Ellis' fury at the table that night and bring us back to being a family.

Instead, my eye caught sight of the recipe for Chicken with Noodles, the dish that I smashed all over the floor in the weeks after the train crash. That night, and still, we desperately missed Mama, but somehow Oliver, wise beyond his years, knew we would be all right.

I knew it too.

I walked back in to the front of the shop and looked around. Maybe this wasn't the life I had always dreamed of, but I knew now that I could be full and happy here. Mama had always told me that I needed to find happiness in today. I had been waiting my whole life—waiting to be older, waiting for the war to be over, waiting for Ellis to get a job. Wouldn't it be a shame if I ended up with nothing to show but waiting?

I set the recipe book down and tied my apron tight. I joined my father at the counter and called the next customer.

● ● ●

And Willow Grove is where I stayed. Over the years, Papa remained adrift, having aged forty years in the days after the train crash. Oliver's worry-filled cling turned into a surly rebellion as he got older, and he caused trouble in town on more than one occasion. I tried to give him all the love that he was missing, but surely fell short. He was robbed of his childhood and his mother's love and nothing I did seemed to make up for that. I worried he wouldn't make it out of high school, but luckily he did and was accepted at a nearby college.

Papa paid his tuition and when he left, I hoped that he would find his confidence and maturity at the university. He found Marion, a sweet girl who seemed to perk up his sullen demeanor. After they both graduated, they bought a house about an hour away from us in Skippack. It didn't last with her, though, and Oliver eventually married Robin. She was much younger than he and quite beautiful. I worried for Oliver, but I forgave Robin everything when she had those two baby boys.

I had wanted a family of my own, but despite Virginia's insistence on my finding a man to marry, my heart seemed forever closed off to the idea. Unwilling to be hurt again, or perhaps, as I only admitted to myself during the darkest of hours, I still loved a troubled man who had married another and was making a life in California.

Over the years, my desire for him and the vast life I had wanted when I was young faded. I didn't consider staying in Willow Grove as settling for a mediocre life; it was just my life. One of my choosing.

Papa and Oliver had needed me. That was indisputable. I reminded myself of this whenever I felt like I had given up too much. Even if I hadn't done the best job, I had tried and could live with my efforts. Had I simply abandoned them, read about them from letters across the vast expanses of the United States, or heard nothing, could I have been truly happy? Either way, my heart was torn between the men in my life, and I had chosen the two who needed me more. There was solace in that.

And then Oliver's sweet sons were born and I poured everything I tried to give to Oliver into them. Though they had a mother, I could see the heartache in their faces when Robin walked out my door, leaving them with me often without an estimated return. Maybe I hugged them too tightly, or was too lenient with them, but they deserved it, and I wouldn't have denied them anything. Especially sad-eyed Corey, who needed his mother's love seemingly more than his older brother Hank. Hank was good-natured and agreeable always, and that was easy for Robin. But Corey seemed to try her every nerve and I was happy to give her a break from him and love him in her stead. His little voice filled the house with sunshine again.

Papa passed away on a bright summer day soon after Robin had Hank. Papa went quickly and quietly, seated in a chair outside in our backyard. I was feet away, chattering at him while tending the blackberries. His head lay softly at his shoulder and I knew he was finally with Mama again. And I was alone.

His services were small, just me, Ivy, William, Oliver, Robin, baby Hank, and a few folks from town. I mourned and missed Papa's presence, and the purpose that came with it.

Ivy, with wrinkles creasing her sad eyes, looked longingly at Robin's sweetly sleeping bundle. She refused to hold Hank when Robin offered. Perhaps it was too much for her empty womb. I stood next to Ivy in the pew and laid my hand over hers, now dotted with age, when we stood for the hymns. Without a family of her own, silver-haired Ivy would go home with William to a life full of social obligations. Though she entwined her fingers with mine there at the church, she had chosen to build a life in Chestnut Hill, and I knew she would bury her suffering once back in her beautiful, well-appointed home.

I hugged Oliver and Robin outside on the church steps and invited them over for cake. They declined, saying that it was naptime for the baby. I planted a big kiss on Hank's chubby cheek, insisting that they come for cake another time soon. Before leaving, Oliver squeezed my shoulder and planted a small kiss on my cheek. "What will you do now, Tish?" he asked.

"I don't know, Ollie. Anything I feel like, I suppose." I gave him a small smile and brought him in for a long hug. "Please do come by for that cake soon," I said softly.

"We will," he assured me as he looked me in the eye. "And Thanksgiving. You are hosting Thanksgiving. Christmas too, maybe. Robin might serve us tofu otherwise."

I agreed, happy to be a fellow conspirator.

I returned to the house on Berrell Road, full of sunshine and summer breezes, feeling a bit like the birds that swooped and sang outside the open windows. Without Papa, and with Oliver now a grown man, my duties were suddenly fulfilled. I was free to do anything I pleased. I could live anywhere I chose. I would never live in California, but now I didn't particularly want to. This house was home.

Lost in time and memory, I had trouble picturing Ellis' face. All I could conjure were his hands. I could see them, rough and hearty, and imagined them resting paternally on the shoulders of a son that wasn't mine. Though I still felt sadness at the missed opportunity of us, I wished him every happiness.

Everyone was kind at the delicatessen, having heard the news of Papa's passing, but once it was closing time, I went home to a quiet house full of extra things. It was time to move on and so I began the task of packing up the items left behind.

I had attempted to do this with Mama's things years ago, but Papa became so agitated that I stopped altogether. His eyes turned cold and he would shake his finger at me, like an old miser protecting his gold. Sometimes when I would knock on his door to announce breakfast, I would find him fingering an old coat of Mama's, his eyes focused on something in the distance.

For years, I left him with the physical remains of her personal items, and now there was twice as much—his and hers—to go through. I packed trunks full of clothing that was decades out of style, laying their belongs inside together, as they were now in the Hillside Cemetery. Hats that were stiff and not of today's fashion, and delicate shoes that were beautiful but worthless on my large feet went into the trunk, along with belts, sashes, and stockings. Even after all these years, I could smell Mama as I rummaged through her things, her scent diffusing into the house, sweet and deep, tinged with my childhood.

Once their bedroom was emptied, I worked my way around the house, finding long-forgotten gloves and handkerchiefs along the way. I moved to the main floor, passing one of her still lifes. Those would stay. The onions and carrots she painted with me by her side would grace the walls for as long as I lived here. As I stood in front of it, I laughed, feeling suddenly like Papa in my coveting.

I would continue to paint, of course. There seemed little time for it, but my love for the process lingered, even if my subjects were homegrown fruit and not mountains, and even if they only ever graced the walls of my home.

I walked in to the kitchen. Though all of the things in here were originally hers, they had grown to be mine too.

We had worked together in here from the day we moved in. I learned everything from her, and though I worked under her direction in the beginning, we soon were working together, and then I was finally capable of it myself. I opened all the drawers and the cabinets, flaying them like fish. Our pastry cutter. Our rolling pin. Our paring knife. Our wooden spoon. Each of these held her imprint, but also mine. I closed the cabinet doors and slid the drawers shut. The kitchen contents would remain intact, and I would use them every day. As I grew older, the house would be home again for my nephews, who spent much of their precious childhood here, filling this old house again with love.

Though I would eventually update the appliances and the facades of the cabinets, I never replaced or fixed the floor. I left the gouged tile there, feeling its broken truth with my wrinkled bare toes each morning as I made my coffee, secure in my decisions and grateful for my life.

CHAPTER SEVENTEEN
Molly

The morning of the dinner party, I worked inside to the sounds of Corey outside mowing the lawn. I riffled through Aunt Tish's book, rereading the recipes I had chosen. I would never know Aunt Tish like Corey did, but if food held memory—like the iced oatmeal cookies held the memory of my mother—maybe by cooking the food she cooked, I could get to know her in some way. For the dinner party, I decided to serve Oyster Fritters, Chicken and Noodles, and Orange Feather Cake.

Hayden slept while I furiously prepped, knowing my time was limited. Flour flew all over the kitchen, mingling with oyster liquor and orange zest. It was a mess, but I was thrilled to be back at it. I sang to myself while the mixer whirred for the cake, the chicken simmered, and the fritters fried, all in harmony.

I set the table after Hayden woke up, holding him in one arm. As I placed each utensil on the table, I held it up to him and said its name. "Fork, Hayden. This is a fork." His chubby digits flailed in the air before bringing them as a fist back into his mouth.

Corey finished his yard work about an hour before the guests were to arrive. After his shower, I passed Hayden off to him while I went to take mine. The fritters were staying warm in the oven, the chicken was ready to be served, and the cake was cooling on the counter.

"Just open the wine, babe?" I called to him as I rushed up the stairs.

Dressed and presentable, I returned to the dining room. Corey had turned on some music, lit a few candles on the table, and opened a bottle of my favorite white wine.

"You have him for a bit longer?" I asked. "There is some last-minute cooking I need to take care of," I said.

"Sure," Corey said. As I passed by, he grabbed me and stole a quick kiss. "Little man and I are going to have a beer. I'll answer the door when everyone gets here."

Back in the kitchen, I mixed up the tartar sauce, dipping my finger for a taste. When the balance of mayonnaise, relish, and lemon juice was just right, I took the bite-sized oyster fritters out of the oven and arranged them on a plate, giving them each a dollop of the sauce. I sprinkled freshly chopped chives over top and brought the plate to the family room. Corey was letting Hayden gum the upright beer bottle and I shot him a stern look.

"Stop giving our baby beer. I thought that was a joke. And don't eat too many of these before everyone arrives," I said in a stern but mocking tone, as Corey was poised to pop one into his mouth. "Hayden is off to bed promptly at seven, okay? Don't get him too riled up."

"The beer will help him sleep," Corey said, laughing. I just shook my head at him and hoped he truly was joking.

Back in the kitchen, I ladled the chicken and noodles into a large serving bowl. It would stay hot with a lid, and so I placed it on a trivet on the table. I also brought in a bright green salad and crusty dinner rolls.

The doorbell rang promptly at six—I expected nothing less of Hank and Jocelyn. Hank let out a low whistle as he came in the door. "Looks great, kids," he said. "I haven't seen this place look this good in years."

While Jocelyn took Hayden from Corey and began fussing over him, Hank walked around, poking his head into every room. "Kept the old paintings, though, huh? I like it." He made his way into the kitchen and I followed. "Where's the beer?"

I grabbed him one from the fridge and pulled a wine glass out for Jocelyn. We made our way back to the family room and I handed her the glass, now filled with chilled Sauvignon Blanc.

"The house really does look nice," she said.

"Thanks, Jocelyn," I said, reveling in the high praise from a tough critic.

Soon, Liz and Christy arrived with their husbands. It turned out that Liz's husband knew Christy's husband and so they shook hands and greeted one another, happily discussing how they came to be at the same dinner party. I smiled and thought *small town.*

Christy grabbed an oyster fritter and whispered to me, "Is that the sister-in-law with Hayden?"

"Yup," I said. "How are the oyster fritters?"

"Fabulous. And fat free, I'm sure. Don't tell me otherwise!" With a smile and a wink, she moved to get more wine.

The clock in the foyer chimed loudly, ringing out seven times. I collected Hayden from Jocelyn. "I'm just going to put this little man to bed, and then we'll sit down to dinner," I said.

"Goodnight, Hayden," Liz called. "Sleep late for Mommy tomorrow morning!"

I lifted Hayden's pudgy arm and made him wave it at our guests. Up in the stillness of his bedroom, I turned on his mobile and the music that I hoped would soothe him to sleep. I changed him into his pajamas and gave him a fresh diaper. We settled into the rocker and I began to nurse him. While the party sounds floated up to his room, I relished our togetherness. I didn't want to rush back to the party, a feeling that surprised and comforted me. I took my time with him, and when he was asleep I lowered him into the crib, patting his tummy and smoothing his hair. I crept out of his room, closing the door softly behind me. With the video monitor in hand, I joined the rest of the adults downstairs.

I poured myself a glass of wine and we ate the chicken and noodles, creamy and dotted with bright peas and carrots. The salad cut the heaviness of the meal and cleansed our palates for the next hearty bite. For dessert, I served the loaf cake, fragrant with orange, and sweet against the tart lemon curd glaze and blackberries. We talked and the wine flowed.

As the last bites of orange cake were eaten and forks clattered down on empty plates, I went to the kitchen to get the coffee pot and offer more cake. I brought out a bowl of candy also, Mary Janes. I watched Corey's eyes land on them and a smile curve slightly on his lips. He unwrapped one and looked up at me, his mouth silently forming the words, "Thank you." I smiled at him and nodded slightly.

"Whoa," Hank said. "Remember these, Corey? Aunt Tish always had Mary Janes for you! Where did you find them, Molly?"

"They were in the bulk section at the grocery store; thought I'd buy a few. I hear the house was rarely without them," I said.

"Did you get peppermints too? They are my favorite," Hank said.

"Next time," I said, smiling.

Everyone helped clear the table. I stood at the sink as the dishes were brought in and everyone crowded into the kitchen.

"Leave them, Molly," Christy said. "Come have another glass of wine with us before we have to go. The grandparents have Delaney, but we should head home soon."

"I'll have another glass," Liz said with the enthusiasm of already having had a few.

"Yes," I said smiling. "I'll think I will have another. Jocelyn, how about you?"

"No, but we had a lovely time. The babysitter is on the clock. We should go," she said.

Hank nodded in agreement. "Did you know babysitters charge twelve dollars an hour these days? Expensive, huh? Maybe that's why Mom always brought us here to Aunt Tish's when she went out. Saved them a bunch of dough, I bet."

"Aunt Tish was more than Corey's babysitter," I said. Corey slipped his arm around my waist.

"You know, speaking of dough, I saw you fixed the kitchen floor," Hank said, pointing to the floor where the deep gouge was. "It looks perfect now."

"Nothing's perfect, but it's ours," I said.

Corey smiled at me. I knew he was happy in this house, and it turned out that I felt happy too.

Acknowledgements

I am forever grateful to Linda Breckenridge, Heidi Duffy, Diane Schweizer, and Bob Schweizer who encouraged me to never give up on my dream. Throughout this project, Courtney Gawthrop, Tina Baliban, Tina Hadgimallis, and Erica Heck were my sounding boards, and I am incredibly thankful for their friendship. Thank you also to my first readers, Bethany Meyer and Kelly Greenleaf, who read early versions and still said I should continue.

Much appreciation goes to Colleen and Mike Harter, who helped answer all my home improvement questions, and the Upper Moreland Historical Association, whose digital newspaper archives helped greatly with my research of Willow Grove in the early 1900s.

I'd like to thank my editors, Helen Mallon and Susan Helene Gottfried, for their insight and invaluable advice. Thank you to Gary Miller, and the hardworking people at Morgan James who brought this to fruition.

This book couldn't have been written without the unfaltering support given by my amazing husband, Stew, who worked hard to allow me the incredible gift of a year dedicated solely to writing.

I am indebted to and inspired by my little ones, Stewart and Alice. My heart is full of gratitude to be their mother, and even though I am not perfect, they help me learn to be a better mother every day.

About the Author

Heather has a degree in Art History from the George Washington University and a degree in Culinary Arts from the Restaurant School at Walnut Hill College. In her free time, Heather is the Archivist for the Upper Moreland Historical Association. She lives in a historic home in Willow Grove, Pennsylvania with her husband, two young children, and an old cat named Bananas. This is her debut novel. Visit Heather at heathergreenleaf.com

Morgan James
Speakers Group

We connect Morgan James published authors with live and online events and audiences who will benefit from their expertise.

Morgan James makes all of our titles available
through the Library for All Charity Organization.

www.LibraryForAll.org

Printed in the USA
CPSIA information can be obtained
at www.ICGtesting.com
JSHW022325140824
68134JS00019B/1304